"Author Patricia C. Jackson has crafted an intriguing suspense novel with romance, action, espionage, and mystery at every turn."

"...Jackson pulls quite a few surprises that land at just the right time in the plot. I was also impressed with the dialogue, which really moved the exposition forward and characterized the wide cast very well. Overall, I would highly recommend Mask Weavers For Hire to any reader seeking a character-driven mystery with plenty of thrills throughout."

- Reviewed by K.C. Finn from Readers' Favorite

"In general, Mask Weavers For Hire felt real and compelling..."

"Patricia C. Jackson has a way with words; she describes her characters and scenes with beautiful metaphors and poetic lines that had me craving more: "Ashes, cinders glowing red-hot would lay at the door of my soul...""

- Reviewed by FolusoFalaye from Readers' Favorite

"Amazing scene setting, rising tensions, and filled with the great atmosphere, a reader will be drawn into Patricia C. Jackson's world and on more than one occasion be forced to wait with bated breath to see what unfolds."

"Gripping, entertaining, with a good solid character base. Questions, discovery, and mystery will keep you hooked from cover to cover."

- Reviewed by K.J. Simmill from Readers' Favorite

"The author's style is relaxed and readable with the action moving at a fast clip that makes the reader constantly turn the page to find what happens next to their character. I thoroughly enjoyed this book and can highly recommend it."

- Reviewed by Grant Leishman from Readers' Favorite

MASK WEAVERS
FOR HIRE

Patricia C. Jackson

Matchstick Literary
1-888-306-8885
orders@matchliterary.com

Acknowledgements

In loving memory of my mother Sadie, father Ray and Wanda my sister. To The Girls Club for their loving friendship and laughter. To my husband Farrell and my son Andy I love you both. To Marilyn for her many hours of help, encouragement and faith in me.

Chapter 1

"Compliments of the gentleman over there, Ms. Carla," said the waiter, setting down a glass of wine. He tilted his head in the direction of the man sitting at the other table, then smiled and stepped away.

The man was wearing a dark suit that definitely looked to be on the expensive side. The Windsor knot said it wasn't his only one. He didn't appear to be the timid type. An air of self-confidence saturated the very seat he occupied. When we made eye contact, he picked up his glass and walked over to my table.

Great, I thought. *Just what I don't need tonight, Don Juan on steroids.* I glanced at my watch and realized that Sarah was late, even later than was normal for Sarah. When I looked up, he was standing next to the seat across from me.

"Excuse me, my name is Daniel. I don't mean to be intrusive, but I noticed you seemed to be dining alone tonight. Would you like some company?" His voice was soft and low, almost a quality of intimacy. "I have always found conversation makes the food taste better."

"Actually, I'm not dining alone. My friend is joining me, but she is late. I expect her any time now."

"I hope everything is okay with your friend. The weather is moving in quite rapidly. With a little imagination one could envision the Antarctic out there." He paused, looked at me, and smiled. "Have a lovely evening." He turned to walk away but stopped when I spoke.

"Thank you for the wine."

"My pleasure," he said.

My head had begun to feel fuzzy. *Two glasses of wine on an empty stomach, it's definitely time to order something to eat.* I called over the waiter and ordered one of my usual choices. A little while later, as my plate was set before me, my cell phone rang. It was Sarah. Unusual tension strained her voice.

"Carla?"

"Yes, Sarah, are you okay?"

"I'm okay, but the car isn't."

"What happened?"

"Some guy slid through the intersection and hit me."

"Slid through the intersection?"

"The streets are awful, absolutely covered in ice."

"I'll come get you." I shifted to grab my purse.

"No, that's okay. Ben was working late, and I managed to catch him before he left the office. He's going to come by and pick me up. You really should think about staying in the city tonight, Carla. That's what we're going to do. We got a room at the Great Eastern. Could we have breakfast instead of dinner?" She laughed that infectious laugh of hers, and I knew she really was okay.

"That's not a bad idea. I'll call you when I get checked in at the hotel. You're sure you're all right?"

"Yes, I'm fine. Even the EMTs said so. I'll make reservations for you. Talk to you when you get settled in."

As I put down the phone, I saw Daniel look over inquisitively. This time I really studied him, took stock of the man. He was tall, approximately six foot two, slim build, high cheekbones, dark hair, athletic looking with the appearance of intellect. What more could a girl ask for? The guy wasn't asking me to have his baby; he just wanted a dinner companion. What harm could there be? I motioned for him to come over.

As he approached the table, he asked, "Was that your friend? Is she okay?"

"Yes and no. She's okay, but there was an accident. Things are worked out, but it does appear like I'll be dining alone. Unless your offer still stands?"

"I would appreciate the company," he said and sat down across the table from me.

Daniel was different. I couldn't quite put my finger on it, but there was a quiet intensity about him. The way he observed me and took in his surroundings with an awareness that suggested he never missed a thing.

He started the conversation with a bit of his past. He said he had been a chaplain but had moved away from his faith. Without further explanation, he quickly went on to another subject, as though that was more than he had really meant to say. The Daniel that sat across from me and the image I had of a chaplain—white hair, older, mild-mannered fatherly type—didn't match up in any way, but then how many chaplains had I ever known.

"So, Daniel, what do you do now?"

"I'm a consultant broker for clients who want to acquire art and antiquities. I spend much of my time overseas."

"Art and antiquities—findings from the ancient world?"

"Yes, I guess you could say that."

"It sounds like an interesting life. With so much travel I assume you're bilingual?"

"I speak a few different languages. What about you? What do you do, Carla?"

"I'm a psychiatrist. My work consists less of the material things of our world. I focus on people and the most intimate parts of their lives inside their minds." The statement didn't seem to shake Mr. Self-Confidence at all.

What I did not share with Daniel, or rarely anyone, was my own unspoken language. On some level I had always inherently understood that perhaps I was just a little different. As children we are innocent and open, accepting of everything, even what we don't understand. However, as I grew, I quickly learned that even children become uncomfortable with you when they think you know if something is going to happen before it does. Over the years, I used my gift in my practice as an artist uses a paintbrush—a tool spreading across the canvas, lifting hidden color to the surface to provide better interpretation of the situation as a whole. I could never explain the sometimes-elusive anomaly that made me aware of things unseen. Therefore, I simply accepted my gift of silent language and kept it private.

Daniel's conversation with me became a dance of inquiry. The man definitely didn't have two left feet. His abilities in that arena were supple and apt. He was charming and pleasant. I glanced down at my watch. The late hour surprised me.

"Daniel, I'm sorry to end our evening; however, it's late, and I have a seminar to attend in the morning."

"In that case, may I stop by the hotel in the morning and have breakfast with you?"

"I believe that can be arranged. I must admit you were right—the conversation did make this evening much nicer."

Daniel smiled as only a man can when a woman has told him he's right.

"Your friends Sarah and Ben, they sound like an interesting couple. Perhaps I'll have the opportunity to meet them as well." We set a time and agreed to meet in the dining room of the hotel.

As I started to leave, the maître d' approached me. "Bryan had to go home early. I'll have one of the men bring your car around."

"No, that's not necessary. I'll be fine." He nodded and handed me my keys.

***

Stepping out of the restaurant, the Boston cold wind grasped me with frigid fingers, forcing me to pull my coat tighter around me. Streetlights illuminated the falling snow, drifting down through the naked trees, now dressed in sheets of ice. The trees stood elegantly, as though they were awaiting a winter gala.

Walking across the parking lot toward my car, I could feel the accumulation of ice under the snow. As I reached the car, a voice came from behind me.

"Hey!"

Expecting to see Daniel, I turned around. Two men were walking toward me. One man was short and heavy, the other approximately six feet, both in their midtwenties. The latter held a knife. I could see the blade flash silver in the dim light.

"Hey, you got something I want." He grabbed my purse. As he attempted to pull it off my arm, we both slid on the ice. The strap twisted around my arm, his body up against mine. The strong pungent smell of liquor and sweat permeated his body. Slamming me against the car, his fist came down against the side of my head and shoulder. My feet went out from under me, and I hit the ground hard. Now pinned between the front tire of the car and the attacker, he drew back his foot and slammed his heavy boot into my side. The sharp intensity of the blow took my breath away.

Suddenly my attacker was ripped away from me. I looked up, but I couldn't believe what I saw. It was like something out of a Hollywood stunt scene played out in front of me. Daniel gave street fighting and martial arts a whole new meaning. I heard a cracking sound—an arm? A leg? The sound a turkey wishbone makes when you break it on Thanksgiving Day, followed by agonizing cries of pain.

A black SUV sped into the parking lot, sliding in beside the two men that Daniel had beaten to the ground. The back door flew open, and they climbed in with screams of discomfort. The vehicle spun out, slid one direction and then another, just clearing a lamppost before exiting the lot. Crimson blood lay splattered across the virginal white snow around where Daniel stood watching the SUV speed into the night.

He came over and helped me to my feet. "Are you all right?" he asked, looking me over. He looked and sounded like a man that had just taken a leisurely walk in the park. His voice was soft and steady. His clothing wasn't even ruffled. He reached down to pick up my purse and handed it to me.

"Yes, I think I'm okay." For some odd reason I felt no pain, just numbness.

My body began to shake. I didn't want Daniel to see or know how frightened I really was. He walked over and picked up the knife. This time it didn't flash silver in the light. Bloodstains darkened its blade.

"Toys of the maladjusted," he said as he slipped it into his overcoat pocket.

"Chaplain?" I inquired. He only smiled.

"Let me help you into your car. I'm so sorry, Carla, I should have walked you to your car. I'm going to follow you to the hotel. I'll call the police on my cell phone. They can meet us there and take the report. Wait here, I'll get my car."

***

It was only a few moments before Daniel pulled up beside me. He was driving a little Lexus sports model. Somehow, I wasn't surprised. The concept fit him. He motioned me on and then pulled in behind me. Sensible people had long since left the streets, so traffic was light. Pulling into the hotel parking lot, I saw a police car. The officer got out of his unit and met me halfway.

"Dr. Van Doran?"

"Yes, and you would be?"

"Miller, ma'am. Officer Miller. Have you been injured?"

"I'm fine. Just a little shaken is all."

Daniel joined us. "I called in the report," he said.

We sat in the back of the officer's car as he took our report. Daniel took the lead. He was strictly factual. He filled in details before the officer asked the question. I couldn't help but notice a distinct minimizing of his involvement in the situation. One would never have known there was blood or screams of pain. From his explanation, it appeared the men had thought better of their situation and chosen to leave without much of a fight. Was he that modest? The Caped Crusader fighting for honor and justice? His mannerisms dictated that I follow his lead. I concurred with his description of the evening's events. The officer finished taking notes, and we all parted ways.

Daniel watched me as I entered the hotel, making sure I was safely inside; then his car pulled away onto the street.

**

The Eastern Hotel had been a grand lady of her day and had recently been renovated at considerable cost. However, the integrity of the interior design remained the same, old-world classic that spoke of another time when things moved more slowly. One could experience the overstated elegance of the moment: the crisp white tablecloths and waiters filling drinking glasses, the ringing sound of ice against the crystal, and the thick plush carpets that softened one's step.

My legs felt like Jell-O as I walked across the lobby of the hotel. The desk clerk was a young man with dark-rimmed glasses, intensely devouring a very thick book. He was no doubt a student attempting to earn extra money for college expenses. After checking in, I asked the clerk to call up to Sarah's room and tell her I'd arrived. A few minutes after I got to my room, there was a knock at the door.

Sarah came to my room in her flannel pajamas, no makeup. A petite five foot one inch, ruffled auburn hair, dark eyes. I had a flashback of our days in college: the sleepovers when we stayed up until the early morning hours cramming for exams. We exchanged hugs and agreed to fill each other in on all that had happened in the morning over breakfast, and she returned to her room.

After trying, I found I couldn't sleep, so I stood looking out the window at the lights of the city. *Had Daniel been a chance encounter or something more? My mind keeps going back to tonight's dinner companion, Daniel Walters. What is that tapping at my awareness? He was charming and personable. Why do I feel there is so much more that exists but is not within my vision? Was this man truly a chance encounter or something more?*

Chapter 2

Sitting across the table from Carla in the restaurant tonight was so different from studying the good doctor's profile. Her background information was all there. What they hadn't captured—what the ink and paper had failed to reveal—was her engaging personality, the sound of her voice, and Carla's classical beauty, thought Daniel.

Just thinking about Carla, he could feel his heart quicken and his breathing deepen. Of course, he had done his reconnaissance long before tonight's encounter: observing her from a distance and monitoring her daily routine. It was easy to recognize Carla's discipline and concentration of purpose in all that she did. There was something about her strength and drive that was intriguing and exciting like no other woman he had known. At five thirty every morning she went for a run under the streetlights. Her body was that of an athlete, lean and strong, legs that went for miles—the kind of legs a man envisions wrapped around him. She was the epitome of a professional yet possessed that soft, feminine mystique. She was stunning, with long blonde hair, delicate features, and full lips that smiled often. Her eyes were the most entrancing violet-blue that immediately captured your attention and drew you into her.

Arriving home, Daniel turned his attention, not without difficulty, to fitting the key into the lock. When the door opened, a little gray schnauzer sat waiting.

"Hey, Major, where's that master of yours?" Daniel heard the sound of two beer caps popping open and looked up to see Nicholas standing before him. That government persona still had not vanished from him, although he had been retired from the service for three years.

Years ago, Nicolas had been "Mr. Incognito." He had appeared to be the most ordinary of men—average height, average build, hazel eyes, and an olive complexion. Nicolas could crash a party, stand in the middle of the floor for an entire evening, and no one would remember he had been there. Age had since changed that. His full head of hair had turned a striking silver white, and it was as though that one characteristic had transformed all his other features, making him quite a handsome man. Now the moment he walked into a room he stood out as a memorable figure. Mr. Incognito had become unforgettable.

Daniel had learned a lot from Nicolas over the years. They sat down on the couch in the living room, drank their beer, and reminisced about a few old cases before Nicholas went on to ask me about the evening's event. He had previously filled Nicolas in on a few particulars about his current case.

"So I know our agent was at the intersection tonight," said Nicolas. "Tell me, did he play loose and nice with the doctor's business partner and let you and her have the table to yourselves?"

"Yeah, he managed to intercept the business partner. She was a no-show," Daniel replied.

"Right, and what *didn't* go well?"

Daniel didn't answer for a moment. Knowing Nicholas, he knew that was more of a statement than a question. How did he know something out of the ordinary had happened? Daniel couldn't come up with an answer, so he said, "Okay, I'll ask, how do you know the evening's events didn't go exactly as planned?"

"Well, Daniel, unless you have become a complete slob at the dinner table and that's ketchup on your sleeve cuff, which I don't believe it is, that might lead one to think everything didn't play out as it should've."

Daniel looked into his eyes and saw a spark of appreciation for the game of espionage and knew the same reflected in his own eyes.

"Carla got mugged in the parking lot of the restaurant," he conceded. "You're kidding?"

"No, I'm not kidding, and I honestly feel bad about it."

"You do." This time Nicholas's voice was flat, no audible ring that identified the end of his sentence as a question or statement. His radar was always razor-sharp.

"Anything you want to tell me, Daniel?"

"Yeah, as a matter of fact, there is, and you're the only person that I know will understand what I'm about to say." Nicholas put down his beer and leaned back against the sofa, and Daniel continued. "She's a deadly combination—brilliant and beautiful. I always thought the boys did a good job on the bios, but . . . I don't know how to explain. It wasn't just her looks and quick wit. Something about her made me feel some kind of déjà vu, but it wasn't where we had been, more like where we are going."

Nicholas picked up his beer again, this time taking two very large gulps before setting it down again. "You need to be very careful with this one, Daniel. She is truly dangerous. Women like her come out of nowhere. You know what happened to me on that street in Paris. I was on an assignment, and she walked past me. She had nothing to do with anything. I tell you, she just walked past me, and the rest is history."

"Tell me that story again, about you and Jacqueline."

"Okay, but first I need a professional answer from you. What do you think this Dr. Carla Van Doran knows?" Nicolas prodded.

"I don't think she knows a thing. I also have the profile on her ex-fiancé, Richard Dupree. He's a textbook sociopath, smooth and ruthless, with a good cover story. It appears he's an attorney involved in some high-stakes mediation, if you get my drift, so it looks like his years in college paid off in a weird sort of way. The good doctor has been set up, no doubt about that."

Nicolas looked concerned. "He's experienced?"

"Yes, and he, and those he's working for, know just about everything. They know the gardener worked for the professor and the gardener stole the chip. They traced the gardener to Colette, the professor's neighbor, and Richard believes the gardener either gave the chip to Colette or stashed it somewhere in her house."

"What happened to Colette in all of this?" Nicholas asked.

"It appears she had an accident. She fell down a flight of stairs and broke her neck."

"Okay, so they believe either Colette had the chip or it's back somewhere in the professor's house."

Daniel nodded. "Right again. Colette and the professor lived next door to each other, and they had become friends. Once the professor died, the trail went cold. That's why they made it so convenient for Carla to buy the house the professor had lived in. Working deep cover, Richard had become her fiancé, but she broke it off with him. We don't know why, but they remained friends and they still see each other."

Nicholas picked up his beer again and said, as though working it all out, "That way the ex-fiancé has access to the house." He paused. "You think he's the best they've got?"

"Yeah, but he can't do anything too dramatic. The way events took place forces them to play things long-term. The clock is ticking, and time is running out."

"What type of work did this Colette do?" Nicolas asked.

"She was a sociologist and sometime ago did profiling work for the government. She hadn't had any recent assignments. Before the alleged accident, they brought her in for questioning under the guise of updating files. She was solid," Daniel confirmed.

"And . . ." Nicholas questioned.

"And? What?" Daniel said.

"I haven't been away from the game that long, what else did she do?"

"Oh, you're going to love this. She was, shall we say, semiretired, had an office at home."

"Yeah, and?"

"Sex therapist."

"No way. Now this case is getting more interesting," Nicholas said with a broad smile as he lifted his beer can in a salute.

We sat in silence for a moment, and then Nicholas said, "Getting Dr. Van Doran into the professor's house, now there is an eloquent setup. It's creative, I like it."

"That's always been your style, Nicholas, creative."

"Hey, don't knock it. As I recall, that kind of thinking bagged us a few cases. Now science is making the game of espionage a lot more interesting. Micro Science is giving the tech boys a whole new vocation. Those satellite babies and drones, now they're no joke. Piece of work, no doubt about that." He gestured with his empty can toward the kitchen. "You got another beer in there?"

Daniel went to the refrigerator and pulled out two more beers. Sitting back down on the couch, he handed one to Nicholas. As Daniel sat back down, he said, "Tell me about Jacqueline again."

Nicholas began, "I swear, Daniel, I think it's the romantic in you. Okay, I was on an assignment in Paris. It was just an ordinary day. I was walking down the street, and I saw her coming toward me. As soon as I saw her, it was as if I already knew everything about her. We were going to be together; it was just that simple. Oh yeah, and did I tell you we're taking the grandkids back to New York this week?"

"Yes, you told me. I've heard of love at first sight, but was it really like that?" Daniel questioned.

Nicholas smiled. "Yes, actually it was, and a man can only pray to be lucky enough to find it. I'm not saying Jacqueline and I haven't had our difficulties. However, she has always been there for me, even with the long hours of my absence without explanation. She's always been the love of my life."

Daniel opened a package of potato chips, put them in a bowl on the coffee table, and took another drink of his beer. "It's a little scary, Nicholas, but I think for the first time I know exactly what you mean."

Nicholas put his beer down. "The doctor?"

Daniel sank back into the couch. "Never thought it would happen, not to me, not like this, but I swear to you I know she's the one."

There was a quality of caution in Nicholas's voice. "You know this violates all protocol, Daniel. You've had enough years; you've seen men go off the deep end. But I know in matters of the heart you're a blind man walking. You're going to need someone to talk to, and I'll be here for you, just like I always have."

"I've been grateful to you for that, you have taught me everything I know," Daniel confided.

Nicholas brushed off the compliment and changed the subject. "I'll be back from New York in a couple of weeks. Try not to get into too much trouble before I get back."

"Yeah right." Daniel smirked.

Totally ignoring Daniel's remark, Nicholas continued, "Did you notice that last windstorm took a couple shingles off your gazebo?"

"Actually, between airports and pond hopping, I've been gone so much I'm doing good to remember where my house is," Daniel admitted.

Nicholas said, "When I get back from New York, I'll come over and do some repairs for you. Of course, I'll expect my regular payment will be in the refrigerator."

"You've got a key, and you know where the fridge is."

"It's about time Major and I head for home." He rose from the couch and went to gather his coat, brotherly smacking Daniel on the shoulder as he went past. "See you when I get back."

Nicholas hesitated at the door then turned around. "Daniel, the water could run deep, be careful of the iceberg."

Chapter 3

The phone ringing pierced through my otherwise peaceful sleep.

"Dr. Van Doran, your 6:30 a. m. wake-up call."

The seminar for extrasensory perception I would attend today leapt to the forefront of my mind. Unlike the usual professional educational hours I was required to take, in recent years I had indulged myself with the pleasures of exploring the unscientific and unmeasured. I already had a keen understanding of the subject matter—ESP had been a part of my life for as long as I could remember.

Standing up to head for the shower, I became intensely aware that the previous night's Hollywood scene on ice had come with the price of an aching body. I looked into the mirror and was shocked at my reflection. The number of cuts and bruising far exceeded what I would have imagined. With all the adrenaline that had been pumping, I hadn't felt the total impact my body had taken. Fortunately, my conservative clothing and some makeup would cover most of it up for the day. Reliving the incident through repetitive concerned questions and explanations really wasn't what I had in mind for the day.

Dressed up and seminar papers in hand, I made my way along the hallways to the dining room, needing a little time to settle in and gather my thoughts. I've always found the concept of entryways, doors, and portholes of time and space to be entered and exited at our own free will fascinating. Depending on where we pass through or walk into, one step could change our lives forever.

I stopped short of the doorway to the dining room. To my amazement, there sat Daniel with a newspaper and coffee. As I approached him, he was immediately aware of my presence. He looked up at me from his newspaper. His eyes then darted around the room in one swift flash and then back to me. Now I had his undivided attention. He stood to greet me. As a smile appeared across his deeply suntanned face, I sensed a definite shift in his energy field; he had dropped his guard and felt warmer and more open.

I felt an involuntary smile of my own answering his. "You're early," I said.

He pulled out my chair for me and waited until I was seated before taking his own. "I really wanted an opportunity to spend a little time with you before your friends joined us. I thought we connected on so many levels. I'm going to be out of the country for two to three weeks, but when I come back, I would really like to see you. Would you be interested?"

From my side of the conversation, I realized there was a pregnant pause. That was *the* question; it had come so quickly. Here I was, Dr. Van Doran, self-proclaimed morning person, cranium-functioning and all that, set back on her heels. I simply wasn't prepared. I wanted to see him; I just hadn't expected that to be the first topic of conversation. After a few more seconds, I managed, "Yes . . . yes, I would love to see you again. I enjoyed our evening, the beginning and the middle, however the end left a little to be desired. Perhaps we could engage in something a little less physical next time?"

As I looked into his steel-blue eyes, I couldn't help but notice how the hue now matched the blue pinstripe suit he was wearing, like a chameleon adapting to its surroundings. There was a great deal more to this man than floated on the surface. His mannerisms were always socially correct. What was he really like under the veneer of perception?

His mood faltered, and he said with some audible guilt, "Carla, I feel the need to apologize again."

"No, Daniel, you were the one that saved me from a fate that could have been a lot worse. These kinds of things happen."

"I promise it will never happen to you again, not when you're with me." From last night's performance, it was obvious he could deliver on his promise.

"You said you were going to be out of the country?"

"Yes, I'm going to Egypt and then on to some remote areas."

"Egypt? Isn't that part of the world rather dangerous nowadays?"

"I don't often get to choose where the business takes me."

"Are you out of the country often?"

"A few times a year, in years past a lot more, but I have earned my semiretirement from abroad. So, would it be permissible for me to call you when I get back?"

As an answer, I took out one of my business cards, turned it over, wrote down my cell phone number, and handed it to him. "It's unlisted," I explained.

A serious look spread across his face. "That's okay, I'm an agent for unlisted phone numbers. I'll only sell it to pot and pan distributors, and the travel agents that call at the dinner hour." I laughed, and he held his solemn expression for a few moments before joining me.

Our laughter quieted to smiles, and he glanced around the room before nodding at the doorway. "I think that must be your friends coming to join you," Daniel stated.

As I looked over his shoulder toward the entryway, I realized the mirrored wall in front of him had caught the reflection of Ben and Sarah. Even positioned as he was, once again nothing had escaped Daniel's watch.

Ben looked as though he was ready to take on the world—broad shoulders, five foot ten inches, slender build, and every hair in place. The man always managed to look like he had just stepped out of a Ralph Lauren photoshoot. The only thing missing was "*Road to Success*" tattooed across his forehead. Then there was Sarah: flamboyant, spontaneous, and always just a step ahead of Ben. The self-appointed greeting committee and ambassador to the world.

Daniel stood as Ben and Sarah approached our table. The fragrant scent of Sarah's French signature perfume played in the air as she walked over to Daniel, close to him—in his space. "So this is the hunk you met last night." She gave him a complete visual once-over. "Nice, very nice." Daniel chuckled and turned to Ben to shake hands. Then he turned his focus back to me.

The waiter, an older man appearing well suited to his trade, set a glass of water before Sarah. She leaned forward, and her soft pink cashmere sweater designed to display cleavage fell open just a little more. She loved discreetly provocative clothing, loved walking up the line of tease.

She looked up at him for a prolonged moment and, with a trace of the syrupy-sweet Georgia accent that she weaved around northern boys when she wanted their attention, said, "May I have my coffee now, please? That would be high test of course with caffeine. I really am in *such* need." Her breasts no doubt captured his imagination; he stumbled over something that remotely sounded like confirmation of her request. She looked at me and smiled. We both knew how much she did enjoy her games.

"My car can be repaired," Sarah said, "but you know, I thought it was really strange, that man at the intersection, I saw him coming. He didn't attempt in any way to avoid me. It was like the whole thing was in slow motion. He was looking at me, but he didn't make any attempt to avoid me."

"Maybe the guy just froze," Ben said. "I'm just glad no one got hurt." Ben had always been the stabilizing force in Sarah's life—the right man at the right time.

Throughout breakfast, Ben and Daniel ran the gauntlet of conversations, from sports to politics and US foreign policy. Sarah seemed to enjoy the boys bonding for reasons I was quite aware. Ms. Matchmaker was already envisioning evenings together.

After roughly an hour, at a lull in the conversation, I interjected, "I hate to break this up, but my seminar starts in half an hour. I really must go."

As we stood up to leave, Sarah was less than tactful with her reconnaissance for information. "Daniel, I do trust we will be seeing you again?"

"Yes, I believe you will," he answered while looking at me. His smile told me he was definitely planning to follow up on that statement.

This time Daniel walked me to my car. He opened my door, and as I turned around to say goodbye, Daniel leaned down and kissed me on the lips. It was a tender kiss, unexpected but nonetheless pleasurable. A crisp breeze carried the smell of his cologne, masculine and clean. His black hair glistened like raven feathers in the morning sun. His complexity intrigued and fascinated me. I had always prided myself in the ability to read others. When the surface did not avail itself to me, sometimes my empathic senses prevailed, but here he stood before me and there still remained a veil between us.

***

Arriving home after the seminar, I made a hot cup of herbal tea, knowing that was going to be the extent of my healthy holistic experience. I was all too aware of the seductive and sinful dark chocolate that waited for me in the pantry. After indulging myself with the veracity of a pagan goddess and licking the chocolate off my fingers, I picked up the papers from the seminar and checked my messages.

Daniel's voice was affectionate and warm. "I'm at the airport, just getting ready to leave. Hope your seminar went well. I'll call you Thursday, eight o'clock your time."

Chapter 4

As usual, my Mercedes-Benz was stuck in gridlock on the freeway in morning traffic. The local radio station gave updates regarding an accident just a few miles ahead. As a doctor of psychiatry, I did at times admit to observing my fellow man with a sense of serendipity, surveying my fellow freeway companions in the cars around me; I had even come to recognize each of them. There he was with his electric shaver and the brunette with her morning makeup ritual. Oh, yes, not to forget Mr. Handsome. The man that checked out everything on the freeway that didn't look like it had a hairy back.

I was definitely getting out of this rat race just in time to save my sanity. That week I could sit behind the wheel of my car and feel satisfied with the progress Sarah who is my business partner and I had made. The property we wanted to lease would be available within the month. My heart raced with joy at the mere thought of it. No more half-hour travel time on the freeway just to get to work. A short ten-minute drive was all it would take to get there. The drive into the city was otherwise routine and uneventful.

I laid my briefcase down on my desk and looked at the day's appointments. I had been doing this work so long that the stories remained the same; just the faces changed.

My first appointment was Jason, a young teenage boy, bipolar with adolescent hormones raging. If I could have only convinced him of the importance of staying on his medication. However, in true bipolar fashion, from time to time he saw his life through rose-colored glasses and took himself off his lithium. Because his IQ was quite high, his parents had agreed to allow him to enter the university at an early age, hoping that keeping his mind engaged would keep him out of trouble. The strategy had not been totally successful.

Jennifer, my second appointment, was the most interesting case I had encountered in some time. The child had been in counseling, first with one counselor and then another. Her parents, Mr. and Mrs. Stevens, were typical upper-middle-class professional people. Her father, Jack, owned his own business, and her mother, Carlotta, was a classically beautiful lady and ever civic minded. They lived in the socially correct neighborhood, *"the old home beautiful"* story. As a psychiatrist, I had been down this road before. If everything was so perfect, why was this child sitting in my office? One couldn't point the finger at the rough seas of puberty in this particular case. Her parents had signed release forms for her school counselor, previous psychologists, and doctors. She fit very well as the teenage unruly, oppositional defiant. However, there were too many large black holes in this jigsaw puzzle.

Throughout the assessment process, Jennifer presented well. She possessed some of the genteel qualities of her mother. There was also the undercurrent intensity and drive to achieve, reflective of her father. Jennifer's IQ was off the charts. She also was at the university, sixteen years old and in her third year. I suspected she had been held back for social reasons. I had worked with children possessing abnormal high IQs before, but nothing like this child. Collective public opinion assumes children like Jennifer must glide through life easily, but lack of experience and maturity impacts with the velocity of a high-speed collegian, making meeting expectations of society difficult for these particular children.

***

In the late afternoon, Jennifer, a new patient referral, entered my office. She had long light brown hair, and the clean, scrubbed look that courts innocence. She was a plain-looking child, not one that stands out in a crowd. Her quiet demeanor indicated she preferred it that way.

Following her normal procedure, she walked across the room. A Newton's cradle sat on the windowsill. She lifted and released the first silver ball in a row held by clear wires and started the balls into their click-click motion.

"I'm sorry I'm late, Dr. Carla. My girlfriend has a sister that goes to the high school, and she got grounded, so she can't drive her car. I gave her a ride home, so she didn't have to ride the big Twinkie."

"The big Twinkie?" I questioned.

"Yeah, you know, the school bus."

"Right," I acknowledged.

She sat down in the brown leather chair in front of my desk. Jennifer was normally a soft-spoken child.

"Dr. Carla, the sky is turning dark, and it's really raining hard out there."

Was she afraid of storms? "Well, Jennifer, at this time of the year there are no tornadoes. That's a good thing, right?" There was no significant reaction from her.

An unscientific tool I had on my desk was a small basket of colored stones, along with various other toys, as my clients perceived them. I had come to enjoy my basket of stones. I knew before the client ever chose a stone which one would be picked up, but what I didn't know was how it would be handled. This little game garnered a great deal of insight. Jennifer constantly picked up the pink stone. Her thumbs rubbed over the smooth, small stone, always in a backward motion—away from the issues at hand. Jennifer seemed to be energized by the storm. She wanted to tell me about a movie she and her girlfriends had seen with her friends, the undesirable ones, from the "bad families," as her parents referred to them but didn't get the chance to say more.

The unseasonable storm had become more intense, gathering dark, rolling clouds. Wind and rain lashed against the window. Sounds of thunder roared in the distance. I turned in my chair toward the window in time to see a large bolt of lightning flash across the sky. Then I recognized Jennifer was no longer describing the scene from the movie. When I slowly turned around, in her other hand was the large black stone. She held it, moving her thumbs forward with rhythm and severe intensity. Had the stone been rough, her thumb would be bleeding. While studying her face, our eyes met.

"Numbers . . . numbers, I have to have the key . . . numbers? Or they'll all fall down. Give me the key. Numbers? . . . Numbers?"

The large black hole in the jigsaw puzzle had grown larger than before. What was going on? The severity of the storm, the imbalance of nature's rhythm, must have brought this to the surface.

Thunder crashed around us, vibrating the glass in the window so intensely that the silver balls became unbalanced and could no longer hold their rhythm of movement. Lightning lit up the whole office. The lights flickered and then went out. We sat in the quiet dark for seconds that seemed like hours. Jennifer sat in her chair, staring at the silver balls.

The lights came back on. I was still facing Jennifer. Her eyes were wide open. Her face vanished emotion into that place where we hide ourselves from others. She looked down at her clenched hands and then opened them. For a moment she stared intensely at the black stone. With a gesture of panic and fear, Jennifer released both stones back into the basket. I needed time to reexamine her records with new perspective.

Her eyes had always appeared to hold a world of knowledge beyond her years. It was like holding nitroglycerin in one's hand and not knowing where to set it down. Oh yes, it was exhilarating. My ordinary day had become something new and challenging. I always marveled at the human condition in its various forms. This child sitting before me, what genetic tumblers had fallen into place that brought her from her mother's womb a genius?

***

On my way home from work, I stopped by the kennel to pick up Kinsey. I had inherited Kinsey from Colette, my neighbor. She had been a spark of light that I truly missed in her passing. Colette was a free-spirited person, no doubt from the time she was born. Psychologist turned sex therapist in her retirement years. She had insisted that I should consider the idea for myself long before the time came to cash in on my 401K.

Colette had just acquired Kinsey before the horrible accident. She didn't have any relatives to inherit him, so I took him. I was just so not a Rottweiler person, perhaps a small Yorkie, but the whimpering and big brown eyes got to me. The truth of the matter was I still saw Kinsey as that fat, roly-poly, falling-over-his-feet, lovable puppy that came home to live with us.

He blended into the house quite well under the watchful eye and tutoring of Devin, my Siamese cat. Devin had taken it upon himself to raise this small, clumsy bundle of undisciplined matter. Devin even corrected behavior when necessary. This had become a source of entertainment and amusement as time had progressed. The elephant and the chain had nothing on those two. We pulled into the driveway. My cleaning lady, Maria, had parked her car to the side. Richard, my ex-fiancé, had helped me find this house. It was a great deal more than I could have afforded on the open market. The previous owner had been an older man, a professor of science at the university. The proceeds of his estate went to a niece living in Germany. She just wanted her money and a quick settlement, leaving many of the professor's belongings still in the house.

Chapter 5

Kinsey was anxious to get out of the car and be home to see Devin and Maria. As I entered the house, I heard the sound of Latin music, tapping on the eardrum, like cinnamon and spice permeating the air. The house was always alive with the zest of Maria's spirit, the smell of fresh-brewed coffee, along with baked goodies I had long since quit attempting to resist. The cookies sat on the marble-topped kitchen table awaiting my ever-appreciative guilty pleasure.

I picked up the mail from the table in the foyer: advertisements and bills. Advertisements rated right up there with unsolicited telephone calls that one gets during the dinner hour. As I walked down the hall toward the kitchen, the advertisements went into the wastepaper basket beside the umbrella stand.

As I entered the kitchen, I observed Maria pouring a cup of coffee for me. Her long, dark hair came down past her shoulders, lying in curls, soft ringlets around her face, framing what would be a sculptor's delight. Her expressive eyes hid nothing; a poker player she would not have made. Maria's nature was open, warm, and caring.

She had on her favorite, slightly oversized red sweatshirt. She wore her blue jeans tight, discreetly emphasizing her other attributes. Her looks could turn a man's head, but her mannerisms always garnered her respect. She turned down the music, which could only mean one thing. Maria was very thorough in her fact gathering. Monday morning gossip had been especially juicy, and I knew I was going to be privy to the most intimate details. After all, I hadn't called her Watson from time to time for nothing.

I sat down in my chair. Maria didn't even start with the small pleasantries of "And how was your day?"

"The CIA was over at Nelson's house today."

"You mean the Nelsons that bought Colette's house? They haven't even moved in yet."

"Yes, yes," she said. "They were looking for something; they even brought in a dog."

I slumped back in my chair. "They're looking for drugs! There goes the neighborhood."

"Slow down, you don't have it right. You know Alisha Davis down the street?"

"No," I replied. "Not really."

"Well, Alisha's brother works in the detective bureau downtown. He said they are looking for a chick." I was well accustomed to Maria's accent and at times mixed-up English vocabulary, but I wasn't getting it.

"A chick?"

"That's not the big news. They don't think the fall down the stairs was an accident. They think Colette was murdered."

"Murder? Chick?" I began to realize I was sounding like a parrot. "Maria, what are you talking about? A chick? A baby chicken?"

"No, no chicken, not like that. You know, *chick*, the little things you put in cell phones, computers, the little things that make them work," she said, impatient at my lack of understanding.

We were at our customary "I am to figure it out" stage.

After a few seconds, I realized what she was trying to say. "I think you mean *chip*, not *chick*."

She looked at me for a prolonged moment. "Whatever. You do know this English not easy language, right?"

"Right, Maria."

"Anyway, the detective, he thinks Colette was pushed down the stairs. He has always thought this."

"Well, Watson, did you see the CIA remove anything?"

"No, I don't see them take anything out. I think the thing may be still in the house."

"The chick?" I corrected myself. "I mean chip?"

"Yes," she said, "that thing."

"Maria, you're making my first assumption about the drugs sound better by the minute. Surely, they don't suspect Colette was involved in anything like, what, espionage?" Maria tilted her head sideways and frowned, which meant, *I don't have that word in my vocabulary.* "Okay, Maria . . . spy."

"You mean like the handsome Bond man 007?"

Thank the powers that be—she watched TV. "Yes, well, something like that."

She put down her coffee in disgust. "How you get there?"

"Think, Maria—a chip, the CIA. What else did you hear?"

"They believe it was one of Colette's clients. Maybe a man, he said he has a sex problem and he goes to Colette about his problem. Maybe he just uses her for place to hide what they are looking for," Maria explained.

"Come on, Maria, this information isn't the type of thing that is talked about on the street."

Ignoring my inability to perceive the whole picture, Maria continued, "Alisha Davis a nice lady. I let her borrow your picnic basket last fall. She was to bring it back this morning, but the hospital called her to volunteer today."

My head was spinning in more directions than I cared to think about.

"Maria, what does my picnic basket have to do with Colette?"

Maria had been sitting on the edge of her chair, her arms resting on the table. She picked up her coffee cup and leaned back in her chair. I understood very well the body language and the look; I had been insensitive to one of the rules of good gossip: get all the details first, ask questions later. In apologetic acknowledgment I waved her on.

"Alisha say she had recipe for me. She was to put it on top of picnic basket and leave in pantry at her house. She said she would leave the back door unlocked. She told me to go down and pick them up. So I go down and I am in pantry when I hear her brother, the detective, come in with another man. They are in kitchen. They sit at the table and talked all of this. Her brother, he is upset about the CIA. They are involved now, something about not sharing information. That's how I know. I hear straight from the man." She threw her hands up in the air. "I know I am not supposed to hear, but I am in pantry, and the only way out is through kitchen. I just stay very quiet until they leave."

I sat for a moment, taking all the information in. Finally, I said to Maria, "I bow to your accuracy and professionalism and apologize for my inappropriate attention to detail. I'll try to do better in the future. Touché."

"Touché, what does that mean?" Maria asked.

"It's French . . . for 'your point.'"

"You don't teach me French now, okay?" she protested.

I allowed myself a chuckle and nodded, but quickly turned serious again. "Maria do you think anyone saw you go into the house this morning?"

"No one saw me," Maria said.

"Have you told anyone what you just told me?"

Her face held tension. Her dark eyes were wells of apprehension and concern.

"No one but you," she replied.

"Maria, you mustn't tell anyone, and I mean *anyone*, what you heard. If Colette was murdered and there is something the government wants back, it is definitely not a game we want to be involved in."

She nodded in understanding and retreated to another room to finish her duties.

After Maria left, I reheated my coffee in the microwave, picked up the bills from the table, and went to my office. It was pleasantly warm from the fire Maria kept going in the fireplace in the winter months. I often worked on my case notes in the evening, and Jennifer's folder was on top of the files, but I couldn't rein in discipline of thought. My mind was racing from one thing to another like an Olympic contender attempting to participate in all events at the same time. I sat down in the large, overstuffed chair in front of the fire, placed my coffee cup on the table beside me, and pulled a soft yellow throw around me. My addiction lurked in an ornate wooden box on the end table that housed my lovely dark chocolates. It was undoubtedly the proper time to indulge in comfort food.

Devin leapt into my lap and curled himself up. His warmth and the gentle vibration of his purring were eternally comforting. Kinsey had taken his place beside the fire. It was so quiet and peaceful that it was hard to believe something as sinister and intense as murder could have actually happened across the backyard fence, and to my dearest friend, Colette.

Sometime later, I was awakened by the sound of the grandfather clock in the hallway chiming the hour. The realization that I had been dreaming of Colette shattered my tranquil awakening. It was one of those odd, disjointed symbol dreams. I was in a plane high up in the sky, looking through something at the land below. Flashes of black geometric forms, letters, and numbers came across the sky. Hearing Colette's voice behind me, I turned around and there she was, looking like a vibrating hologram. She handed me a gift-wrapped box. The wrapping on the box was for a child's birthday. She put her fingers to her lips, signaling I mustn't tell what's in the box. That dream was definitely going to take some time to decipher.

"Come on, Kinsey. It's time for you to go out before we go to bed."

I let him out the back door, and Devin and I waited for him to come back. The moonlit night cast shadows across the yard. Kinsey made his routine check all the way around and then came back in. As Devin and I watched him, for the first time I was truly aware of Kinsey's size; he was no longer a puppy, now a full-grown adult Rottweiler patrolling his territory. Somehow I found great comfort in that awareness.

The three of us went upstairs to my bedroom. Pictures of family and friends were displayed on the bureau in lovely antique silver frames. Weekend treasure hunting at antique shops and garage sales had relinquished their bounty. One of the pictures was of my mother, my father, and me at the airport. As an only child, there were no siblings standing beside me, just loving parents—that did not come back. Headlines in the newspaper had told of the crash of a small private plane. My maternal grandmother, Mary Colleen, became my guardian. She tried to help my five-year-old mind wrap itself around the reality of what had happened. The child in my memory had difficulty understanding. "They are not coming back. How long are they not coming back?" I questioned.

"Forever," she had stated in a soothing tone.

A week later, in the middle of the night reality came to me, the child, as I stood in the doorway of my grandmother's bedroom.

"What is it, child?" Grandmother said with a fond look.

"Are you going to leave me forever?"

"No, I'm not going anywhere for a long, long time," she said with quiet empathy.

She took me into her bed and held me in the warmth of her arms.

"Carla, Grandmother will teach you many things, and in time you will come to understand that our loved ones never truly leave us."

She kept her promise. Over the years, my own abilities awakened, grew, and flourished within that realm, seldom visited by others. She had always been my compass and safe harbor.

My grandmother was clairvoyant. She saw me in ways I could not see myself. In the summer when it was hot and humid, she would brush my hair and pull it up off my neck into a French braid. She would tell me stories about my father's Dutch ancestry.

"He gave you a good physical body," she would say. "It's important to balance the physical with the mental. One day you will call upon your physical body to sustain your life. Discipline will reward you." So I ran in marathons and maintained a regimen at the gym. I had a good diet—most of the time. Baked goodies, pies, warm cookies, and rich chocolates admittedly called to me often. My hearing was acute, but my willpower with food not so much.

There in my bedroom where I had my private quiet time, I felt closest to them—those that had passed on. Sometimes they visited me in dreams. I was aware of their presence in my daily life. Mary Colleen even dispensed wisdom from time to time. In my youth, she had taught me how to understand my gifts.

"Your gifts are from God," she would tell me. "You should use them wisely for the benefit of others." I would be a healer one day, of that there was no question. She had told me that I would grow strong in ways I could not imagine. I would need to be strong for those I loved. She hadn't needed to tell me what I had inherited from her side of the family. It was most evident in her deep violet-blue eyes and my gift of extrasensory perception. Both had been passed down from generations of her Irish ancestry.

There was the other assortment of pictures: Colette and I on vacation in the islands. She was a free spirit in every sense of the word and the closest thing I ever had to what I thought having a sister would've been like. She was definitely family. Then there was the picture of impulsive, sweet Sarah in our college days, and of my office manager, motherly Marcy. She ran my professional world and kept me sane. Marcy insisted Sarah and I needed to get out of the office from time to time. "Call them health outings," she would say, "but you girls really need them."

A dream journal lay on the table beside my bed. While the scenes from that odd dream were still fresh in my mind, I recorded them. The dream had been in vivid color, which spoke to me of reality in some form to come. I would unscramble the symbols later.

Devin, shades of the Red Baron, had perched himself on top of the armoire. He could survey his world, which consisted of his house, me, Kinsey, and of course, Maria. In true Siamese fashion, he ran the household and everything in it. He did so with grace, style, and flair. Kinsey took his place on the floor at the foot of my bed.

Chapter 6

On Saturday morning, Maria stopped by to help me with some additional cleaning. She looked tired.

"I no sleep well last night," she said. "I kept thinking one question after another."

"What kind of questions? Give me an example?"

"The professor, the scientist you bought this house from."

"Yes, what about him?"

"Colette talked about him. She knew everyone in the neighborhood. She said they had fun talks, she called them debates." Knowing Colette as I did, that could mean a number of things.

"What would they debate on?"

"I don't know, but I do have a question. Carla, you said when you first looked at the house, a lot of the professor's things were still here."

"That's right, they were," I acknowledged.

"You don't say anything about his papers, his files. He kept an office at home just like you do. Where did all those go, and who did they go to?"

I sat contemplating her astute question then realized I didn't have a clue. So many of the professor's things were still in the house. It was odd that the file cabinets had been partially emptied. He would have had a computer; that was also gone.

Many of the professor's books were still on the bookshelves. Some of his clothes and personal possessions remained in the house—some, but not all. Why would that be?

"Another thing, the square gold locket I found between the cracks in the floor of the attic. If the sun hadn't hit it just right, I would never see it. You said the professor must have given the locket to his wife as a gift, but what about the symbols inside the locket?"

"Yeah, the engraving on the inside was really different. It was a mixture of science symbols and something I'd never seen before."

"Do you still think they were love messages to his wife?" Maria questioned.

"To tell you the truth, I really don't know what they were."

"They don't put pictures inside," she remarked.

"Okay, Maria, let's start with Richard. He handled the professor's estate."

"Carla, you know Colette was right. You keep the ex-fiancé; you never get a new one."

"I'm working on that." I turned and picked up the phone. I had the number well memorized.

The phone rang, and Richard answered. We exchanged pleasantries for a time.

"Richard, last week Maria gathered up some of the professor's things, clothing and so on, that had been stored in the attic; she is going to take them to the Salvation Army. Maria asked me what happened to the rest of the professor's things and I didn't have an answer for her."

I could hear Richard clear his throat. "I went through all his personal papers to find the bank statements to pay any outstanding bills. The paperwork helped us find his niece in Germany—things an executor must do to settle an estate."

"Okay, I got that, but what about his computer and the file cabinets? They were empty."

"Two men from the university stopped by to pick up the professor's research papers and computer. Everything went so fast from there. I told his niece I would get an appraisal for the contents of the house. When she found out there was a buyer, she just wanted to get the whole thing settled."

"Do you happen to know what the professor's research was about?" I questioned.

"Well, science isn't my field, but the best I could get out of it was something about the transfer of energy. Even his peers found it difficult to understand his theories, and most of what he did was experimental. He did some work for the government from time to time," Richard stated.

"That's interesting." The word "government" made my nervous system queasy nowadays. "The two guys that came for his things they were from the university, you said?"

"Yes, that's what they said," Richard acknowledged.

"They didn't happen to have on dark sunglasses and bulges under their jackets by any chance, did they?" I asked.

We both laughed, but that moment of silence on the other end, I thought I knew what it was. Had Richard asked for ID, or had he taken them at their word? I couldn't help but notice he deflected the question and changed the subject.

"By the way, Carla, when are you going to be having another one of those Friday night dinners?" Richard asked.

"As a matter of fact, Maria and I had just been talking about that. How does two weeks from now sound? We can get caught up on things then." I really didn't want to give him time to ask any of his own questions.

"That sounds good," he said. "I have an out-of-town trip, but I'll be back before your Friday-night dinner."

We said our goodbyes and hung up.

"Things are looking better, Maria, however, I do believe we are entitled to buy a license for paranoia. It's unnerving, particularly when the incident takes place practically in your own backyard." She looked more relaxed, but the dark circles under her eyes confirmed the fact she had not been sleeping well. "Take the rest of the afternoon off, you could do with the rest."

After Maria's car pulled away, I went back into the dining room. The professor had acquired many beautiful antique pieces of furniture for the house though I had purchased most of what was there. The cherrywood dining room furniture was my favorite. The dining room table could accommodate as many as ten people. Maria would help me get things ready and prepare the food for the Friday dinner. It really wouldn't take long; we had it down to a fine science. To see us in action, one would have thought we invented the assembly line.

Later that night, I sat in my office going over some case notes when I realized my thoughts had drifted off again. It was becoming a habitual behavior and an annoyance. I had given up my yoga. Perhaps I needed to reconsider that decision. There's that dream circulating in my head again. What was in the box Colette gave me? It wasn't just a box; it was a child's birthday gift-wrapped box.

Another fifteen minutes had passed, and I was still sitting there attempting to analyze all the aspects of that dream. I made a bargain with myself: one more hour of real work and I could get up from my desk. In the kitchen, cheddar cheese and a cold beer would be my reward.

I separated some of the papers on my desk and reached for the paperweight. As my hand reached out, it was as if a bolt of lightning hit me. *What on earth?* I sat straight up in my chair, instantly reliving that day in Colette's office. I could see and hear her clearly.

The figurine on her desk was of an abstract art sculpture. Father, mother, and child intertwined, round, smooth. It was a heavy piece. She had always used it as a paperweight. Colette noticed me admiring the piece.

Knowing my appreciation for art, she insisted on giving it to me as a gift. She said it appeared at her front door with a note from one of her clients. She never saw him again and didn't know what happened to him. He just quit showing up.

Leaning back in her chair with a smile, "I received it as an unexpected gift," she had said. "Now I'm giving it to you. One day you may spontaneously give it to someone else. That's the best kind you know, spontaneous—like a good sexual climax."

I could hear her laughter echo in my head as I pulled my hand back away from the sculpture, sat back, and stared at it. *Dear Lord in heaven, tell me there is nothing hidden inside that thing.* I picked up the stone piece and turned it over: the sculpture looked solid. I put it under the light on the desk to get a better look. It appeared uniform in composition and texture. I ran my fingers over the sculpture and noticed a slight difference in the texture. The bottom felt different. I went to the kitchen, took a knife out of the drawer, and scraped the bottom of the sculpture. White bits of plaster began to show up on what should have been a brown stone surface.

I took father, mother, and child sculpture to my workbench in the basement. I turned the piece over, made a small hole in the center, and attempted to look inside with a flashlight, but the hole was too small. I made the hole larger and rammed the flashlight to it again. *What is that taped to the inside?* I poked and prodded with a pair of tweezers until it popped out. There it lay on the workbench. A *chip*. I couldn't believe what my eyes were seeing. It had been in Colette's house, and now it was in mine.

I sat in the quiet, staring at the sculpture's dark, gaping hole. The phone on the wall over the workbench rang, shrill and piercing. The sculpture dropped from my hands onto the wooden bench with a deep, dull thud. I jerked up the phone's receiver as though it was a fire extinguisher in immediate need.

"Hello."

"Carla, it's me, Maria. You sound out of breath."

"I took Kinsey for a run, we just got back in." That was a lie, but what was I to tell her? The recess bell just rang, and the devil had come to play.

Apparently, she bought it because she continued, "I'm going to the store tomorrow, is there anything special you want me to pick up?"

"Wouldn't hurt to have an extra couple bottles of wine for our Friday-night dinner."

"Okay, I'll add that to the list."

After she hung up, I realized I was still sitting here holding the phone. Obviously, my brain was overloaded and having a meltdown. With trembling hands that had but a moment before been so confident, I put the chip back inside the sculpture.

It must have taken an hour to dig through all those boxes still packed away in the basement. Eventually, I was able to find enough of my pottery tools and supplies. My attempt at repair was anything but professional; however, it would have to do for now.

At least one part of the dream made sense. This was just a key that would unlock the other symbols. I had to know more about the professor; somehow his work was definitely connected to Colette's death. I could feel sickening realization in the pit of my stomach, followed by waves of anxiety.

How long would it be before the government connected my friendship with Colette? Naïveté—perhaps they already had. What would that mean? My flippant remark to Maria came to mind: "We have a right to our license for paranoia." I sat there wishing I had never felt the need to make that statement.

Cheese and beer somehow just didn't seem like enough. I had been keeping some old brandy for special occasions, and that night's discovery definitely qualified as a special occasion. I went back upstairs and poured myself a generous portion, something to settle the nerves.

A plan needed to be put into place. I needed to approach the situation as a strategist. Swirling the amber liquid around in my glass, I began to formulate my agenda.

I needed to know more about the professor. That was paramount. Colette's client, the man who had left the gift of father, mother, and child on her doorstep, there was no way I could find out who he was. Had he even used his real name? The professor, on the other hand, was a different story. One of the couples that came to my Friday-night dinners could be invaluable. She was a secretary at the university, and her husband was a professor.

The hour was getting late, so I let Kinsey out for his patrol expedition while I finished my brandy. It took Kinsey a little longer to come back. Perhaps a cat had run across the yard and Kinsey was fantasizing himself as the great tracker. He pounced on the back step with a loud thud. I opened the door and let him in. As I turned out the light in the foyer, Devin sprinted up the stairs and sat at the top of the landing in regal pose observing our ascent. I often wondered, as he sat there, did he see Kinsey and I as physically challenged, clumsy in comparison to his own sleek, smooth movements? He definitely had a superiority complex, no doubt about it. Perhaps he pitied us.

Chapter 7

I put on my nightgown. It was pink, soft, and fell all the way to the floor. What is it about the feel of material wrapping itself around our bodies on a cold winter's night that gives us comfort and makes us feel cuddly and warm? If the government was investigating, what could they know about me? I stood before the full-length mirror and thought about my life. *How had I become the person I am?* My friends, associates, and acquaintances had all seen exceptional suitors come and go from my life. The question that lingered among them: *Why had she not committed to one of them?* Only Colette knew the answer to that.

In college, I had immersed myself in my studies, prioritizing that even over a social life. It wasn't until I had been working on my doctorate and could see daylight at the end of the tunnel that Philip came into my life. I loved him, truly loved him. We had set up housekeeping in a small apartment off-campus. Our wedding date was set for the fall of that year. I came home early one day to hear the television on a channel playing what must have been a soap opera, full of moaning and groaning—not exactly Phillip's preference of entertainment. I stood in the middle of the living room floor and then realized the television was off. The sounds were coming from our bedroom.

I walked through the bedroom door and saw them on the bed. They were unaware of my presence. It was as though the room existed of nothing but them. All emotion drained from my being. I sat down in the oak rocking chair in the corner of the room, the one my grandmother had given me. As a child I sat in her lap as she read to me, the time of love and innocence, before vision. The wolf in sheep's clothing suckled at the entrée of life. I observed their bodies as they rhythmically rose and fell.

The ultimate violation of trust. My girlfriend, Heather, and my fiancé Phillip's moves and sounds were so familiar. Intimate and mystic were those rituals of love that I thought had been our own, now shared in a lusty betrayal revealed—the garden of Eden's forbidden fruit.

Heather saw me first. I suppose it would have been the classier thing to have done—gotten up and walked out, allowing them to dress. But I didn't. Instead, raw, unreasoned intent dictated my unresponsive presence. Perhaps the betrayal had awakened a newly found sadistic appreciation for revenge. Heather attempted to find her clothes on my bedroom floor. The look of shock in Philip's eyes, his head in his hands, knowing there were no words.

An afternoon of indiscretion had changed our lives forever. That day I came to realize that intense emotion blinds us. Even clairvoyants retreat to dark places. I had not seen that one coming. By the clock, it was only a matter of minutes that my life with Philip, as we had planned it, was over.

After that I threw myself completely into my work. There I was safe, physically and emotionally. Men became my companions and entertained me, but when they grew too close, I found reasons to step back, step away. Even Richard wasn't able to break down that door, although he understood me better than any one man had ever understood me. The knowledge that we would always be friends was of great comfort to me.

As time passed by, one constant I will confess to enjoying in the midst of all this was Daniel. He called every Thursday promptly at eight and several other times throughout the week. I had only shared with him the normalcy of my life. We all come to relationships with our own baggage, though renting locker space for storage is quite another matter. From our conversation, it was evident he was doing a lot of traveling. We kept things light, and I was looking forward to his returning to the States.

***

Two weeks later, Maria and I were ready for yet another of our Friday-night dinners. Everyone showed up. It was a full house. Sarah and Ben came early. They had just come back from vacation, and she looked tan and relaxed. Sarah went to the kitchen with me while Richard and Ben took their drinks into my office and made themselves comfortable, relaxing in front of the fireplace.

Sarah had a way of being too direct at times.

"Did you hear from Daniel Thursday? Did he call you this week?"

"No, I didn't hear from him this Thursday." The truth was that week the phone calls had stopped. I consoled myself with a busy schedule.

"Maybe he's on his way back," she said. "Carla?"

"Yes, Sarah, I know you think he's hot. He's probably just involved with his work. So much has been going on around here I've hardly had time to think about him." That was a lie. I was hurt and disappointed that he hadn't called. I thought about him every day and looked forward to hearing his voice. If I said it aloud, would it make my feelings more real? I just wasn't ready for that much reality. Closing the door would be easier.

"What do you mean? What's been going on?" she said as she nibbled at the cheese and olive tray.

I stopped short. Sarah, my lifelong friend—did I really want to bring her into this? She looked at me with interest, the kind that a truly caring friend has for you.

"Okay, if it isn't Daniel, what is it?"

"It's a long story. I'll tell you later."

With an exasperated look, she let the topic go and helped me carry some of the things to the dining room table. The evening progressed well. Several conversations went on across the table at the same time. Everyone was relaxed and had a good time. My dinner guests, the professor and his wife, were of little help. They had seen the professor on campus a few times but didn't know a great deal about him.

I went to the kitchen to get more wine for the table, and Richard followed along to give me a helping hand. As he was pulling the cork on one of the bottles of wine a guest had brought, I asked him, "By the way, I never did know exactly what it was the professor died of."

"It was a heart attack. He was in his eighties."

That was straightforward, I thought.

Richard stopped and looked somewhat puzzled for a second.

"Something troubling you?" I wondered aloud. "What is it?"

"The professor's gardener, something just didn't ring right about him. He was odd." Richard took a sip of his wine.

"Odd? In what way?" I questioned.

"You said Colette never mentioned him, right?"

"I don't recall her ever saying anything about the gardener. Why do you ask, Richard?"

"Records show he had been in the employment of the professor for over a year. It looked like he just quit showing up. He didn't even request his final paycheck. I don't recall seeing his name in the funeral guest book. You're sure Colette never mentioned him?"

My mind stuck on that one remark: *he just quit showing up*. He must have been Colette's client, the one that left her the gift of father, mother, and child on her doorstep. He definitely had a connection with the professor—she never saw him again.

"You're right, Richard, that does seem a little strange."

Richard looked at me. His mood had taken on an immediate change. He seemed quite happy tonight for some reason.

"Okay, what's going on? Did the lady of your dreams fall into your lap or what?"

"Come on, Carla, you know you're the only lady of my dreams, and always will be."

Richard had a knack for being gallant.

"It's a special night," he said.

"Yeah, why's that?" I smiled questioningly.

"Let's go back into the dining room." He sported a smug, all-knowing look. "You'll see."

We went into the dining room. Everyone was standing with their wineglass in hand. I was confused.

"What's going on? Are we toasting someone?"

"No," Sarah said. "We are toasting something."

"Really? What thing are we toasting?" I questioned.

"The lease to our new office," Sarah said. "No more half-hour drive on the freeway, Carla. The lease is on the table in front of your chair. I've already signed. We're just waiting for your signature."

I turned to Richard. "You sly old fox, that's why you were so interested on when I was going to be having my next Friday-night dinner." Richard was always at his finest when he thought he was in the driver's seat.

When the evening ended, Richard was the last to leave. "I'll be gone for several weeks," he said. "I'm going to New Orleans, a negotiation settlement. I'll give you a call as soon as I get back."

I looked at Richard, the man that would negotiate settlements. His premature gray temples gave an air of sophistication; he had a fastidious approach to detail, right down to his manicured fingernails. In his closet, pairs of shoes appropriately coordinated with each power suit, of which he had many. Beneath the smooth, warm, polished exterior lay a sharp contrast: ruggedness, a steel-driven approach to life.

"Have fun," I said. "Take lots of pictures. You know how Maria and I like to live vicariously through your photos and travels."

"I'll definitely do that, sweetheart, you can count on it. You will be in your new office by the time I get back. I'll see you there and take you and Sarah to lunch."

***

The next week flew by. Thursday was moving day. Everything was boxed and ready for the movers, so I looked around at what would be an empty office within the hour. A soft knock on my door brought me back from the mental wave of ecstasy I was riding. Jennifer stood in the doorway.

"What are you doing here, Jennifer?"

"My mom said you were moving." Jennifer walked across the room toward me. Her eyes were searching over all the boxes. "My file is in one of those boxes, isn't it? I'm going with you." She handed me a business card. "Mother gave this to me this morning." It was one of the new cards Sarah and I had the printing shop make up. The new address appeared as 44 Terrace Lane. Jennifer couldn't have been clearer: *You're not abandoning me, right?*

"That's right, Jennifer, you're coming with me. I can give you directions."

Jennifer smiled. "Oh no, that won't be necessary. I am quite familiar with the neighborhood. We used to live there before they built the new house. Trust me, I know it inside and out." She sat on the corner of my desk with a look of disgust. "Good old upward mobile dad." Her voice had the cut of sarcasm. "The old neighborhood was just fine, I loved it there, but not enough social climbers to satisfy my old man, I guess."

Old man? That didn't sound like Jennifer. Her new vocabulary was odd and unsettling.

"I take it it's a school conference day. Does your mom know where you are?"

"I'm going to meet her at the mall. Big sale going on, and you know Mom. I'll definitely be hitting her up for some tag names. Well, I have to go. See you at your new digs, Dr. Carla."

The movers came in as Jennifer was leaving. They were quick and efficient. I stood and stared at the empty room. Clients' faces and names flashed across my mind—people's lives I had been able to make better. It always meant a lot to me. I thanked God from time to time for my place in life. I walked out of the door for the last time, put my keys down on the receptionist's desk, said my goodbyes, and left.

I pulled into the parking lot of our new office. The moving truck was already there, and so was Sarah—both waiting for me. When she saw me, Sarah got out of her car. She represented the poster child for what every woman loves to hate. Size 8 with the appetite of a lumberjack. When we went to restaurants, she was blissfully unaware of such concerns as calorie count. Unashamedly and with malice of aforethought, she announced to the waiter that he could save himself a few steps and just bring an extra basket of bread. She was an absolute jewel.

Sarah held a large bottle of champagne in the air with one hand and gestured to the moving crew with the other. "I invited them to join us for some celebration bubbly." Clearly the men had already become acquainted with Sarah.

One of the guys looked to be approximately six foot two, and the other six foot four with shoulders appropriately proportioned. Sarah looked exceptionally petite and delicate standing there between them like an innocent, harmless child. They were the ones that were going to place the furniture in the office at her direction. Yes, indeed, they were prime beef on the hook, no doubt about it. I had actually seen the trauma unfold on other occasions: blank stares from shoe salesman caught in her web. When Ms. Precisely Right was through with the movers, they would deserve all the bubbly they got.

Chapter 8

Sunlight streamed through the windows of the office overlooking Chicago's Golden Mile. A young man with a crew cut and bulging muscles opened the mahogany doors, announcing in a voice that rang of military order and history. "Richard Dupree, sir."

Richard stepped into the office. His deep blue eyes locked on to the man in the Armani suit sitting behind the desk. He studied him for just a moment then said, "You're back I see. Well, Kurt, how was your flight over?"

Kurt picked up his Havana cigar. "Little stopover on the way, otherwise smooth flying."

Richard shook his head and smiled. "You know those cigars are going to kill you one day." There was an irony in Richard's voice. The two men looked at one another with an evident comradeship, history that was unmistakable.

Kurt leaned back in his chair. "You're kidding, right?"

"Yeah, Kurt, you're right. If the couscous, towel heads, and the snipers didn't kill us, we're going to live forever."

Richard sat down as Kurt poured him a drink. "Still like it straight up?"

"Yeah, works for me. How's the good old oil boys doing?"

"Cartel is alive and well, paying the bills. Richard, you have always been our best man on the ground. We have a couple new players Stateside." Kurt moved two photos across the desk. "You know either one of these men?"

Richard picked up the first photo and studied the man's face carefully.

"No, can't say I've seen this guy before. What's his story?"

"His name is Ivan Petoskey. Father was Russian military. Mother was Chinese from a unique family with connections—friends in high places with money. He is also the man who turned gardener."

"He has some colossal nerve to come play in our playpen. That's downright arrogant," Richard said.

Both men laughed as they sipped their thirty-year-old scotch.

"Thought you would see it that way. Richard, you have carte blanches. Find him a permanent resting place, the sooner the better. You'll have all the information you need before you leave."

"Consider it done." Richard picked up the other picture. "Now what about this guy?"

Kurt was silent for a while. "You've never seen this guy before?" he asked.

Richard looked up, then back at the photo, his intense, piercing eyes searching each feature, flaw, and characteristic. Years of assignments flew through his mind.

"No, who is he?"

"His name is Major Daniel Walters. We have been working on this assignment for three years, my gut tells me we're really close. This Walters, he's made connections with Carla."

"What?"

"When you didn't contact me, I knew this one had got by you. Carla hasn't mentioned him?"

Richard could feel his face flush, his heart pound a little faster. "No. This Daniel Walters, has he connected Carla to the chip?"

Kurt flicked the ash from his cigar into the ashtray and leaned forward. "That's about the size of it."

"Who is this guy?"

"An agent buried deep under layers of Homeland Security, and he's seeing Carla. Keep focused and professional, Richard. You know you can't let your emotions do your thinking for you. We arranged for Carla to be in that house for a reason."

Richard bristled. "That's right, and she's still there under my control."

"The good major didn't just fall out of the sky, Richard. We don't want him to know of our presence. As far as Carla is concerned, you're going to continue to be the good ex-fiancé and friend. We need to keep it that way. In our trade craft the honeypot operation doesn't work if the queen bee has left the hive."

"Like I said, Kurt, she's under my control. This isn't anything I can't handle."

"Listen, Richard, don't underestimate Daniel Walters. Make no mistakes. He's experienced, been trained by our government, and he's been around under the radar. This guy's no joke," Kurt cautioned.

"So, this Major Walters, he's Stateside?"

"Not exactly, he goes abroad from time to time. He's flying into New Orleans this week."

"New Orleans? Commercial?" Richard asked.

"Yes, just like any good little citizen racking up flyer miles. He's going to be meeting someone. We want to know who and where. Keep that camera lens on long range, he may have a perimeter around him. We don't want to get burned on this. Richard, I like money as well as the next man, and I intend to have my share. I'll probably end up with a few other guys' shares before this is all over." Kurt leaned back in his chair with a smug smile.

Both men laughed and raised their glasses in the air.

"We have to get there first, Richard. We need to get that chip in the right hands, get our money, and get out of the game. Let the politicians, military, and the moneymen fight it out from there."

A gold inlaid hourglass sat on the desk. Kurt lifted it and turned it over. The sand began to slip through the center.

"What's on that chip," he said, "could destroy the entire world as we know it."

Both men sipped their drinks in silence for a while as they watched some of the sand filter its way to the bottom. Transparent images gripped their minds, but the magnitude of their thoughts could only be held for a moment.

"Yeah," Richard said, "makes a man wonder, doesn't it. Money without worth or money without a place to spend it?"

Kurt took another puff of his Havana cigar.

"We have to get there first." He poured himself and Richard another drink.

Richard acquired the information he needed, left the office, and checked in to the hotel. After dinner, he went to the lounge and pounded down a couple more drinks. A very attractive brunette with the kind of body featured in magazines teenage boys drool over sat down beside him. Her intentions were more than obvious. His mood was dark and less than interested; his cutting, sarcastic remarks sent her on her way.

What he needed now was time to think. That remark in the office: *Don't let your emotions do your thinking for you.* Kurt had recognized something, something he hadn't. He had pressed Carla too hard about the engagement and setting a date. That's when she backed off, backed away. He knew her history and he knew better. He wanted her to agree and make the game real. That's what Kurt saw—the truth—and what he now had to admit to himself. He had never spent so much time in deep cover before. His fantasy life had become real, and Carla was his woman. The short assignments were less complicated and supplied immediate gratification.

Focus on the crosshairs. A slight squeeze on the trigger or a quick slice across the throat was much simpler, clean, and direct. Kurt was right. Walters hadn't just landed on Carla's doorstep one day. Richard ordered another drink. The bartender poured, hesitated for a moment, and then moved on down the bar. Why hadn't she told him about Walters? He didn't fit into her world of academia. She felt comfortable around the scientific nerd types.

Had he touched her, laid beside her, and tasted the sweetness of her body? Carla would have to understand: *No man takes what's his.* He could feel fire of aggression in his belly. Richard ordered another drink. The bartender sat it down in front of him but didn't move away this time. He gave him that "well, buddy, you want to talk about it" look. Richard rolled his eyes, laid down a wad of cash, and went up to his room.

That night sleep eluded Richard. He couldn't shut his mind down. Visions of Carla and Major Walters were seared into his brain. Long-range lens? He scoffed. *No way.* He wanted to be close to Daniel, close enough to see his eyes and watch how he moved. Close enough to have the scent of the man. Every good tracker and hunter understood the need. He would be at the airport when Daniel arrived.

***

Daniel put his briefcase in the overhead compartment and took a seat on the aisle. After the plane was in the air, he tilted his seat back and watched the different cloud formations drift away. Carla had been so much more than he had expected. One day, he would have to tell her what only the professor and the professor's niece knew. All the others were dead. Even the government only knew half his story. He felt like a man living in two worlds at the same time. The professor would have enjoyed helping him unscramble the dilemma. Perhaps he would have given him a dissertation on time travel, spot theory, and so on just for kicks. He still missed his uncle's counsel, humor, and dedication to his beliefs.

The flight attendant, a young man appearing to walk a little light in his shoes, bent down over Daniel with a pearly white smile, premature salt-and-pepper salon-cut hair. "Can I get you something to drink?"

His congeniality was perhaps just a little more intense than he had learned in flight attendant Class 101.

"A cup of coffee would be nice. Black, please."

The young man returned quickly with Daniel's coffee. "Are you going to be in New Orleans long?"

"I'm meeting my wife," Daniel said.

He looked down at Daniel's hand. No wedding ring or suntan evidence there ever had been one.

Daniel's recovery was instantaneous. "Reconciliation."

"Congratulations. Enjoy your time in New Orleans," the airline steward responded.

Daniel sat reflecting on how automatic his reactions were, what years of experience had taught him. This was the man he had become.

He closed his eyes. Creative imagination let him envision what a normal life with Carla would be like. He would stay with the department but sit behind a desk. He could shift down on the adrenaline. Suburbia: a dog and cat, normal hours, just like real people. As soon as this assignment was over, he would tell her everything he could.

The pilot's voice came over the speaker giving landing time and weather. As they set down on the runway, Daniel's mind returned to his duties: the report he would give to his contact. In the airport, he heard the speaker's announcements of arrival and departure times. He looked around, seeing tourists, businessmen, and families.

Stopping by the newsstand, he picked up the *New York Times* and a New Orleans paper. The salesclerk at the counter was busy ringing up a purchase for two giggling teenage girls. Daniel walked over and laid his newspapers on the counter. Richard, dressed in a pilot's uniform, stood in an alcove behind the magazine rack just adjacent to the newsstands. He observed Daniel's every movement, even the sound of his voice.

New Orleans—the spirited lady rising up from her knees. She would expel the taste of nature's rage and man's mistakes once more. Water and oil had been heavy weights on the arms of her economy. The magic and ambiance were still playing in the streets. Daniel and another man sat at a table under an umbrella and listened to the musician's melodies, notes ringing out from open doors. The area was crowded with the flow of people. Small shops with bright-colored merchandize displayed in their windows. A small, dark-haired child holding a rag doll stood in a doorway beside her dog.

The man sitting beside Daniel took off his sunglasses, reached down, picked up a small cardboard box, and placed it on the table. Daniel took the lid off the box and looked inside. He reached in and appeared to be examining its contents but did not retrieve it from its container.

Daniel looked at the man and smiled. "It's perfect. Good job," he said.

"How about the next time you want us to go shopping for you, perhaps you could come up with something domestic?"

"Isolationist, how un-neighborly of you. What about the world market and our contribution? Haven't you heard? The world is flat," Daniel responded.

"Funny, I do need to tell you it wasn't perfect when we found it, but our artisans did a nice job."

The men sat drinking their drinks. The clear blue sky and heat from the sun called for another round. Somewhere in the distance behind a lace-draped window, the sound of a cameras shutter lens: *click, click, click.*

Chapter 9

Saturday morning Kinsey brought his leash to me, and the weekend ritual continued as it had since he was a puppy. I guess in the beginning I thought he needed a break from the taskmaster Devin with his overseeing discipline and such. The little guy needed an ally, and he had become my constant companion on early morning runs and weekend errands. We were on our way to the new office to put some finishing touches in place. Sarah wouldn't be coming in until Monday morning. I had gathered some things from the house to take to the new office, including treats and a water bowl for Kinsey. I put some books in a box on top of my desk at the house. There was that paperweight—father, mother, and child—staring back at me. *Would it be a good idea to take it with me to the new office?* I wondered. The thing would then be out of the house. How many other people could it put in harm's way?

It had been so easy to put this dark demon on the back burner. If I were honest, my procrastination had been out of fear and self-preservation. There wasn't a book I could have gone to that would have told me what to do. No life experience dictated an answer. For the time being, I continued to leave the potion simmering in its caldron, along with my questioning thoughts of Daniel. I hadn't heard from him. Where was he? What had happened to him?

Kinsey and I arrived at the office. It was a unique piece of property. The building had the appearance of a residential area rather than commercial, with sufficient parking nestled among the trees and landscaping. What pleased me the most was the large wall of windows facing the backyard. A privacy fence surrounded the backyard, and shrubs and plants created a lovely garden within.

Sarah and I had sat down earlier and drawn up a serenity garden that would function as a place to take clients out when weather permitted. Could it get any better than that? Truly, there were blessings and I was thankful for them. First things first, I took Kinsey in and left the boxes in the car. Kinsey explored everything, inhaling deeply. One would have thought he was a bloodhound or, at the very least, genetically related to a Hoover vacuum cleaner. After going over Sarah's things and then mine, it was time for him to see the backyard. He investigated every flower beds new arrival.

Opening my thermos of coffee, I looked around at all the files. There was so much to organize and put away. I estimated it would take until noon at least. I went to work immediately, but the noon hour had approached rapidly, making a run by the local fast food seem to be the appropriate plan. I put Kinsey in the car, and he was delighted as we pulled up to his favorite establishment. The employees had long since become accustomed to his greeting their bags of food at the drive-thru window. In the beginning, they were somewhat hesitant, concerned as to whether Kinsey knew the difference between their hands and the good-smelling food in the containers. We went back to the office and dined on our gourmet fare. Kinsey lay in front of my desk, soaking up the sunlight that came through the windows. I could hear his soft, rhythmic breathing and could tell he had fallen asleep. I arranged files for Monday and pulled Jennifer's file, reviewed it again, and laid it on top.

I sat back in my brown leather chair and let the quiet of the room envelop me. It was so very peaceful. I closed my eyes to rest for a few moments, following Kinsey's lead. Some time had elapsed when I awoke to the sound of Kinsey's deep, guttural growl, loud and primal. I had never heard him like that before. He was no longer my sweet, cuddly puppy. He was a full-grown, very angry Rottweiler. I looked up and saw, of all people, Daniel, standing in the doorway with a box from my car in his hands. He stood frozen in place.

"No. No, Kinsey," I said as I got up and came around to the front of the desk. Kinsey had already gotten up and was stalking slowly toward

Daniel. I had been through dog obedience training with Kinsey. He had been a model of obedience, but now it was as though he didn't even hear me. Grabbing his choker chain, "Sit, Kinsey," I ordered, but he didn't sit. I could feel the strength in his body as he moved between Daniel and me. Again, I commanded him to sit. He finally sat, but the muscles in his body were still taut. Daniel slowly put down the box. The tension in Kinsey's body relaxed somewhat.

"Daniel, I'm so sorry, I've never known him to be like this. These are new surroundings for him, and you are a stranger, after all. Come to think about it, his treats are in that box you were holding." Taking Kinsey around to the back of the desk, I ordered him to lie down on the floor beside my chair.

"Have a seat, Daniel, I'm quite certain things are okay now. I have to admit I'm surprised to see you here. I thought you were going to be out of the country for some time yet."

He settled back in his chair much more relaxed than I would have thought he would be. "Some of the loose ends of business were tied up earlier than I anticipated," he said. "I flew in Thursday."

"Daniel, how did you find me?"

"I checked with your office late Thursday afternoon. They gave me your new address. I saw the boxes in your car, and the door to the building was unlocked, so I just brought the boxes in with me. Didn't realize I was invading your watchdog's domain." He glanced over to where Kinsey was lying and then back to me. "I have four tickets to the theater, and there's a new restaurant that just opened near there. I was thinking we could make a night of it. Do you think Sarah and Ben would like to join us? We could get caught up on what has been going on with each other."

"That sounds like a great idea."

"Carla, I thought of you every day I was gone. I would like to have talked to you more often, but there are places where cell phones don't reach. Getting back to camp, conversations with archaeologists, not to mention water and a bath, were luxuries."

"I understand," I said, relieved there was an explanation. "As I recall, you did say your accommodations were less than adequate from time to time. Were you able to locate some of the items you were looking for?"

"Yes, I did. There is a piece that is particularly beautiful. I would like to show it to you tonight. Carla, the night skies were stunning. I do sincerely hope you understand there is nothing I would have rather done than to have shared them with you." His unexpected openness shocked and pleased me.

"I have to admit I really did look forward to your calls, Daniel." I could hear Kinsey behind my chair inching forward. "I'll just put Kinsey out back for right now."

Kinsey was not at all happy being exiled to the backyard. As I came back in, Daniel put his arms around me and brought me close to him. "You feel so good," he said as he ran his hands through my hair. He bent down, kissed me on the neck softly, and whispered, "I love the smell of your body." I could feel his hardness, his need. His hands moved like a man that knew how to take his time, to pleasure, to excite a woman and bring her to passion.

"Before I go, I have something in the car for you." He went out to his car, came back in, and handed me a square cardboard box. "It's a little heavy," he warned.

I took the lid off, reached into the box, and pulled out the contents. There it sat in all its artistic beauty, another brownstone father, mother, and child. My heart leapt into my throat. My years of training had conditioned me. I knew without looking at Daniel he would be reading my response on a variety of levels. I looked straight into Daniel's eyes. "How perfect," I said. "It will go great in my new office. Thank you, Daniel. That was so thoughtful."

"You're welcome. It's different, something you don't see every day. Though if you did, I guess you could always use them as bookends," Daniel teased.

For a prolonged moment, the air hung like a void in time waiting to be filled.

"An excellent idea, however, I doubt I shall ever run across another one like this."

He was playing a game with me—checkmate, cat and mouse. Dropped in the middle of the Amazon, without a sense of direction or knowledge of survival techniques, how did I get here? Only a goddess of mythology could find this amusing. How did Daniel fit into this spectacle of mirrors, allusions, and reflections? Nothing was as it appeared.

Daniel looked so relaxed. "I'll come by the house and pick you up tonight at six-thirty. Maybe, given some time, I can even make up with Kinsey. I have some errands to run. I'll see you tonight."

I stood in the doorway of the office and watched Daniel's car leave the parking lot. There was one thing I knew with every fiber of my being: Daniel was not the predator deeply embedded in this nightmare. He was not the flame under the caldron.

***

I went through my closet like a frantic, hyperactive adolescent on her first date. *What should I wear?* I looked at one garment after another. A pantsuit? No, too businesslike. Perhaps a dress? No, one too long and the other too short. *I could call Sarah . . . no, I'm an adult, I can handle this.* I picked up the phone. Sarah answered.

"Daniel's back in town. He has four tickets to the theater. He wants you and Ben to join us tonight, and he wants to try out a new restaurant that's just opened."

"We would love to! How are you going to dress?" Sarah asked.

"I don't know what to wear tonight. Are you on your computer?"

"Yes," Sarah responded.

"I want you to look at these outfits." A few moments later, Sarah had her screen up and we were on video chat. "See the gray pantsuit? What do you think?"

"That depends, are you planning on getting rid of him or keeping him?"

"Keeping him?"

"Yeah, Carla, I've known you a lot of years, and I haven't seen you look this interested in a long time. Come on, it won't kill you to say you really like this guy."

I relented. "Okay, I think I do."

"Then the gray suit is definitely out."

I held up the black dress before the computer screen. "This one?"

"Too long and conservative. You aren't going to a funeral. Let the guy see a little leg. I can tell you exactly what to wear: that blue dress you bought last fall. The material is soft, has a low neckline, a tight waist, and a flowing skirt. That little dress can go see his mother and then go out on the town. It says 'I'm not cheap, but I definitely like a good time.'" Sarah laughed with enthusiasm.

"Sarah, you're outrageous."

"Yes, ma'am, that's why you called me. You do know Sunday morning I expect a call from you with all the details."

***

As I descended the stairs, the doorbell rang. I opened the door, and a large bouquet of red roses greeted me. I invited Daniel in. Kinsey stepped between us and growled, baring his teeth. Obviously, he hadn't forgotten the day at the office. Daniel's handling of his food bowl evidently was still a primary concern to him. I took hold of his choker chain and pulled him back.

"Daniel, the flowers are so pretty. Thank you. I'll just put them in some water. Come on, Kinsey, come." He followed me reluctantly down the hall, looking back at Daniel like a cross bear that had just missed his evening meal. I put him in my office and closed the door. I could hear him whimpering on the other side. Daniel was still standing in the foyer.

"I really do apologize for Kinsey's behavior."

"Don't apologize, he's only doing what his nature dictates. To him I am an intruder. He's just protecting what is his. If I would hold his treats, what else would I do? It'll take time, but I'll definitely need to mend some fences between us. Actually, I like him, he's spirited." Daniel walked over to me with a warm smile "He'll learn to like me, just as you will come to love me."

What assurance he had about himself. How confident he was. Maybe that's what he saw and liked in Kinsey, the ability to be aggressive when necessary. He put his arms around me, drew me close, and tilted my face up toward him. He kissed me with such tenderness. His hands moved gently down over my body, anything but controlling and dominating. How could this man invoke such emotion? It was as though my body was in direct opposition of my mind's logic. I could feel his warmth, strength, and passion.

"Carla, things happen to us in life we don't count on. You're one of those things. I wasn't looking for someone to be in my life. I do need to finish some business dealings. Then I can put my life in order in such a way that you and I can see more of each other, get to know one another. I really would like that, would you?"

The man had the most uncanny way of catching me completely off guard. My day's work consisted of dragging facts out of people. His quick straightforwardness unraveled my sense of order.

"Daniel, you do understand, I know there are things about your life you haven't shared with me."

"I know, Carla. My work and our timing could have been better in some ways, but in other ways . . ." He hesitated as though there were things he wanted to say and couldn't.

"After your work . . . should I use the word *assignment*? After it's over, can you be completely open with me?"

"Carla, I'll tell you everything I can. I know you're concerned. After all, we humans are the most lethal thing on the planet. I can tell you now–you will never have to fear me. I would move heaven and earth for you. I need you to trust me, believe in me. I'll make everything right for us, I promise you. I need to catch a plane in the morning. I need to tie up some loose ends here in the States. I'll only be gone for a few days." He reached into his jacket pocket and pulled out a square black box, handing it to me. "Open it," he said. "Open it now."

His excitement was plain to see. He was anxious and pleased with himself, assured I would enjoy what he had brought to me. I opened the box, and there lay a beautiful antique necklace. The light from the chandelier above me illuminated the shimmering luster of the gems. The artisanship was superb. Even to the untrained eye, one could see this wasn't an ordinary piece. The quality and workmanship was truly beautiful.

"I hope you like it, the moment I saw the piece I knew it was yours," Daniel beamed.

I walked over to the mirror in the foyer and held the necklace up to my throat. The dress Sara had suggested was made for this piece. He walked up behind me.

"May I?" he asked.

He attached the clasped behind my neck. We both stood staring at the necklace. What a gorgeous gift. I had never seen anything quite like it before. My mind transcended time. Antiquity, the ladies that would have worn this piece. What gala affairs had they attended, the cherished women that a man would have lavished such a present upon? I shouldn't take such an expensive gift. However, I mustn't appear ungracious either. He was right. I was incredibly drawn to this piece.

I turned to him. "This is such a beautiful gift. I don't know what to say."

"You don't need to say anything. Please just accept it with my deepest affection." He quickly changed the subject to my home. "These houses are classics," he said. "Carpenters of the time took great pride and care in their work."

The doorbell rang. I could hear Kinsey barking. He was the official greeter and was not taking his demotion lightly.

The first thing Sarah said as she walked through the door was, "That necklace is gorgeous. It wouldn't have been a gift from that handsome admirer standing beside you, would it?"

"Yes, it's a gift from Daniel."

"I do have girlfriends. Does he have a brother?" she inquired, purring like a cat.

"Sarah!" She only laughed.

"One must look after the sisterhood," she said.

Throughout the evening, Sarah appeared to find the necklace as fascinating as I found it beautiful.

***

After our evening out, Sarah, Ben, Daniel, and I went back to the house. I noticed Kinsey's personality hadn't improved much when it came to Daniel. Ben and Sarah went over to pet him as usual, giving him his due amount of attention. Even Devin ingratiated their presence, showing up so they could pay homage. Feeling uneasy about Kinsey's reaction to Daniel, I put Kinsey and Devin in the pantry off the kitchen. I'm sorry to say they didn't go quietly into that good night. They didn't even do so with class and dignity.

Sarah and I got out a few snacks and were in the process of pouring drinks when Ben volunteered to be the tour guide and showed Daniel through the house. He pointed out features of interest. Ben enjoyed being the official tour guide. Most of all, he liked the history, the architectural design of the period. Pocket doors that slid back into wide walls were usually his starting point. The uniquely carved mantels over the fireplaces spoke their own language. The stairway going up to the second floor revealed a large stained-glass window. In daylight hours, the pastoral scene cast a rainbow of light across the floor. There were numerous linen closets strategically positioned for convenience of the household. He always finished up by coming down the back stairway. They had made their rounds and had come back to the kitchen. Sarah picked up the tray of wineglasses.

"Let's go to the family room." She turned around and bumped into Daniel, spilling wine on his shirt. "Oh, I'm *so* sorry," she said as she attempted to wipe the wine off his shirt.

"Hey, that's okay, really it's okay. I'll just go to the bathroom and get this off with some water."

He started across the kitchen toward the bathroom. *How did he know where the downstairs bathroom was?* I wondered. Ben hadn't shown him. Halfway across the floor Daniel paused, maybe in uncertainty, maybe because he just realized what he'd done. Sarah interpreted it as the former and said, "Oh, the bathroom is over there." She and Ben continued into the family room, totally unaware of Daniel's unguarded moment.

Daniel hesitated for just a split second. "Yeah, okay." He was thinking to himself that it had been a beautiful cover-up, not letting her know that he already knew the layout of the house.

Being an observer on the sidelines, one sometimes sees more than the mind wants to absorb. Carla wondered, *Had I really seen what I thought I saw?*

After some conversation, Sarah decided it was time for them to go home. She definitely wasn't feeling any pain. I couldn't quite decide if it was her intention to give Daniel and me some time alone or if Ben was going to have a very interesting evening.

At the front door, I remembered the book Sarah had wanted to read was upstairs. "Sarah, I finished that book. I'll get it for you." I went upstairs to my bedroom and picked up the book. When I turned around, Daniel was standing in front of me.

"They left. Sarah said she would pick the book up later." He was standing so close I could feel the heat from his body.

A little foreplay now had gone beyond what I could have imagined. His hands were lambent flames awakening the flesh. His wet mouth had become a symphony of seduction. As he raised his body over mine, the sensation was electrifying. Our bodies met as though in memory of an ancient ritual of passion and desire. I found myself meeting his hunger with emotion I didn't know existed in me. Not since I had been with Philip—no, not even with Philip.

I felt myself melting yet at the same time becoming the fire. I was that flame that licked at his skin absorbing the moisture and the liquid of his lips. We both rose like the Phoenix but had become the sun devouring one another. Ashes, cinders glowing red-hot would lay at the door of my soul, never again allowing me to go to that hidden place of safety, the place where I denied emotion.

Softly in my ear, he said, "You'll never be alone, my love. I'll always know where you are. You will be in my heart." Excitement and fear fought to occupy the same space within me.

***

Morning was still and quiet in suburbia. He lay with his arms stretched out across my body. His head rested on the floral pillowcase, eyes closed and long black eyelashes against his sun-tanned face. Black hair in a relaxed array, it contrasted more sharply than the morning light that filtered through the bedroom window. The spring leaves of the trees cast shadowed patterns across the comforter on my bed.

The raw passion and emotion he had awakened in me was undeniable. Whatever happened between us, I would be forever grateful to him for that awakening. The scent of his body was masculine and warm. I looked at him as he slept deeply. What experiences in life brought him to be this man? As I went to that place of retrieval, I sensed the professional and the other side rarely shown but to a few—the side of him he had shown to me, as though he compartmentalized his life. Perhaps it was his defense mechanism, a way to cope with an unrealistic reality. The world he must work in and the world he would prefer to live in. I looked at his face, peaceful in slumber. Daniel was definitely the shepherd, not the wolf at my front door.

I analyzed my own behavior and found the anomaly quite interesting. Daniel wasn't the type of man I had customarily invited into my life. I had always chosen the disciplined, intellectual ones that lent themselves to the world of academia and predictable science. Daniel's intellect involved another world. His world necessitated the utilization of power and knowledge; the need for creativity, cunning, and spontaneity. He had the DNA of a man that could walk through a minefield and come out the other side in one piece. A survivor at all costs.

As I lay there, the word *conscience* appeared, not in a sentence or a stream of thought, but as a proclamation of fact. Interesting interpretation oftentimes becomes the devil's playground. That morning when Daniel left, I closed the heavy wooden door behind him. The things we let in and the things we keep at bay.

My morning run with Kinsey was later than usual. The fog and mist of the early morning were gone. The streetlights were out, replaced by the sun. How different things looked to me then, a bright and shining world of new horizons. My old world was comfortable. I liked the certainty, that dependable flow, the steady equilibrium, but I couldn't, wouldn't, go back. Daniel was the new frontier. As I ran, I felt the excitement of a new life ahead.

Chapter 10

Jennifer put the empty coffee cup in the dishwasher. Her mother always reprimanded her, saying, "Jennifer, drinking coffee will make you nervous and high-strung." No, she definitely didn't approve, but this wasn't a problem since her mother, Carlotta, rarely came downstairs before nine o'clock. Jennifer had just enough time to throw her iPad into her backpack and pick up her girlfriend Tiffany on the way to the university.

When Jennifer backed out of the driveway, there it was again, that Jeep Grand Cherokee parked across the street. The houses in her neighborhood had broad side yards along with landscaped, manicure front lawns. Mr. and Mrs. Wallace lived across the street. Mr. Wallace had instructed the landscaper to make some changes that involved the removal of several large trees and shrubs. Jennifer could see through the side yards now to the next street over where the Jacobs live. They were in Europe and would be gone for a few months. From her bedroom window, she could see the Jeep. The back door appeared to have a white mark across the side. Perhaps there was a security service doing routine surveillance at odd hours. If that was the case, then why were they sitting on her street? As Jennifer passed by, the man inside the vehicle turned his face away from her.

Jennifer drove on to Tiffany's house and pulled in alongside the curb. While she waited in the car for Tiffany, she looked down at the sterling silver ring on her hand. Jennifer ran her fingers over the onyx then pressed the tiny button on the side. The top of the ring opened to reveal the secret compartment, which remained empty. Jennifer remembered the day she found the ring in a small antique shop; it had cost a lot more money than she had wanted to pay.

A raspy little voice in her head told her one day she would find something valuable and of great meaning to conceal in the hidden compartment, away from prying eyes. Jennifer wore the ring every day and told no one of its camouflaged space, not even her best friend, Tiffany. Sometimes it's nice to have a secret. A private tiny niche unknown to others, a world all your own.

Tiffany got into the car and immediately offered Jennifer one of her Pop-Tarts.

"No thanks."

"I'm sorry there's no strawberry."

"What?"

"I know you like the strawberry ones, but we didn't have any this morning."

"Oh, no, that's okay." Jennifer half smiled toward Tiffany.

"What's going on, Jen? You look a little preoccupied this morning. You and your mom have another fight?"

"No, everything is fine. Or I think it is." Jennifer adjusted her seat.

"Earth to Jennifer, it's me, Tiffany. What's going on?"

"Remember when we went to the mall and you made a remark about a vehicle sitting beside my car?"

"Yeah, sure, what about it?" Tiffany said, ripping of the Pop-Tart wrapper.

"Describe the vehicle to me."

"What?"

"Indulge me," Jennifer stated.

"Okay, yeah, it was a Jeep, and I pointed out it had a white mark across the side. It looked like it might have been paint or something. So much for my excellent memory. Now give, what's going on?"

"Tiffany, I think I have seen that same Jeep for the last few weeks, but it could be my imagination." She was quiet for some time. "Well, what do you think?"

Jennifer stopped for the traffic light and turned around to look at her. She was biting her lower lip. "Earth to Tiffany?"

"Yeah, yeah, I got it. I just didn't want to add to your concerns. Jennifer, did you realize that Jeep was behind us all the way to the health club when we picked up your mom?"

"No way, you didn't say anything about that."

"Well, it didn't seem important at the time. Remember, I used your rearview mirror when I put on my lipstick and you said to use the mirror on my side, the one on the sun visor."

"Yeah."

"Well, that's when I saw the Jeep behind us. It was back a ways, but, Jennifer, I'm telling you it was definitely that same Jeep. Why would it be following us?" Tiffany questioned.

"I have no idea." Jennifer took a deep breath.

"Have you ever seen that vehicle anywhere else?" Tiffany asked.

Jennifer really didn't want to answer.

"Well, have you?"

"Maybe . . . yes . . . well, I think so."

"Where?"

"Off a side street by Dr. Carla's office, in front of Jacob's house, and this morning on my street."

"Have you told anyone?"

"No."

"Why not?"

"Look, it's probably just a coincidence," Jennifer said, knowing she didn't believe that for one moment.

"Coincidence or not. You really need tell someone."

"I don't want to come off looking like some kind of weirdo. Being known as a science nerd is quite enough."

"I don't like this one bit, but it's your call, Jennifer. Promise me if you see that Jeep again, you'll tell me."

"Okay, okay, I promise."

Because of Jennifer's advanced academics status, she had managed to talk her way into the science lab. Jennifer kept research data and did various other tasks assigned to her by the professor. It was Wednesday night and her turn to work in the lab after evening classes. When she reached the lab, there was a note on the door: *Jennifer, I have a meeting I must attend tonight.*

Professor Bronson had given Jennifer a list of duties he wanted her to perform. There was more work to do than usual, so she called home to let her parents know she would be running late.

After entering the updates on research data, Jennifer finished the last entry into the computer-organized and arranged files for the next day. Locking up the lab, she then walked down the long hallway. She couldn't help but notice everyone had apparently gone home. None of the classrooms were in session, only darkened rooms. There was an eerie quietness about the place at night.

Jennifer had parked close to the building. As she walked down the sidewalk, the lights of a vehicle came into view. Her heart skipped a beat. *No, that can't be . . . but it is.* The Jeep. Jennifer stepped off the sidewalk and ran toward her car. The Jeep picked up speed then came to an abrupt stop between Jennifer and her car.

The side door opened, and a man stepped out. He walked over to Jennifer, and their eyes met. His face was grim. He had the kind of nose sported by boxers, but not very good ones. A scar ran across the side of his face, another over his left eyebrow. He had on dark clothes, was of a medium build with a head full of thick black hair. He reached out for Jennifer, but she stumbled back. He tried again, and in a stern, low voice he ordered, "You're going to get in *now!*"

A booming voice came from behind Jennifer. "Hey! We got a problem here?"

As she turned around, she saw Nathan, the security guard for the university, and standing beside him was David, an officer Nathan was training. Rumor had it that Nathan had been an MP in the military. Other more reliable sources suggested that perhaps his involvement had been a bit more involved, Special Ops. Whatever the case might have been, Nathan was a huge man—the kind of guy you instinctively knew you didn't want to challenge, in or out of uniform.

Scar Face glared down at Jennifer, then back at Nathan and the other officer. "No problem, Officer, we just thought maybe the little lady had a problem with her car." Before anything else could be said, the man got back into the Jeep and they pulled away.

"David, did you get that license plate number?"

"Yeah, sure did."

Nathan looked at Jennifer. "You're the science lab tech, aren't you? Jennifer, isn't it?"

"Yes," she confirmed.

"Do you know either one of those men?" he asked.

"No . . . well, I think I've seen the Jeep around, but I don't know them," Jennifer stammered.

"Here's my card, Jennifer. It has my cell number. If you work late again, give me a call, and I'll keep an eye out for you."

"Thanks, Nathan, I'll do that."

"How far do you live from the university?"

"About ten minutes."

"Okay, David can defend the fort. I'm going to follow you home and make sure you get there safely." He tossed a cluttered key ring to David. "Be back in twenty minutes. Write up the incident report while I'm gone."

***

As Jennifer entered the house and closed the door behind her, Nathan's car pulled away. Her mother and father were in the family room. The TV was on, playing a rerun of "Masterpiece Theater." She could see her father was in his favorite chair. On the table beside him was a glass half full of his favorite drink.

In the last few years with the down economy, there had been less lavish vacations and fewer shopping trips to the high-scale retailers, though the country club membership had remained in place—keeping up appearances for a businessman was still essential. His drinking had increased, and the alcohol made him dull. Many times he would fall asleep in his chair, and later she would hear him in the hallway stumbling to his bedroom.

Jennifer snuck past the family room and down the hall to her own bedroom. She changed and got into bed, immediately turning on the electric blanket. There was a kind of chill in the air she had never felt before. Tiffany had said she needed to tell someone. Who would she tell? Her mother? Jennifer knew what that would bring down on her head. Just like when Jennifer had gone to her mother about what her father had been doing to her. Jennifer's mother would tell her she was a bad girl and she had brought it on herself. Her mother hadn't changed; she was still the self-absorbed, shallow, needy creature she had always been. No, she had never found safety there.

The thing Jennifer did have confidence in was her own mind. In the quiet of her bedroom, she questioned that perfect mind, the one that had never previously failed her. Photographic memory, like a steel trap, allowed things to always come so easily, flowing in and out of her brain with a rhythm so natural. She never quite understood how others struggled with the obvious.

Jennifer lay there and admitted to herself her own fears. Jennifer's mind wasn't so perfect. What about that crack in logic she had seen on that day? She had put her gym shorts in the washing machine at the last minute. Water was running on to the clothes, and as she looked down into the machine, on top of the water floating freely were black symbols and numbers all jumbled up in the water. Jennifer stared in disbelief. She put her hands in the water, and the numbers and symbols slipped over and through her fingers. Jennifer turned around to see if anyone else had seen what she saw, but no one was there or had been there. No one but her. Jennifer turned back around and looked down into the water to find it clear, no floating symbols or numbers.

Now in her room, Jennifer had broken out in a cold sweat at the memory of it. Her stomach muscles tightened; she thought she was going to throw up.

Jennifer had to admit it wasn't the first time that had happened. Her exceptional mind, "the perfect vessel," as the professor had referred to it. That was what set her apart and made Jennifer who she was. Jennifer hadn't told Dr. Carla about the repeated appearance of the black numbers and symbols. That was so far on the other side of the spectrum, the kind of thing a crazy person tells their shrink. Was she really losing it? Maybe she had overloaded herself with activities, but it had never been a problem in the past. Jennifer turned on the light next to her bed, took out a pen and paper, and began to write down all her activities.

Jennifer's physical energy level was never in question. Of late, she had been thinking about the professor and his wife. The thoughts made her melancholy and admittedly sad. Jennifer's loss of them and the move from the old neighborhood had taken its toll. Depression depletes the energy level, but that wasn't the whole story; Jennifer knew that.

She began to assemble a list: university, excelled schedule along with electives; music lessons; sports and clubs; the night science lab; volunteer service. Jennifer examined the list. *Maybe it is too much.* Balancing her activities had never been a problem in the past; however, she'd never had that Jeep following her around with a man in it that looked like Mr. Mafia, mobster for hire. Now there was a seed of thought for an entrepreneur: mobster for hire. She could've definitely used one of those tonight to get that guy off her back. The question was why was he there–why her? What could he have possibly wanted from her?

Jennifer needed to get away from there. Away from everyone and everything to somewhere she could think. If she gave undivided attention to the situation, then maybe she could force her mind to unlock the secret. What did those symbols and numbers really mean? Jennifer turned the notepad over and wrote, "PLAN B: Money, transportation, direction, and a confidante." She could get money out of her savings at the bank. Transportation and a confidante . . . Jason, a classmate and also a patient of Dr. Carla's, would certainly understand. Direction? Well, three out of four wasn't bad. She would work on a destination tomorrow.

Chapter 11

Jennifer arrived early at the university and stood in the hallway beside room 206 waiting for Jason. He was tall and thin with wiry, long muscles. His loose, curly dark-brown hair appeared to reflect his own nature, that of a free-spirited mustang. He often raced from one subject to another with the energy of a bucking bronco. His interest and knowledge were broad and extensive.

Jennifer had first met Jason in the waiting room of Dr. Carla's office. When she went for her appointments, she looked for his red pickup truck in the parking lot; it was always the shiniest vehicle there. When she turned around to look down the other end of the hall, Jason was standing there just looking at her.

She was the epitome of everything he felt he was not or could ever be. She was so altogether—a brilliant mind attached to a stable, steady emotional base. When he talked to Jennifer, it was as though she could express his thoughts and feelings better than he understood them himself. She had always been kind to him, even when rumors flew of his rebellious behavior. Some of those rumors were justified, others fabricated beyond even his recognition. His computer skills, however, were no joke. The federal government wasn't exactly laughing either. That was how Jason had managed to end up with his very own probation officer—a federal performance computer analyst, no doubt with an outrageous clearance grade.

"Jason, I need your help," Jennifer demanded.

"Okay," Jason muttered.

"You don't even know what it is I want yet," Jennifer taunted.

"Doesn't matter. What do you need?"

"I want to take a road trip."

"Okay," he said.

She couldn't help herself. The temptation to play with his mind was too strong. "I'm not planning on coming back."

"Are you pregnant?" The question ricocheted through the air like an out-of-control missile.

"Why would you say that, Jason?" Jennifer slapped his shoulder with her hand.

He only shrugged. "What other reason could you possibly have for wanting to run away? Jennifer, you have it all, always have had . . . I guess I really don't need to know why, that's your business. When do you want to leave?" He held out his hands.

"I'm sorry, Jason, you have every right to question. I'm asking a lot from you. I'm scared, and I need to get away for a while. Someone's following me. He even showed up at the university."

"You mean like a stalker? You want me to bring my gun?" Her shocked look amused him. "Really, it's okay, Jen. My dad is an outdoorsman, a State Ranger, he taught me a lot. Maybe there are some things I could teach you about survival."

His words hit the very core of her being. "You may be right about that, Jason, in more ways than you know, but I have a plan. I've thought this all through."

Jason looked down at her petite little body so in contrast to her four-star general attitude. "I'm sure you have," he said with a broad smile.

"We need to follow my plan. There are things you need to do, Jason. The first thing is that you tell no one, and I mean no one, what we are going to do. Do you understand?"

"Got it . . . no one."

"Meet me in the parking lot after your last class. I'll fill you in on the details then." Their eyes met. A road trip with Jennifer had given his dull day a dime's luster.

After his last class, Jason sat in his truck waiting for Jennifer. His mind analyzed every aspect and possibility, every word she had said to him. In her eyes there was fear, but there was determination in her voice. What was going on? Who or what had done this to Jennifer?

His cell phone rang. Looking down at the caller ID, he saw it was his probation officer. How convenient. With any luck, maybe this phone call would suffice as an office visit.

"Hello."

"Jason, it's Mike, how are things going?"

"Fine."

"Look, I'm calling because the day you are to report in . . . well, it's like this. As you well know, Homeland Security has no sense of humor, and my calendar looks like a Chinese jigsaw puzzle. Pardon the pun. How about our making your report same time next month?"

"Yeah, that works. Nothing much going on with me anyway— university, home, that's about my life. Boring as all get out." There was a moment of silence on the other end.

"Still taking your lithium, right, Jason?"

With a touch of sarcasm in his voice, Jason said, "Obviously. Like I said, boring."

Mike cleared his throat. "Just remember, Jason, you don't have a great deal more time with me and then I'll be out of your hair. Just keep on keeping it together, okay?"

"Right, counting the days." As Jason hung up, he saw Jennifer coming across the parking lot.

Jennifer got into Jason's truck.

"We need someplace we can talk."

"Okay, how about my house? Mom's at work," Jason replied.

"Okay, that'll do."

His house sat at the end of a tree-lined street. Jason took Jennifer to the kitchen, opened the refrigerator door, and got out a couple Cokes. "We have some frozen pizza. Would you like me to put some in the oven?"

"No, I don't think I want anything else right now."

"You want to see my bedroom?"

"Sure, is it a man cave?" Jennifer smiled.

"Yeah, you could say that." Jason blushed.

The house was a split-level. His bedroom was downstairs. Jason couldn't believe his luck. Not only was Jennifer in his house, but also she was even going to look at his bedroom with him.

He opened the bedroom door, and they stepped in. Sunlight was coming through two large windows. Jennifer's eyes made one search around his room: an unmade bed, desk, reading lamp, and computer. Some clothes in a laundry basket on the floor. She had to give it to him. It was better than what her sister, Caroline, had managed to do. Surprisingly enough, his room was filled with books, pictures, and hunting gear—the room of someone who sincerely enjoyed the outdoors. On the walls were pictures of Jason and his father on various hunting trips. There was a picture on his desk of his mother, father, and Jason. They were all sitting together and smiling, undoubtedly in better times for the family.

Jennifer picked up the picture and held it in her hands. She turned to face Jason.

"I'm sorry about your mom and dad not being together anymore. They looked like they were really happy."

"It's okay. Actually, they've been talking a lot on the phone lately. They're trying to work things out. How about that? I even heard them talking about counseling."

Jason pulled his desk chair out for Jennifer, and she sat down. He sat across from her on the side of his bed. Jennifer looked at him. He knew there were a lot of wheels moving in that pretty head of hers. He could tell she was having difficulty knowing just where to start.

"There are things I haven't told Dr. Carla," she said. "I'm beginning to remember things, but I don't know where they are coming from or why. I keep seeing black letters and numbers, things I can't make a lot of sense of right now. Jason, I think someone else may know why these thoughts are coming back to me. It must have something to do with the old neighborhood, the professor and his work. I'm scared I'm losing it. Do you think I'm losing it, Jason? We're friends, you can tell me the truth."

"No, Jen, I don't think that. Some of the work you have been doing with Dr. Carla may have something to do with this. You like her, right?"

"Yeah, I do." She nodded.

"Your volunteer work at the university science lab could have triggered something. The guy that showed up at the university, what did he look like?"

She thought for a moment then smiled. "Okay, imagine a grumpy hit man working for a Colombian drug cartel."

"You're kidding, right?" Jason gave her his full attention.

"No . . . actually that's about as accurate as it gets," Jennifer stated.

Jason pulled a pillow over and leaned up against it. "Wow! Jen, that doesn't sound good."

"I don't know that taking off is the right decision, Jason. I just know I need a safe place for a while to think things out."

"Jen, if distance and time to figure things out is what you need, my dad's place would be the ideal solution. Out west would give you plenty of distance from this place and all the time you need to sort things out. You'd be safe there."

"Your dad?"

"Sometimes for his work he goes into the back country for weeks on end. He has a trip coming up. He wouldn't even know we were there. When do you want to go?"

Jennifer laid out her organized agenda for departure. "I need to get money out of the bank. I'll pick us up some new cell phones."

"I can get the cell phones and some more ammo." Jason caught Jennifer's disagreeable look. "Really, Jen? If that drug-cartel-looking guy comes after us, you'd better well hope we have something more than our toothbrushes with us." Jason began to feel the excitement of adventure.

"We need to do this on a Friday night," Jennifer said. "That way we won't be reported as absent from school and it will buy us some extra time. I'll tell my mom I'm staying over at Tiffany's house to help her with an upcoming test. She'll buy that."

Jason thought for a moment then said, "I can come up with a cover story for the weekend, and I'll keep the truck full of gas ready to go. If we drive it straight through, we can be off the road and at my dad's place before anyone questions our whereabouts. So we're on for this Friday?"

"I'd like to give it a little more time to see if any of the pieces come together. Maybe this was just a weird set of circumstances that will play themselves out. If I tell Dr. Carla . . . but, Jason, it will be so hard. There are things I don't know how to tell her, but she may be the only one that can help me find the answers. I really don't know what else to do."

Jason looked at Jennifer and felt her pain. "You know I'm your friend," he said. "I want to say something, and I don't want you taking it the wrong way and getting upset with me. You asked me to be honest."

Jennifer had no idea what was coming, but it had to be better than this "no answer to anything" situation she found herself experiencing. "It's okay, Jason, you can say whatever you want to me."

"This thing about the numbers and the letters, that has to be coming from somewhere. I think you're on the right track with letting Dr. Carla help you."

She looked down at the floor and didn't reply.

"Look, Jen, I know this is frightening to you, but maybe you have something about the professor locked away in your mind. Maybe it's just a way of holding on. We all deal with loss in different ways."

"I really do miss the old neighborhood and the professor and his wife. Could that be all this is?" Jennifer disclosed.

Jason shrugged. "If Dr. Carla can turn a key for you . . . well, maybe it would be better for you to find out what the numbers and letters are about before you encounter the man in that Jeep again. I'm not saying it all goes together, but what if it does?"

Jennifer's voice was quiet and uncertain. "There so much . . ." She didn't finish, as though she wanted so very much to say more but couldn't. She sat up straight, pushed her hair back away from her face, and took a deep breath. "I'll try."

"Jen, you're the bravest person I know. You can do this. After you see Dr. Carla, let me know what's going on."

"Okay, I will. You keep that gas tank full." She smiled.

No one spoke for a few moments. Then Jason asked, "The professor and his wife, what were they like?"

"They were so good to me, she was loving and kind . . . they never had any children of their own." Jennifer remembered their warmth.

"And the professor?"

"He was terrific. He didn't treat me like a little kid, not even in the beginning when I was so young. He taught me about science. I mean some way-out stuff, Jason. It was like being on a fast track to the most exciting frontier you could imagine. With my IQ, I caught on quickly. I guess he figured that out earlier on. Being with him was so exciting. He taught me how to think outside the box. For the first time in my life, I had to work hard to keep up. I began to understand what I could really do with my own brain. As I got older, he let me work with him on some of his theories. I looked forward to every hour I spent in that house with the professor and his wife." Jennifer's eyes filled with tears. "The only thing I feel really badly about was the gold locket."

"What gold locket?"

"The professor and his wife gave it to me one year for my birthday. It had been hers and she had worn it often, but she wanted me to have it. The professor had some of his science equations engraved on the inside for me. It was a square gold locket. The last time I remember having it was at the professor's house. His wife, Erika, had become ill with a breathing problem, so I had taken some boxes to the attic for her. I thought I lost it up there. I even went back up to look, but I couldn't find it. The professor assured me it was in the house somewhere and would show up. I hated that I lost the locket . . . it really hurt. Have you ever lost anything that really made you hurt inside?"

"Yeah. When my mom and dad separated, and I couldn't make it better for them. We weren't a family anymore, and there were so many miles between us. I knew if they would just talk to each other, they could work things out. I love my mom, and I miss my dad so much. I miss all the things we did together as a family. They are talking a little more now, which is a good thing. It still hurts, but working with Dr. Carla has helped some. I have to give her that."

"Jason, I know sometimes you quit taking your meds. You did that so your parents would notice and maybe talk to each other more, right?"

"Yeah, but I realized that maybe if I kept my act together, my parents could focus more on each other."

"That's pretty perceptive, Jason. I always knew you had a good heart."

"Jen, do you think the symbols in the locket have something to do with the man in the Jeep?"

"Yes, I do. I understood some of those symbols and other things the professor was working on before he died, but not all. Someone else is holding the key that will unlock the mystery and make sense of all of this. I know that sounds crazy, but it's all I've got." Jennifer came over and sat on the bed next to Jason.

He tentatively pulled her over to him. She didn't resist, and they lay back on the bed. He bent down close to her, felt the warmth of her body, and smelled something clean and sweet in her hair. His lips brushed against her neck and found her body tasted of sweet vanilla. He wanted to do so much more than just hold her. He wanted to play out his fantasy: hot, steamy sex, her physically wanting him just like girls wanted the men on those late TV shows. She was not like the other girls he had been with. They were all easy and uncomplicated. Some of them could have written the scripts for those late-night shows. She had come to him for help, had asked him for it. He could see the vulnerability in her eyes and knew he couldn't take advantage of her, not ever. She seemed more relaxed now.

Jason kissed her forehead, closed his eyes, and said softly into her hair, "Everything's going to be all right, Jen. You know I'll do whatever it takes to keep you safe."

Chapter 12

Marcy had been our office manager since Sarah and I began our practice. Her organizational skills were phenomenal. She kept us on track with our daily schedules. With an eagle eye, she oversaw our personal lives with such enthusiasm it would have made a mother superior proud. Marcy placed Jennifer's file on my desk as she remarked, "Jennifer called. She's tied up in traffic and is going to be a little late."

Within fifteen minutes Jennifer appeared in the doorway carrying a lovely tray of assorted cookies. She sat them on my desk. A catering service would have been envious.

"Jennifer, that's a lovely arrangement."

"I made them myself. I'm actually quite good at baking."

Interesting. This was the first time I had known Jennifer to acknowledge her own attributes, and she did so with enthusiasm and pleasure. I looked at the tray again and recognized the traditional pattern on the Springerle, German biscuits scattered among a variety of other cookies. I picked up a multicolored cookie from the tray and asked, "What is this one called?"

"They're church cookies. I call them stained-glass windows," bragged Jennifer. Taking a cookie herself she and I indulged with some pleasure.

Our session was longer than normal that day. We discussed issues related to boundaries and security.

"Dr. Carla, could you make my next appointment in the morning?"

"That can be arranged, but why are you asking?"

"I have a doctor's appointment the same day." She immediately picked up a black stone from the basket. An unusual choice for her. She looked around at the office. "I like your new office," she said, being socially polite. "Did you add some new plants?"

"As a matter of fact, I did." Her body language was uptight and tense. "What is your doctor's appointment about?"

"I want to get a work permit. Some of the girls said it would be a good idea. Get us out of the house when summer comes. I know Mother wants the doctor to give me a drug test."

"Are you using drugs, Jennifer?"

"No. You know something, Dr. Carla, if I was using, I would tell you. I have always been straight with you." She sat forward in her chair, almost aggressively. "Do you know that? Do you believe me?"

"Yes, Jennifer, I do know that about us."

"A lot of athletes don't use drugs," she said. "Because they want to play the game, some scholarships make that possible. I don't use because I know what my IQ is and I have no intentions of frying my brain."

Undoubtedly, she had her priorities straight. "You're apprehensive about the doctor's appointment, why is that?"

Jennifer moved around uneasy in her seat.

"What all does the doctor do when you go for the exam?"

"Regarding a work permit, I'd say it's pretty routine: check your heart, blood pressure, eyes, you know, 'open wide.'"

Her hands tightened down on the black stone as she reached for the pink stone in the basket. She held one stone in each hand. Obviously, my terminology had triggered a response.

"Does the doctor do that thing?" She was squinting her eyes, making creases on her forehead.

"What thing?" asked Dr. Carla.

"You know . . . the other thing," Jennifer said, tilting her head to the side, shy.

"You mean a pelvic exam?"

"Yeah, *that* . . . is it a part of the routine exam?" Jennifer replied.

She had turned to stare out the window. "On vacation we go to the country. My parents have a small farm there. It's safe in the woods.

The animals, rabbits and deer, they're safe there too." Her breathing had taken on a deeper, heavier rhythm, making her heart pound faster in her chest.

How strange. It was as though her clothing had taken on the qualities of stiff cardboard—something she could hide behind: not at all representative of the soft pastel sweater she was wearing.

She continued, "There are no people there to hurt you."

"Is that right, Jennifer?" My interest was piqued. I leaned forward.

"That's right, I can just be me," Jennifer responded softly.

"When someone comes to hurt you, who are you then?"

There was a long silence. Out of her mouth, a male voice announced his presence: "I'm going to take care of this one day."

"Who are you?"

"Aaron," said the male voice coming from Jennifer.

I remembered once Jennifer let me read a short story she had written for her English creative writing class. It related to futuristic space travel, and a character named Aaron was the protector.

"I'm Aaron, I want to speak to you."

Jennifer sat completely still. All of her body except her eyes faced the window. Her eyes watched me.

"Aaron?" I whispered.

"Yes."

"I want you to tell me who hurts Jennifer."

"The changeling," Aaron said with caution.

"And that would be the one that becomes . . . someone other than themselves?"

"Yes."

"Who is the changeling?" I asked.

"Her father. He's been doing it for years." Aaron grimaced at the apparent thought.

"What does he do?" I laid my pin down on the desk.

"He sneaks in at night and gets in her bed. Sometimes he holds his heavy hand across her face. I really am going to kill him. I'll have a plan, a way to do it."

"Do you have a plan now?" I asked.

"No, that will take time. I want it to be clever. He's deserving of that. I want to take my time and enjoy the process."

"Aaron, do you know I'm here to help Jennifer?" I folded my hands.

"Yes, we know," Aaron responded.

"Who else have you told about this?" I asked.

A steely cold look came across Jennifer's face. She threw back her head and laughed. "Now, Doc, that's a real classic for you . . . oh yes, you're going to love this one. She told her mother, good old Mrs. Community-Minded, but she couldn't have her world messed up like that now, could she? It got really ugly. Her mother wounded her."

"How did she wound her?"

"She heard Jennifer's words, as though they were spears driven into the flesh of her king."

The raspy voice of Aaron took on a sinister tone of laughter as he said, "Hear ye, hear ye, good citizens of the realm. What say ye be the status of a queen without a king? Jennifer's mother saw herself tumbling down from her coveted royal pedestal. She became enraged, striking out, slapping Jennifer in the face. Pushing her backward as though she were a vile creature not worthy of being in her presence." Aaron paused. "You know, Doc, unseen scars of physical trauma linger on in all of us. What we hide behind, so others will not see, becomes the fiber of our being."

I could sense, feel, taste the strong, thick bitter bile of Aaron's raw, unchained power. A holy man performing an exorcism would have his work cut out with this one. I recognized the essence of what Aaron could be truly terrifying.

"That confrontation was years ago," he said. "Now Jennifer's concerned, worried . . . frightened."

"What is she frightened about now?"

"Her younger sister, Caroline, we know the changeling is going to go there one day. That's when I'm going to have to take care of him."

"Aaron, I want you to promise you won't do anything to Jennifer's father without talking to me first. Can you do that, Aaron? Promise me, okay?"

The raspy voice replied, "You got it, Doc."

"When you formulate a plan, you will tell me," I firmly demanded.

"When that day comes, Doc, I will tell you. You know Jennifer loved your house. She was safe there," Aaron remarked.

I couldn't have heard him correctly. "Whose house?"

"The gold locket. She lost in the attic. Looked and looked but never found it. They had given it to her. Had some very special symbols put inside, just for her." Aaron smiled.

I felt like Jennifer wasn't the only one in my office in need of help. This couldn't be happening to me. Could he be talking about the locket Maria had found.

Jennifer stared at the lamp on my desk. The two stones that had been in her hands were now back in the basket on my desk. Her hands were moving back and forth on the arms of the chair. The deep monotone voice of Aaron continued, "It felt so cold and smooth."

"What was cold and smooth?" I was confused. My mind was still in the attic where the gold locket had been found.

"The table with the marble top that sits in the kitchen. The cookie dough rolled out really nice on it," Aaron continued.

Was I dreaming? This had gone beyond bizarre. "What are you talking about? How do you know about the marble tabletop in my kitchen?"

"The professor's wife taught Jennifer how to make cookies on that table. Lots and lots of Christmas cookies. They sang 'Silent Night' in German. Erika, the professor's wife, taught Jennifer German."

My mind was now racing in directions I previously had not contemplated. I couldn't recall anything in her paperwork indicating that she ever spoke German. Spanish, yes, and a class in Chinese, but not German. The professor's wife wasn't the only one who had taken an interest in Jennifer.

"Jennifer's aptitude and love of science came from the professor, didn't it?"

The gruff voice raised an octave. "That's her secret. It will always be her secret."

My mind was having difficulty wrapping itself around what I was hearing. This was like being caught up in a swirling vortex. "Why does it have to be a secret?"

The voice became soft, reflective. "You don't understand. She never had anything that was her own. She couldn't have a diary to journal her own thoughts. She didn't have any privacy—school papers and even phone calls were monitored on the extension."

In the distance, I could hear church bells ringing the hour. Jennifer sat abruptly upright and looked about the room as though she was searching for something, then cocked her head to listen more closely.

"What are you looking . . . listening for?"

"Numbers? . . . numbers? . . . letters jumbled, tumbled, and they all fall down." Her body slumped backward into the chair, apparently exhausted.

Long before its time, the innocent part of her being had been violated. Like a premature baby comes into the world before it is ready, the precious undeveloped time was taken from her, stripped away. Erika and the professor were hers. They fed her soul. I nearly fell out of my chair. Talk about the lights going on in Vegas.

"Jennifer . . . Jennifer?"

She looked up at the ceiling, then at her hands, finally meeting my eyes.

Marcy opened the door slightly, saying apologetically, "It's about Jason. The university is on the line. They're having a problem. They want to talk to you. This is the third time they have called. They're quite insistent."

"I'll take the call." I looked directly into Jennifer's eyes, knowing she wasn't going to remember anything about what she had told me. "Jennifer, what's the name of that doctor you're going to see?"

She cleared her throat. "Dr. Towner."

"I'll check out some things for you about this appointment." Towner was the family doctor, and I had signed a release for information in my file. We had collaborated on cases before. "Wait in the waiting room for me. I'll be able to have more information for you, and in just a minute

I'll have you come back in, okay?" This would give me time to unravel my brain and establish a plan on how to proceed.

"Okay." Jennifer hesitated at the door. Turning back to me, she said, "You know Jason is his own worst enemy, right? The other kids don't understand him, but he doesn't understand himself half the time. The others make him feel like an outcast because he's different. They all live in their own made-up worlds, so how different is he, really? I like him." She had said it to me as though I should understand her approval sanctioned his rite of passage. She continued, "I understand why Jason doesn't like to take his medication. It changes him, and then he thinks he isn't who he really is."

"That's an interesting observation. Tell me, Jennifer, how does the medication change Jason? Who is he really?"

Looking toward the window, Jennifer appeared to be thinking. Silence filled the room, and just when I began to believe Jennifer wasn't going to answer, she turned and looked at me.

"I understand," she said, "that the medication is in his best interest. It helps him make better decisions, and it balances his emotions. But when he speaks, his words sputter out like a kitten that can only mew when it wants so desperately to roar like a lion." Without another word, she went into the waiting room and left me in my chair to ponder the teenage boy who wanted to feel the onset of manhood.

Marcy handed Jason's file to me and cleared her throat.

"I know, Marcy. This morning is starting off a little rough, but look at it this way: its job security."

She gave me a half-hearted chuckle and said, "That's what I've always liked about you, Carla, your inconsistency in the face of reality. I'll give it to you though, you are one tough gal in the trenches."

I picked up the phone to take the university's call. It was Leah, Jason's counselor. Jason had attempted to forge a medical note of excuse in order to get back into classes. At this point he was in the dean's office. His mother had recently changed jobs, and Jason wouldn't or couldn't remember the name of the company where she worked. Leah wanted to know if I had updated material so she could contact his mother. Jason's probation officer somehow had gotten information regarding his creative forgery on a doctor's prescription pad and was on his way. Ironically, the note somehow had disappeared, and Jason was claiming no knowledge of its existence. I gave Leah the phone number and assured her we would connect later in the afternoon so she could bring me up to date on the details of Jason's tiptoeing through the fields of psychic anarchy.

The university had more than once gone out of their way to help Jason. Leah was prepared to tell his probation officer there wasn't a problem. Jason's psychology professor found him to be an interesting study and had told Leah he was going to let Jason back in class. It would be my guess that note was riding around in the professor's jacket pocket, never to be seen again.

The phone rang a few times before Dr. Towner's secretary picked up. Evidently, their office was having a busy day too.

"The doctor had an emergency," she explained. "He's not in the office. Is there anything I can help you with?"

"When do you expect him back?" I asked.

"Not until later this afternoon," responded the secretary.

At this point, my frustration barometer was off the charts. "Tell him to give me a call as soon as he returns. It's very important."

I heard the tone of utter exhaustion on the other end of the line. "I got it," she said. "Very important."

"While you're writing that down on your message pad, would you put a smiley face beside it, please? With strands of hair straight up? The look one would have if you had stuck your finger in an electrical socket."

There was laughter on the other end. "Yeah, it's nice to know you're not in this boat alone," she said. "I'll see to it that he gets the message as soon as he gets in."

I went out to the waiting room to get Jennifer, but she wasn't there. "Marcy, where is Jennifer?"

"She left. She said to tell you she was okay with everything and would call you later."

I went back to my office, picked up Jennifer's file. What had I missed? I had reviewed the file several times. I went back through the body of work then realized she had given me the answer. That day in my office before the moving men came, what had she said? "We used to live in that neighborhood, before the new house was built." I picked up the file again and went back through some of the older data. There it was: 118 Ravenswood Place. One street over from my home.

I called Jennifer's home, assuming her mother would answer. After the way things went at the office, I felt the need to speak to Jennifer. It was her father, Jack, that picked up instead.

"This is Dr. Van Doran. Is Jennifer there?"

Her father, normally Mr. Personality, was edgy. "No, she isn't, and she hasn't been here today, ran away, I suppose. We called the police and told them she's missing. They said they had a report from Children's Services." The longer he talked, the more enraged he became. Do you know what that little brat said about me? How could she do that to me? I have my reputation, my business! How do you think this is going to look? I never thought she'd tell, never thought she would do this to me . . ."

I quoted his last sentence back to him. "I never thought she'd tell, never thought she would do this to me."

There was silence on the other end. He knew he had said too much. He had said it all.

"You're twisting my words. I didn't say that . . ." Jack said desperately.

"Yes, you did. I simply repeated to you exactly what you said to me." By this time, he was screaming out of control.

"This conversation is over! Don't ever call here again!" He slammed down the receiver.

Obviously, I wasn't the only creature on the planet under stress. With the receiver still vibrating in my hand, Marcy appeared in the doorway.

"There's a Detective Connors here to see you."

"Send him in."

A very large man walked through the door with a full head of chestnut hair streaked with gray. I would say his personal view of himself was that of a dedicated, knowledgeable detective. His mannerisms were casual and confident.

"Come on in. Have a seat, Detective."

His trench coat was wet from the rain that had not stopped from the night before. He sat down and folded up a mini black umbrella that looked like it could not have done little more than cover his head. He looked around as though he wanted to place the umbrella on the desk but must have thought it would be inappropriate.

"Go ahead," I said. "This desk is well seasoned. It's had everything from tears, soda pop, and vomit on it. A wet umbrella isn't going to hurt a thing."

A slight smile crossed his stone-serious face. Placing his umbrella on the desk, he scooted back in the chair and was silent for a moment. His dark brown eyes darted quickly around the room. Like a man that looks at a woman, in a split second he recognizes her as a woman. The detective had just conducted a rapid cognition known as thin slicing.

"I like your style," he said. "You're direct."

Marcy entered the room with two cups of coffee. "Do you take cream or sugar?" she asked.

Looking somewhat impressed at the prompt arrival, he said, "Black's fine, thank you."

Marcy came around my desk and leaned over. The scent of her rose perfume hung lightly in the air as she whispered in my ear, "Would it be all right to offer doughnuts?"

I laughed out loud. "Yes, Marcy, that would be fine. Thank you."

She left the office. By then, Detective Connors was giving me the body language and look that said *What was that about?*

"Trust me, Detective, it will all become clear in just a few moments."

He took a sip. "Good coffee." Relishing his cup, he then got out his notepad.

About that time, Marcy returned with the most sinfully delicious plate of assorted doughnuts.

Connors took one look at the doughnut tray then laughed. "Okay, I got it. Marcy, you're really a good girl."

"Forget it, Connors. She's in my will," I said.

We exchanged what information we could regarding Jennifer's Children's Services abuse case. Detective Connors said he would check back with me later. I did my own thin slicing with Detective Connors. Sizing him up wasn't hard. He was in the right profession. He had the personality, experience, and most importantly, he had not lost his compassion.

Chapter 13

When I got back from lunch, I checked my voice mail. Richard had made reservations at one of our favorite restaurants. Sarah and Ben would be joining us. Dinner and a few drinks after the week I'd had definitely sounded like a good idea.

The Italian restaurant where Richard, my ex-fiancé, and I were to meet Sarah and Ben resided in an older part of town. The warm evening had brought people out to sit on the stoop and talk to their neighbors, while children played on the sidewalks.

As we sat at our table, Sarah's voice resounded with excitement. "Guess what? Ben is starting up his own consulting business. He's been working on it for over a year. Now it's really going to happen."

Richard was quick to praise Ben's endeavors. Sarah went on to explain all the new horizons and possibilities that would be opened for Ben to explore.

"This calls for champagne," Richard said, summoning the waiter.

Suddenly, Sarah leaned forward in her chair. "Carla, that man at the table in the corner, do you know him? The one in the leather jacket. He keeps looking over here."

I glanced over. "No, he doesn't look familiar to me."

Realizing I was paying more attention to my champagne than to the question at hand, Richard turned to look and quickly turned back around.

"You know him, Richard?" I asked.

"No, never saw the guy before. Though it's understandable that the man would look at this table, considering the two lovely ladies sitting here."

Sarah raised her glass. "I'll drink to that."

When acquaintances of Sarah and Ben's joined us, Richard excused himself to make a phone call. Sarah carried the conversation quite well, basking in the pleasures of Ben's entrepreneurship. I took the opportunity to go to the restroom and freshen my makeup.

The powder room provided a red satin-covered settee and a large gold-framed mirror. The room was decorated to reflect the era of the speakeasies, flapper girls and their stylish bobbed haircuts and ruby-red lips.

I stood up and noticed through the slightly opened window elongated, shadowy reflections of two men silhouetted against the building next door. I walked over to the window and looked down to the alley below. Garbage cans lined the brick wall.

Two men stood at the bottom stairs of the restaurant. A slight breeze ushered in the aroma of steaks sizzling on the grill. Light shining from the open back door of the restaurant clearly revealed it was Richard and the man in the leather jacket.

What are they doing down there? Before my mind could formulate a logical response, the man took a swing at Richard. In one swift movement, Richard stepped back, deflected the blow, stepped behind the man, and held him by the neck until his body went limp. Mr. Leather Jacket slumped to the ground.

Two harvest-moon-illuminated eyes peered out from between the garbage cans. An arched-back cat stealthily stepped forward, the only apparent witness. Somewhere in the distance the sound of the ancient city groaned on under the weight of evolution and man's crippled humanity. The shadowy figures appeared more grotesque than before, with Richard dragging his prey to the back stairs. He laid the man's head on the staircase. How convenient for the coroner.

As I tried to catch my breath, my stomach muscles tightened. A corset from Queen Elizabeth's day could not have been more restrictive. I hurried back to the dining room and took my seat. Richard entered the dining room, passing by the table where the man had sat. He didn't even look down at the half-empty wineglass or food remaining on his opponent's plate.

As he approached our table, Ben asked, "Did you get a hold of the man you were trying to reach, Richard?"

"Yes, I got a hold of him. Final arrangements with the gardener," Richard affirmed.

Ben had an admiring tone in his voice. "Richard, you're always prepared ahead of time. No doubt that is what has made you the successful attorney you are."

Richard didn't miss a beat. His voice and mannerisms presented as energized and engaging. "Times are always good with old friends who truly know us," he said as he motioned for the waiter to bring another bottle of champagne. He raised his glass. "To Ben, Man of the Year."

Our champagne glasses clinked together with a high-pitched, clear ring, as if the glasses themselves, in some symbolic way, wanted to clean the air from the event of evil that had invisibly surrounded us. Richard had always been good at theatrics, timing, communications, and setting the mood. I just hadn't realized the extent to which he had mastered the art.

***

On Saturday I took my morning run earlier than usual. I had lain in bed awake. Visions of Friday night's dinner with Richard kept running through my head. Unfortunately, the fresh air and exercise did little to calm my frayed nerves. I could call Sarah and tell her what happened in the alley, tell her everything, but what good would that do? The only thing I knew was Richard was involved in something dark and sinister. Sarah would insist that I break it off with Richard. She would tell me this whole thing was just too dangerous, and she would be right. Involving Sarah would only be releasing some of my own stress and anxiety. I couldn't stop seeing Richard. Frightening as he was, he was still the only connection I had to what happened to Colette.

After my run, I was downing my second cup of coffee when the phone rang. I looked down at the caller ID: it was Dr. Mel Towner, Jennifer's doctor.

"Good morning, Mel. Do you have some news about Jennifer?"

"Carla, the next time your message says 'call right away,' I'll remember to do that. Jennifer's mother was concerned about some health issues; it was just to have been a routine examination. Some things came up that I thought Children's Services should be aware of. The caseworker said she had already heard from you. Jennifer told my receptionist she needed to go to the car to pick up something. I guess we should have known better. We don't know where she is."

"Don't beat yourself up too much, Mel. She pulled the same car scam on me earlier." I realized, however this played itself out, it wasn't going to be easy for anyone. Lives would be changed. "Thanks for the call. If I hear anything, I'll let you know."

I put some rye bread in the toaster. Such an ordinary thing to do. What had happened to my ordinary life, the one real people live? Schedules, routine, oh, for the days of boring. I would've given anything to have those days back.

If the hand of evil had reached out for Colette at the top of the stairs, I would see her vindicated. Richard was frightening me in ways I could never have imagined. Not only was he not the man I thought he was, but also he was the only possible link I had to find the truth about what really happened to Colette. As treacherous and unorthodox as it was, he remained my only road map. I realized I'd returned to the house as though it were a cave, a place to hibernate and let the chaotic world pass by.

Chapter 14

Sunday morning, I went downstairs. The sunlight streaming through the kitchen window greeted me. Dressed in cotton pajamas and fuzzy pink slippers, I got cream cheese out of the refrigerator and popped a bagel into the toaster. The coffeepot stood ready like a good soldier. Hearing a soft tapping on the kitchen door, I opened it to find Detective Connors and invited him in. Naturally, I was looking at him with more than a little interest and curiosity considering the early hour.

"I was in the neighborhood. Just thought I would stop in."

"Right, of course you were."

He only smiled and nodded. Kinsey came up to Connors like he was a long-lost friend. Conner bent down, patted him on his head. "Coffee smells good," he said as he looked toward the kitchen table. "No doughnuts?"

"We'll be having bagels this morning," I replied, handing him a plate of bagels.

In a most matter-of-fact way, Connors made it quite clear he knew who my male acquaintances were. It wasn't Daniel, the newest person in my life, that seemed to interest him. It was Richard. Connors presented himself in such a relaxed manner I could hardly take offense. I watched Connors and thought how strange it was. We hadn't known each other long, but it was as though he had been my friend for a very long time. There are times when things go between people, things that aren't said, but they are there and understood. That was exactly how I felt about Connors.

"Carla, when I first came to your office, I saw the picture of you and Colette on your bookcase and knew that you knew her, that you had to have felt the loss. What else you knew or didn't know at that point was a mystery. I was there regarding Jennifer, your client. I didn't know you. There wasn't any way to approach the subject of Colette. I needed to know more about you and the people around you. I got ahold of some of my old military contacts. Technology sped up the process. Richard definitely has networking powers that are unique, to say the least."

I poured him a cup of coffee and sat a toasted bagel on the plate in front of him. I could feel the rhythm of his energy pattern like an identifiable signature, steady and strong. Connors was built like a football player, a fullback. The kind of guy you want running interference for you. Something had drawn him to this particular case, but without a doubt he had his own reasons and hidden agenda.

"Do you find yourself working long hours often?" I asked.

He looked up from the cream cheese he was putting on his bagel. "Not unless it's a pretty interesting case."

"What kind of cases do you find pretty interesting? As in, what brings you to my door this early in the morning?"

A broad, easy smile came across his lips. He relaxed back into his chair. "The good Dr. Carla would analyze me, would she?"

Without realizing it, that was exactly what I was doing. I felt like a sleepwalker caught with her hand in the cookie jar. I could feel the heat from my own embarrassment.

"I'm sorry. I apologize. Can we chalk that one up to social inapt occupational hazard?"

His laughter was robust. "Yes," he said, "I needed that. Like a jolt of strong java, quick and to the veins. I don't usually get that kind of honest, rapid response this early in the morning. "I understand completely. Trust me, I truly do. Without realizing it, I have found myself interrogating my friends on occasion. Real eye-opener, isn't it? You know, Carla, at times our occupations are not so different. It's only in degrees. We extract information. The velvet glove and the anvil." He sat studying me for a moment. "Okay," he said. "Now it's my turn. Carla, how did you meet Richard?"

I thought back to that day when I saw a very handsome man come into the room.

"Richard and I met at the courthouse. I was there as guardian ad litem representing three young children. Their parents were going through a nasty divorce, and custody issue had gotten quite heated. I was waiting in one of the witness rooms when Richard came in. I was sitting at the table reviewing my notes, and he asked if he could use the other end of the table to review some of his case notes. We got to talking, and it all went from there.

"I thought you would have asked me about Daniel. I haven't overlooked the fact that you deflected and didn't answer my question. Without doubt I know we connect, Connors. I'm as sure of that as I am that I'm sitting here. You know how and why. Are you going to share that information with me?"

"Carla," he said, "when I was sixteen, I knew three things. I liked girls, football, and I was going to be in law enforcement, just like my dad. After college, military, I applied for Homeland Security, got a job in DC."

"How did you end up here?"

"My wife's family. DC wasn't working. When I came home from work, she would ask me about my day." He laughed, but not that robust laughter he had when something tickled his funny bone. "You know the old saying," he said. "If I tell you, I'll have to kill you. Well, she didn't think that was funny. My job began to weigh heavy on my marriage. I knew she was right. I needed to dial back on the adrenaline. I'm not going to lie to you. There are days when I miss the rush, the razor's edge."

He took another sip of his coffee and then set it aside. He leaned forward and asked, "How well did you know Colette?"

"I knew her well," I said. "You're good at asking questions, Connors, but you're not answering any. How well did you know her?"

"She had one tattoo," he said, "and I know where it was."

I almost choked on my bagel. Colette and I had gone to the Caribbean for vacation. She sat on the beach in the sand. The royal Creole princess in her creamy soft light tan body. I, on the other hand, generously lathered on suntan lotion, as though I owned the factory it came out of. In the cabana while putting on her swimsuit she made mention of her tattoo, which was in a most private place. It was a small red cherry. She said she had lost a bet with her lover.

"What was the bet about, Connors?"

His eyes lit up like the Fourth of July. "We had a discussion," he said. "I told her what I was capable of. She questioned my abilities to perform the task in question. I said I could do that. She said I couldn't. I won, she lost. She loved cherry pie, so I thought it appropriate."

No doubt, he definitely knew Colette. That day at the beach was vivid in my mind. Colette had a sadness in her voice I had never heard before. "Carla," she said, "If you ever find him, that man that makes you feel that way, I'm telling you, girl, tell him you love him, and you'll never let him go." I realized later she said, "No man was going to love me like that man loved me. What I gave up . . . I went back to reclaim him but was too late. He had moved on, got married. Couldn't mess with him like that. He deserved better." I knew that was one conversation I wasn't going to share with Connors. It wouldn't have been fair to either one of them.

"Connors, Colette was my friend. Not just any everyday sunshine friends." I realized the moment the words came out of my mouth he wasn't going to understand. I didn't know how to explain the bond we shared. Connors looked at me. He knew I was struggling.

"I get you, Carla." Leaning back in his chair, with a reflective tone he said, "My dad and his longtime partner Knuckles retired from the force at the same time. Once a year they took the wives and went on vacation to Florida. Dad took his boat; Knuckles took his boat motor. The wives did well, whatever it is women do. Dad and Knuckles put the boat in the water, sat there with the fishing line dangling, six pack of beer and reminisced about some old cases they had worked on, back in the day. One thing was certain, they would always have each other's back. I get you, Carla. There is a difference in those everyday sunshine friends and the ones that are always going to be there for you no matter what."

"I miss her a lot, Connors. She had enthusiasm for life—a way of living life to its fullest. Obviously, she was more than a name on a report to you. How did you come to know her?"

"Enthusiasm for life, oh, she was all of that and more. We were both living in Washington DC at the time. That's when I met her. The Navy was doing some interesting things in those days. Some things I had been a part of earlier on. Colette was called in on a difficult case. She did some profiling for us. It was an odd set of circumstances. Things fell into place that normally wouldn't have. She ended up right in the middle of it all."

"Connors, Colette and I talked a lot, but I don't remember her mentioning anything about government work."

He continued as though I had said nothing. "I was young. She was the older woman. I was so in love with her. We had one glorious year together, but then she got a career offer. I wanted with all my being for her to stay with me, but I knew she needed to be free, to follow her dreams. She would not have been happy otherwise. There was no way I could hold her back. I had to let her go. For all her strength, she was as beautiful and fragile as a butterfly in flight."

I sat in total shock at the eloquence and openness of his unguarded moment. "Did you see her here? Did you know she was in town?"

"Yes, I knew she was in town, but what we had was many years ago. That chapter in the book was closed. I'm married now, and I have a lovely family. I left a lot of what went on in DC and the military behind me."

"Your wife, does she know about your past?"

"Kerry knows everything she needs to know. It wasn't until this happened to Colette . . . it's brought so much back. She deserved so much better than to have something like this happen to her."

"Connors, you think Colette was murdered, don't you?"

"I know she was. She was the love of my life, and the feelings a man has for his first love are always remembered with deep affection. Carla, how long have you known Richard?"

"Three years."

"I don't know what all you know, Carla. What I say to you stays between us in confidence, agreed?"

"Yes, agreed."

"To Richard, Colette was dispensable. They put her in the crosshairs. She had no idea they were at her doorstep."

I hadn't told Connors about what had happened at the restaurant. "Are you telling me Richard did this?"

"I believe the words you're looking for, my dear, are 'assassin for hire' . . . at some level, one has to admire him. He's a smooth operator."

"How do you know this, Connors?"

"That is what's interesting about the world of espionage. There is always a door that can be opened. Observe from the sidelines, Carla. Richard is going to pay for what he did to Colette."

I told Connors about what I had seen at the restaurant that night with Richard.

"Then you know what he's capable of," he replied. "You can't walk away from this, you're in too deep. You need to be careful, *very* careful, of this man. He must never know that you suspect him. He is not a novice at putting things aside that get in his way. Be a good actress, Carla, your life may depend on it."

Connors stood, walked over to the kitchen counter, and brought back the coffeepot to pour both of us another cup. When he returned the pot, he bumped it against the countertop.

"Oops. Looks like I spilled a bit. Let me just get that." He took a dishcloth from the rack and wiped up the few drops. *What's this? He's domestic too?* Well, some women just get the good ones.

When he returned to the table, it was my turn. "Okay, Connors, what about Daniel?"

"We're all lethal . . . . soldiers in plain clothes . . . we are talking degrees here, levels of consciousness. It's life, isn't it . . . gray areas. We all get pushed up to the line. The question is, where is the line? Daniel, he's like a good German shepherd. You can put him on the battlefield and then take him home for some R&R with the family. He doesn't devour his own."

"That's some kind of a metaphor, Connors."

He laughed. "Right, but very accurate. Make no mistakes, Carla. Richard is a smooth operator and a cunning, ambitious man. My mother was a nurse. I can remember her saying the only thing she would have changed about her life was her education. She would've loved to have been a psychologist. With a husband on the police force, four kids, two dogs, a cat, and a bowl full of goldfish, I guess there just wasn't time enough for all her dreams." He took another drink of his coffee. "Everything she did, she did well. She was energetic and independent, just like you. Do you know what the hardest thing for that woman to do was?"

"No, what was that?"

"To ask for help . . . yes, I will step across that line for you, Carla. I also know for you to have reached out, to have confided in me, you must be at your rope's end. Now we both know what the other one wants: Richard's conviction for Colette's murder. We must have the evidence, and working together, the time will come. We'll get him, I promise you." Kinsey was lying beside Connors. He looked down. "Well, old boy, it's time for me to head out."

We said our goodbyes at the kitchen door. He reached out, took my hand in a gesture of honor. Words weren't necessary. I had not misjudged him.

After Connors left, I took our dishes to the kitchen sink, picked up the dishcloth, and underneath lay a small revolver. I guess the man had said all he needed to say. I turned off my phone and spent the rest of the day in my pajamas watching movies on TV and drinking Bloody Marys. It was the perfect escape plan for a brain left under the broiler too long.

Chapter 15

Jennifer pulled into the driveway, her mother's car just ahead of her. The door to the back seat was open and there was a grocery sack, so she picked it up and walked toward the house. *What am I going to say to her?* Jennifer just wanted to talk, to explain what happened at the doctor's office. This had to come out, what her dad had done to her. Jennifer knew her mom was going to be upset with her, but he needed to be exposed for Caroline, her mother, and her own sake. What a time for her to have a blinding headache. She felt they had been coming more often now. Too much tension, that's all it was.

Odd, the house was dark. No lights except for the light in the refrigerator door and one nightlight on the wall by the kitchen sink. The pale gray light in the room made objects hardly visible. On the floor was a cookbook and a large broken pot of herbs. Its contents were scattered about. Jennifer put the groceries down at the end of the butcher-block island in the center of the kitchen. *The house is so quiet. Where is everyone?* She walked around the center island and stumbled over something. *What in the world is that?* Jennifer turned on the overhead lights. The bright razor-sharp lighting did not cast shadows but illuminated detailed images of the disjointed array of objects.

Knives were scattered across the island, produce was on the floor, and a glass bottle of salad dressing was broken and dripping down the side of the counter. Jennifer looked down, and there were her footprints on the floor—in *blood*. What a perfectly clear print; how very bizarre. Jennifer put her hand down on the counter to steady herself. Under Jennifer's hand was a knife, covered in blood. *This can't be happening. It can't be real. It has to be like the numbers and letters. If Jennifer closed her eyes and looked away, when she opened them again, this chaos would be gone.* The scene of her mother on the floor with deep slashes across her throat, as though the assailant had meant to decapitate her head from her body. *It will all be gone.* Jennifer opened her eyes, but the scene remained the same.

As she stood there in her mother's blood, Jennifer would have given anything to see the symbols and numbers instead of what she was looking at. All her mother's imperfections seemed so trivial now, so unimportant. Who could have done this? Tiffani was right. She should have told someone about that Jeep. According to forensic evidence, she would be the murderer. No one would believe her. Dr. Carla would believe her. Jennifer knew she had always been straight with her. What had she told her? Had she said anything that would incriminate herself, make her look like she could be guilty? Surely no one would believe such a thing. Jennifer should call the police—but no, what if they didn't believe her? She needed a place to hide—somewhere safe. Jennifer always felt safe in the professor's house, but Dr. Carla lived there now. She had to get out of there and find a safe place. Jennifer needed to wipe away her footprints and any other evidence that she was ever here.

Caroline is at her girlfriend's house. Dad is at the country club. Panic stole her breath. *Are those footsteps she heard? What if she was not in this house alone?* Jennifer could feel someone's presence. What if they were watching her? *Are they watching now?* She picked up the knife and walked to the back door. The house was unnervingly quiet.

***

Jennifer endlessly drove down one street and then another, one country road after another, but she couldn't get that scene in the kitchen out of her mind, couldn't stop seeing it. She wanted to tell Dr. Carla everything, but how could she? Jennifer couldn't believe that horrifying sight; how could she put it into words? She just couldn't. She would hide the car and go to Dr. Carla's house. Jennifer remembered that the basement window never did lock well. She could get in and stay there until morning.

The house looked the same to her, but someone had fixed the window lock. Jennifer forced it just a little, and the breaking sound of glass shattered the silence of the night. She heard something coming down the street. *Oh no, it's a police car.* A raspy voice screamed in her ears: *Run . . . run . . . run!*

Friday 1:30 AM

Jason turned in his bed half asleep as he heard the sound of tapping, again and again. His mind jumped to alertness. *That's an SOS.* Where was it coming from? He sat straight up in bed, and his eyes searched the bedroom. *There, at the window.* Jason tried to focus and make sense of the human form. *Who is that out there, standing in the moonlight? It's Jennifer!* His feet hit the floor, heart pounding, and raced down the hallway to the back door. She came into view as he ran around the side of the house.

"Jennifer? Jen?" He could tell something was wrong. She acted like a rag doll, limp and unresponsive. Jason put his arms around her—she was cold, wet, and shaking. "What happened? Jen, tell me, what is it?"

She buried her head in Jason's chest, her voice hardly audible in a choked, hysterical whisper.

"I tried to make things right. It isn't ever going to be better now, not with any of them. We've got to leave, Jason, tonight. Right now. Is the truck ready? You promised me it would be ready . . ."

Jason could see whatever battle had been fought had left the little general in devastating retreat. "Yes, everything is ready . . ."

Jennifer stood there staring at him as though her mind and body had frozen in time. "I want to go. I want to go *now*, Jason."

"Jennifer, you had an agenda. Your timetable may have changed, but the preparations are still in place. You can't go anywhere like this."

He gestured at her, soaked and trembling. He took her hand. "Come on, we need to get you some dry clothes."

Back inside, Jason sat Jennifer on his bed and went to his closet to pull out a T-shirt, a hoodie, and a pair of blue jeans. She put them on, and Jason bent down and rolled up the legs of the jeans for her. Jennifer stood there before the mirror. The borrowed outfit made her look like a child playing pretend in her big brother's clothes. Jason smiled. She looked at him, then back at her reflection. A slight smile crossed her lips as tears trickled down her cheeks. Jason turned Jennifer toward him and dried her tears. She sat back down on his bed. Jason picked up his backpack and sat it beside her.

"Here, you can look through these while I get ready."

She opened the backpack and looked inside. There were all kinds of things in there, things she could see would be useful. Yes, Jason was resourceful. She watched him as he went over to the gun cabinet, unlocked the drawer at the bottom, and took out a handgun and a couple of boxes of ammo. He sat down beside her and put the gun and ammo in the backpack. Their eyes met, and she nodded in acceptance, no longer rejecting the idea. Jason moved over to the desk and wrote a note: *Mom, I have something I need to do for a friend. The need is real and urgent. I promise you I will be all right. Don't worry. As soon as things are settled, I'll contact you. Love, Jason.*

In the still of the moonlit night, his shiny red pickup truck sped along the highway, driving west.

Chapter 16

Friday morning had become a blur of clients, paperwork, and a report to Children's Services of abuse. Sarah came into my office with two cups of coffee.

"It's time for a coffee break," she announced.

"Odd, you don't look like a St. Bernard, but you know something, Sarah, I love you just the same. You have rescued me from this mound of, dare I say, insanity. I feel like I've been buried alive."

With a smile and nod of her head, she said, "Yes, your trusty champion has come with the elixir of the blessed grain."

"Sarah, this summer coffee breaks will be in the serenity garden. The idea you had for the waterfall sounds really great."

She relaxed back into the chair and lifted her coffee cup. "To the serenity garden. May it be outside, not free-flowing inside like the old office was."

"What do you mean?" asked Carla.

"Didn't you hear about the building?" said Sarah.

"No, I didn't hear anything. What about the building?"

"Right after we pulled out on Thursday, just before noon, they had a water break in one of the lines, and they shut down everything. Everyone had to go home."

"Everyone?" repeated Carla.

"That's right, everyone had the rest of the day off."

Sarah changed the subject to our plans for lawn furniture, but she was like a commercial on television—I had tuned her out. I was engaged in my own thoughts. Daniel had said he got my new address Thursday afternoon, but there wouldn't have been anyone there to give him my new address. Sarah and I finished our discussion about the serenity garden and went back to work.

***

At lunchtime Marcy opened the door and gave me a look over her half-rimmed glasses that said, in her professional Marcy fashion, *now.*

"John Clifton's wife is in the outer office with the children."

"Okay, send her in." I put my papers aside, remembering the first time I saw John. He walked into my office, a striking figure of a man, six foot three. He had come back from Iraq and was being deployed to Afghanistan. His wife Ashley was pregnant with their second child.

"I'm really concerned about her," he had said. "She is emotionally fragile, and I'm going to be so far away. I need to know she's getting professional help."

I saw Ashley every other week while John was gone. Upon his return, her panic attacks became less frequent. They had settled into a stable family life.

"Good morning, Ashley." She was alone. Marcy had evidently opted to take eight-month-old Scotty and was entertaining Brad, the five-year-old. Ashley approached my desk and stood there wide-eyed and visibly shaken. "Would you like to sit down?" I offered.

She put the handbag she had been clutching to her on my desk and retrieved from it a semiautomatic pistol.

I was shocked but knew to remain calm. "Is that gun loaded?"

Her speech pattern was shaky and rapid. "Loaded?" she repeated, almost oblivious to my comment as she looked down at her shaking hands.

"I ask merely because you're pointing it at me. May I suggest you point the gun in another direction? Or better yet, how about just putting it down?"

She laid the gun down on the desk and then sank into the chair, visibly exhausted.

"I had the baby with me when I went to pick up Brad from kindergarten. By the time we got back, the house was dark, and all the blinds were closed. John had rearranged the furniture. He had put our couch in front of the door to barricade himself in. Dr. Carla, he has been acting strangely all week . . . . is this . . . PTSD?"

"Post-traumatic stress disorder," I told her, in hopes the actual words would add some clarity.

She continued, "Troy was John's buddy in Afghanistan. I called him, and he left his work and came right out to the house. He's with him now." She choked up, and tears ran down her face.

"What is frightening you, Ashley?"

She took a deep breath. "Sometimes I think he doesn't know where he is. Worst of all, I can see it in his eyes, that blank look. He doesn't recognize us, and that really scares me. We have two small children. He gets things mixed up."

"What things does he get mixed up?"

"He tells me that I shouldn't come here anymore. That your receptionist, Marcy, is a terrorist, a double agent. Dr. Carla, I think he did some really bad things over there. He talks in his sleep." She buried her face in her hands and began to sob.

"I'll take care of this, Ashley. You and the children will be safe. I'll contact the Veterans Hospital now. I know a doctor there. He can give John an assessment. If it's necessary, he will get him admitted."

"Dr. Carla, how long is he going to be like this? Is he ever going to get better?"

"Ashley, it may take some time. How are you feeling about that?"

"When he was over there, I was terrified. The last time he came home I thought it was over, and we could get on with our lives." She sat quietly. A curtain of silence hung its dark vapors.

I knew John had been deployed three times. During his service, there were extended periods of time that Ashley wouldn't hear from John, as though he had dropped off the radar. Tears streamed down her pale, stricken face.

"Fear lived in my stomach every day he was gone, fear that I would lose him forever. And now it's like he never came back. He's still over there."

Ashley waited while I made a call to Dr. Allen Leve and gave him the particulars. He said he'd take care of things and get back to me later. Then we made a plan: Ashley was going to take the children to her mother's and wait there until she heard from Troy. When she left my office, she appeared calmer and less traumatized.

Chapter 17

In my business, we help people resolve their problems. However, like the shoe cobbler's children, we oftentimes neglect our own. Some of my issues had begun to claw themselves to the surface. I found myself pacing around the office like a caged lioness. The inner voice, the intuition that sits just below the surface of our awareness, was nagging at every fiber of my being. For me, the only way to deal with it was to set the things of the world aside and let it come. Whatever it was would make itself known.

I called out to the front desk, "Marcy, no more phone calls for the next hour, please."

I heard a moment's silence on the other end.

"I don't have anything stronger than coffee, but I do have eclairs?"

"No thanks, the brain and nervous system haven't totally melted down. Just need some meditative time."

"I understand," she said, and I knew she did. I pushed the papers on my desk away from me—a subconscious, subliminal gesture of putting the world aside. I closed my eyes and let go of the present. My body became a sponge, absorbing the yellow light of energy. Upward, lighter and lighter. The minutes drifted away. I had a vision of myself sitting on a bench in a park. The grass so green. An older couple hand in hand strolled by, then a toddler with a new puppy. The park was old, historic in its beauty. I knew where it was. A relatively small area of the city referred to as Germantown. Red brick houses with lovely gardens hidden behind stone walls. Restaurants, small businesses, classic boutiques, and a bookstore at 1347 Strosenstein Street. What did it all mean? I wrote down the address and looked at my watch: 10:05 AM. It would take approximately forty-five minutes to get to my destination. I had Marcy reschedule my day's appointments. "I'll be back by five o'clock," I told her and then headed for the city.

***

The streets of Germantown were narrow and paved in brick. The historical society had been vigilant in their endeavor to preserve the heritage of the area. Tall trees lined the streets, flower boxes hung from windows, and wrought-iron fences framed manicured lawns. I pulled up across the street from the park, got out, and walked through the park. It was just a matter of finding the bench, and within a few minutes I was sitting on it, basking in the sun's heat. The birds in the treetops flitted from branch to branch, their rhythmic songs overlapping one another. On the tips of feathered wings, they invoked the ancient promise of spring. I watched the action unfold in front of me, just like it had when I sat in my chair at the office.

Across from the park was one of those quaint little establishments: a bookstore and gift shop. They offered a variety of coffees, a couch, and a few comfortable chairs. Local people stopped in to socialize. Maybe there was more information there than a GPS would give me.

The bell over the door rang as I entered the bookstore. A small, older lady with glasses that hung on a chain around her neck looked up.

"Good morning. Anything I can help you with?"

"As a matter of fact, there is. I'm looking for an address, Strosenstein Street."

"Oh yes, I know exactly where that is. It's really not far." She took a piece of paper from beside the cash register.

She drew a map for me and then pointed at a spot with her eraser. "You're here. That street will get you there." With obvious pride she went on, "I'm third generation here. Not much I don't know about this place."

The atmosphere was warm and welcoming, but I had all the information I needed for the time being. I thanked her for her help, and the door jingled as I left. Back at the car, her crystal-blue eyes were still with me. The stability of her life, the emotional foundation she stood on was so obvious. I thought of some of my clients. Had they had her consistency in their lives, I'd be out of business.

She was right. Strosenstein was just a few minutes away from the bookstore. Who lived there? If someone answered the door, what was I going to say? Who was I, a realtor looking for a new listing? What if it was someone I knew? As I walked up to the front door, my hands began to perspire. I rang the doorbell, but there was no answer. Mail was sticking in the mail drop in the door. I could just pull it out and look at the name. How much time do you get in federal prison for tampering with the United States Post Office? Oh well, I wasn't stealing. I was just looking. I heard my grandmother's voice in my head: *Rationalization paves the way to hell.* Yes, yes, I know.

I looked around. No one was on the street. I reached for the envelopes, pulled them out, and turned them over. The black typed print leaped from the starchy white envelope, scrambling down my throat, causing a loud gasp. Daniel Walters. My hands shook as I started to put the envelopes back. Wait, who was sending him mail? I looked again, but they were just utility bills, bank statements, and general advertisements. I wondered if inside he kept his wastepaper basket beside his bumbershoot stand. I doubted I would find any useful information from them, so I put all the envelopes back into the mail slot.

I walked off the front porch and could see a brick path that led around to the side of the house. I followed the path, and it brought me to a wrought-iron gate that was slightly ajar. I paused, figured there was no harm in looking, pulled it back, and walked through. The backyard was deep and long, and in it was a patio, some lawn furniture, and a grill. Broken tree branches lay across a red brick path that led to a lovely white gazebo. I sat down in one of the lawn chairs and watched as a red cardinal landed on the stone wall that surrounded the yard, granting it privacy. I looked back at the house and noticed a window was open just a crack. Daniel was out of town and not due back for some time. I got up, walked to the window, and through it I saw a laundry room that contained a washer, dryer, some shelves, and a wicker basket.

I felt an adrenaline rush and shortness of breath. I wondered if this was how thieves feel as they're about to engage in their trade. My mouth felt dry, like a cotton factory had taken up residence there. All the physical indicators of my being were telling me that I was definitely out of my element and out of my league. The window slid up with surprising ease, as though it was mocking me, daring me, or was it giving me a last chance to reconsider my amateur standing? Psychiatrist turned burglar—for some odd, comedic reason, the thought spurred me on.

I stood in the middle of the room and realized I had never in my life thought of doing such a thing, much less involve myself in the act. *What is wrong with me? What am I doing?* Whatever it was, I had to admit there was a rush. Suppose they have a magazine: *Burglars 'R' Us*. Maybe I should take out a subscription. Perhaps *Prison Pen Pals* would be more like it. Okay, now I was scaring myself. I really need to focus.

I walked down the hallway. The polished oak floors led to the kitchen. It boasted of new, modern appliances. Not a single thing was on the countertops with the exception of a coffee maker. A dining nook was to one side with windows through which I could see a bird feeder hanging from a tree branch.

The living room spoke the same language as the other rooms. They were modern and sterile in appearance. An operating room would have been proud to reside here. The rooms were purely functional, including nothing more than what was needed. No paintings graced the walls, nor books, pictures of loved ones, or magazines. It was odd for a broker and collector of antiques not to display memorabilia and cherished items. I knew there was more to this man than his cover story.

I stood at the bottom of the stairs and contemplated my level of intrusion. I had gone this far, hadn't I? It was not the time to turn back, to be weak of heart, with only half the job done. What was upstairs? The master bedroom was masculine in its appearance. In the corner on the floor was a gym bag, boots, and mountain climbing gear. On the other side of the room were air tanks and other diving equipment.

I stepped across the hall to a small office. It contained a desk with a computer and lamp on top, and a chair beside. There was a six-panel, bifold door across one wall. I opened the door, and there it was standing before me from the floor to the ceiling: a humongous safe. The floor had to have been reinforced to support its weight. Now my rational mind stepped forward. The man lived alone. Considering his occupation, he was gone from home long periods. Perhaps it would have been prudent of him not to display items of interest. Nevertheless, I found the austere interior unsettling. It was only in the master bedroom I connected with him. The feeling I got was something out of the mainstream. It wasn't as though I was looking at sports equipment. They were tools of his trade. I would walk away today with that and nothing more. At the head of the stairs, I found myself evaluating and analyzing each room that flashed before me. What was I doing? I could do this later at the office. Even an amateur burglar knew not to kick off his shoes and make himself at home.

A voice from downstairs cracked the silence. "Get back here!" came a man's commanding voice. I froze in midstride. "Come along. We don't have time for this." At the bottom of the stairs was a dog, a miniature schnauzer. I knew them to be territorial yapps. "Come on, you can go outside with me." Yappy wheeled around and followed the voice. I heard a door open and close. Taking two more steps to the landing, I looked out the window to the yard below. The voice and Yappy were in the side yard. The man was strikingly handsome with silver-white hair. He had on blue jeans and a flannel shirt; he wore a tool belt and was carrying a hammer. *If I'm ever getting out of here unnoticed, now is the time.* I sprinted for the front door, noting that I hadn't moved that fast since my college days.

I got out just in time, but then heard the gate on the side of the house clang. I looked down from the porch to see Yappy. He was looking at me barking his head off. The man in the flannel shirt and silver-white hair came up behind him, and we all looked at each other for a moment.

"Brandy, get back here." Brandy dutifully obeyed.

I fumbled for a story. "I'm . . . looking for Greta."

"No one here by that name. You must have the wrong address."

I smiled nervously. "Oh, I must have written it down wrong."

He nodded politely and watched me as I left. As I got back into my car, I was certain of one thing: I definitely wasn't going to be quitting my day job.

Chapter 18

"Last call of the day," Marcy said. "Line 1."

"Hello?"

"Carla, it's me, Allen, just doing a little follow-up with you. That case you referred to me, John Clifton, we admitted him today. He's in the Veterans Hospital now."

"I really appreciate your help, Allen. I owe you one."

"Anytime, Carla."

After hanging up, I thought about all the people and connections we make in life, how the universe plays its own music.

I pulled into the driveway and noticed I was home an hour early. No freeway to deal with made me absolutely giddy. One more hour added to my day—an hour for me to do anything I wanted to do. Devin and Kinsey met me at the door as usual, along with the sound of Latin music. Maria had stopped by to do some additional cleaning and experimental cooking. I picked up the mail from the table in the foyer and went directly to the kitchen.

Maria poured me a cup of coffee. "There is an envelope on the table for you. Richard stopped by and dropped it off. He said they were pictures of his trip. He's going to come by later." Maria sat down at the table with me, looking anxious. She always liked to see the pictures Richard took of his travels.

Richard was talented at capturing moments in people's lives, a child's look of awe, an old man's weathered face looking out at an angry sea. Such expressions he was always able to capture. It gave his photos such depth and interest.

"This looks like Bourbon Street in New Orleans," I said to Maria.

I laid down a few more of the pictures then stopped short. There was a picture of Daniel. How could that be? He was out of the country. *That's just someone that looks like him. That can't be him.* I examined the photo more closely. The man was sitting at a table with another man. Everyone around them was standing and sitting at different tables all smiling happily. One would have thought it was Mardi Gras. The two men in the center of the picture looked as though they were in negotiation for a company hostile takeover. The contrast was striking and intense. Then I saw it—a scar across the back of the man's left hand. That *was* Daniel. The whole thing was becoming more bizarre by the day. Perhaps it would be best not to say anything to Maria. I didn't want to upset her.

"I have comfort food," she announced as she pulled an apple pie out of the oven. Her cooking had character, just like some of the Latin dishes she prepared. Sometimes she would try out one of her experimental dinners on me before unleashing it on her family. She was a true artisan in the kitchen. Sometimes the tingling and stinging on the tip of the tongue, the heat that remained on one's lips, was just the right amount of an explosion of sensations, colorful and exciting.

"I would like to have a piece of that pie now, please," Carla requested.

"But it hasn't cooled," she protested.

"I don't care. I want it now."

"You're as bad as my niece and nephews. They do not want to wait either. You're going to want ice cream with that?" Maria turned to the freezer.

"Of course do you think I would want it any other way?"

"Seeing that I am a benevolent person, I can do that."

"Benevolent? I take it that is another one of your sister's new word of the day."

"Yes, do you like it?"

"Yes, it's a very good word."

Maria cut a generous portion of pie, placed it on my grandmother's china plate, the one with the deep blue floral print on a white background. She sat the plate in front of me. "You could save this till after dinner."

"I presume you're referring to that scrumptious TV dinner that's been hanging out in the freezer for the last month, and yes, I want my pie now."

Without a further word, she plopped a scoop of vanilla ice cream on top of the hot apple pie.

I took the coffee and pie à la mode to my office. A little later Maria came in. She looked at me for a moment. There she was again, fiddling with that cross around her neck. Undoubtedly, something was bothering her.

"What is it Maria?"

"I see you're worried," she said. "I think you don't sleep so good. Why you don't just let the CIA take care of this thing with Colette? I know you want to know what happened to her, but if you get too close, maybe you do uncover the truth. Maybe the truth comes here to our door, and that wouldn't be so good a thing . . . right?"

"We are going to be okay, Maria, I promise you. I would never do anything to put us in harm's way." My brain searched for better words of explanation. How was I going to explain my grief, anger, and the need to fill the empty void with something meaningful, to find closure? The thought of doing nothing for Colette was incredible. "Sometimes there are things in life we didn't see coming, Maria. We need to find a way to make sense of it all. Friendships and separations, even death itself, sometimes hold the other to a sense of loyalty, a need for justice . . . yes, even revenge."

She nodded that she understood and turned to leave the office. In a voice so soft I thought her words were meant for her alone she said, "In my country too."

From my chair, I watched the fire in the fireplace. The wood crackled and popped. I remembered all those precious moments I had spent with Colette. I had shared everything with her, things I hadn't told anyone else. She was that once-in-a-lifetime friend you feel so fortunate to have found. Her dark-brown eyes sparkled with a life of freedom unencumbered by society's rules. Her very special spirit was fierce and compassionate, loyal and steadfast. If it had been my own death that was in question, Colette would have gone to any means to secure justice. In the depths of my own heart, I knew I could do no less. My last gift to Colette: justice, a bond tethered beyond time and space. A part of her would always live within me.

Going to bed early seemed like a good idea. I stepped into the shower, and steam rose from my flesh. My tense muscles relaxed. Lavender shower gel, an infusion of ecstasy engulfed me. Suddenly feeling a sharp contrast, a rush of cold air slapped against my back. The shower door opened to my surprise. Standing there, vulnerable—now without fear. What I felt for Daniel was instinctive, what centuries of evolution had not washed away. Every particle of my being knew the deep, sensual voice that said "You're really easy, Doc. I didn't even have to pick the lock. You should be more discreet about who you invite into your shower."

Without turning around, I held up the bottle of shower gel.

"Lavender smells good," Daniel said as he reached for the bottle.

I tilted my head back and let the water run over my face and hair. I could feel the gel on his hands as he rubbed it into my back. I turned around to face him. I was the center of his universe. Lavender-soaked skin, smooth bodies moved as a choreographed script. Our love a symphony of emotion.

Chapter 19

I spent part of the next evening trying to think of a secure place to hide the sculpture. One nice thing about old houses is there are plenty of nooks and niches about to hide one's bounty. By this time, paranoia was riding on my back like a large, hairy ape. I went to the grocery store to pick up some more wine and cheese. As I stood in line at the checkout, the woman ahead of me was on her cell phone.

"Sammy, get off the phone. I'm talking to your father."

Could my phone at home be compromised? How could I find out? Connors and I had to be under the radar. I got through the checkout line and put my things in the car. *If the phone is tapped, would Richard know about that? I've known him for so long. Why didn't I notice his deflection about his past?* We had a personal relationship. My self-imposed rules about invading another's boundaries had stood in the way. I was so busy, and he was so smooth. Connors had said, "Richard must never know you suspect him." I couldn't walk away and observe from the sidelines now. If I called Richard and presented myself as the helpless damsel in distress, needing him, what would he say? More importantly, what would he do? With my professional training, years of experience, and a focused agenda, I couldn't just walk away. I pulled up Richard's number on my cell phone and hit Call. The phone rang several times. My mind raced ahead in fourteen different directions. *I must sound convincing and desperate . . . that picture of Daniel . . . I still don't have an answer to that one.*

"Hello, Richard. You're back. I'm so glad you're home. Your pictures were great. How was your trip?" *I'm not saying anything I need to say. This is coming out all wrong.* I tried again. "I don't even know where to begin. I need you, Richard. I need your help." I could feel my throat tightening up. My voice became a whisper as I strained to get the words out of my mouth. I began to think I was in over my head, but then I thought of Colette. Warm tears streamed down my face. I could taste the salt against my lips. "I think my phone at home has been tapped. I have so much to tell you. I don't know where to begin. It is all so outlandish, I don't even believe it myself, and how can I expect you to? I do have proof, evidence, I can show you. Oh, Richard, I must sound totally insane. I'm so frightened. I need you, Richard. You're the only one I can truly trust. Can you come to the house now?"

In his true, steadfast manner, I heard him say, "It's going to be okay, I promise you. Carla, you know I would believe every word you said. I'll take care of it, baby, whatever it is, I'll make things right for you. I have an investigator that does some work for me. Insurance fraud and so on. He left some of his tools of the trade at my office. I'll stop by and pick them up and come right over."

Back in the kitchen, I sat out two glasses of wine and a plate of assorted cheeses, my own sanity in question. (*Seriously, am I nuts for doing this? And my patients think* they *have problems.*) I found myself pacing around in the house like a caged animal and checking the clock every ten minutes until Richard's car pulled up. He got a small black suitcase out of the car and brought it in with him. I opened the door, and as he came in, he put his arms around me and held me tight to him. His voice was assuring, promising I would be safe. He was here. I struggled to regain my composure. "Come, let's go into the kitchen, I have some wine and cheese for us."

"It looks like we are going to need it," he said with a warm, confident smile. He sat the small suitcase down on the kitchen table.

"What's in that thing?"

"You said you thought the phones were tapped."

"Yes, it is a strong possibility."

He opened the wine bottle and poured two glasses. "You sit here, drink your wine, and give me a few minutes." He began to pull things out of the suitcase: electronic-looking gadgets of which I had no knowledge. He went over to the phone and took the receiver apart then inserted something into it. He went over the whole room with an instrument of some kind.

"Going high-tech, Richard?"

He nodded. "You could say that. I'm going to check out the rest of the house. Give me a minute or two." When he came back, he sat down at the table and leaned back with an air of accomplishment. "Carla, it doesn't appear your phones have been tapped."

I told Richard about the sculpture. He sat quiet for a moment, waiting, then, looking directly at me, said, "Is that it, Carla? Is there anything else you can remember, anything different, odd? Maybe you met a new acquaintance that somehow feels like they don't fit into the overall scheme of things?"

I saw his aura flash and spike red. Long ago, I had learned to listen to my gut and follow my instincts, even when I didn't know where it was taking me. I had planned to tell Richard about Daniel. Now I knew I wouldn't. Like threads in a fabric coming unraveled, porous, and unable to maintain its structure. This situation itself felt as though it had become unstable. Agenda or not, I felt I was in dark, uncharted water.

"Of late nothing in my entire life feels like what I expected."

"Carla, give me a few days and I'll have your answers." He didn't hesitate. It was like a proclamation of fact. His words were what I needed to hear, but for whatever reason, they rang cold and hollow.

"How can you say that, Richard, do you have a magic wand? A door to open?"

"There are always doors to open, Carla, we just have to decide which one."

"What doors are you going to open?"

Richard sat for some time looking at my face as one would a painting in an art gallery. Studying it as though he had never seen it before, studying in detail, making me feel on edge, naked.

"Carla, we are all mask wearers, all of us. The trick is knowing when and with whom to let the mask down, to show ourselves unconditionally to another person. That's truly living, experiencing life at its fullest. I'm going to share some things with you about my life."

Richard had never openly talked about his past. This was definitely a new twist for him. It was what I wanted, but what was I going to hear?

"I was an army brat. Pretty much on my own, we moved around a lot, new schools, new kids . . . I remember sitting on the steps of one of those schools at recess watching the other kids play. I felt it then: that detachment. They had all grown up together from kindergarten on. I would never have that, and once I accepted that fact, it became easier not making close friendships. It didn't hurt so much when the truck pulled away with all our belongings, waving out the back window of the car as we drove away. You look for the last glimpses of the house, the last sight of the little boy at the curb watching you leave. In later years, it was the beautiful young girl with tear-stained eyes. We moved around a lot. My younger brother Timmy had spina bifida. There were a lot of hospital stays and doctor bills. My mother stayed home to take care of him. He consumed every waking moment of her time. Even as he got older and the therapist told her to allow him to be more independent, she never did."

"Was your father around much? Sometimes career military men aren't home that much."

"He was sort of in and out of our lives. Even when he was there, I could see the toll Timmy's illness took on my parents: physically, emotionally, and financially. I knew I would need money for college, so in high school I took on part-time jobs. Summers were for work, as many hours as I could get. I didn't mind the work, by this time I was well disciplined, seasoned to the task."

"How did your father deal with Timmy's physical impairments?"

Richard didn't say anything more. He just sat there stiffly upright in his chair. The roots of a military background hovered over his being, like an ever-present unseen force. Just like the hotshot hedge fund brokers on Wall Street have that hungry look, Richard had his own appearance. His gut a hard six-pack. Chest, arms, legs, developed to the max. Whether in a suit or casual wear, it was obvious to anyone who looked at him, whatever jungle Richard chose to play in, he was on top of his game. What was not obvious to the untrained eye, what lay just below the surface, the alpha male, cunning, hard, calculating, the edginess of the most primal of predators.

"Richard . . . what happened to Timmy?"

I must stop asking questions. It wasn't safe. Ripping off layer after layer down to the raw quick of his emotions. Do I really want to be armed with his secrets? Just how emotionally unstable could he become? My mouth opened. I just couldn't seem to stop. Professional curiosity drew me deeper into the dark, sinister forest of his recollections. In direct sight of me, Richard looked in my direction as though I was not there, a void in space. His voice a flat affect. No emotion, sadness, guilt, empathy, not even satisfaction. The sensation lay over me like the feeling of cold, unyielding steel.

"Dad had his own room. I think he spent a lot of time in there because he didn't want to see, or to look at Timmy. When my brother wasn't in his wheelchair, he was crawling around on the floor; he was an embarrassment. I hated that wheelchair. I hated pushing him around. He was flawed, he was never going to be right. Funny, isn't it, with my mother I ended up being the rejected one, not him. How's that for irony?"

"What happened to him? Do you visit with him?"

Richard stared into his wineglass and took a deep breath. "He's dead."

"What . . . what happened to him?"

"We were at my parents' cabin, you know, the one I have in the mountains. He was in his wheelchair on the dock." Richard's facial features tightened, and he began to talk through clenched teeth. "Tim asked me to go get him a sweater. He was always asking for something. The water is really deep off the dock." Richard didn't say anything more. He just sat there.

"Richard . . . what happened to Timmy?"

"Somehow his wheelchair went off the dock into the water. By the time I got back, it was too late. My mother blamed me."

"And your father?"

"I think the old man was relieved."

"Relieved?"

"Tim was a sucking cancer on all our lives. I think the old man was glad he was gone. That it was finally over." The stem of the wineglass Richard held cracked and then snapped in two under the pressure of his hand. He opened his hand, and blood ran between his fingers.

A deep coldness came over the room, more than a sweater would have warmed. My gift of silent language, flashes of vision, what had really happened that day on the dock played itself out in living color.

Richard's thought patterns were intrinsically woven into his soul. Staring into the face of evil, a chilling reality, the depth of what could not be redeemed. Now unguarded, Richard had let the last of his pretentiousness fall away, revealing himself, looking at me for a reaction. *Would I, could I accept him for who he really was? His agenda had always been dramatic with a sprinkling of fear. I could feel his sadness. Steel on steel a lonely jazz note . . . resounding like a blue misty night, draped in a widow's vale.* I wanted to change the subject to take us both away from this moment.

"Let me get a towel for your hand."

"It's okay. Just a small cut."

I gave him a towel, and he wrapped his hand. I got another glass and poured him more wine. "You worked your way through college?"

"You could say that. I got Anthony as a roommate. We couldn't have been more different. Anthony was on academic probation, a party boy—fun first, work later. He wasn't going to make it. I was lucky. Grades came easy for me, he had to work for his. He was failing at life. That's where the doors opened, Carla. Anthony's family was very grateful for my taking him under my wing. I was that stability in his life. What the family didn't buy him out of they dealt with in other ways."

"Other ways?"

"I'm getting to that. He asked me to go home with him for Thanksgiving. He had a large extended family. They came in from Cleveland and New Jersey. As I recall, even the state of Nevada was represented."

"An interesting array of people?"

"Sure, you could definitely say that. Doctors, attorneys, a judge, all well established in their professions. Then there was Paul, he was into nuclear chemistry, astrological physics, some way-out stuff. He was one weird dude all right."

"How's that?"

"He keeps a notepad beside his dinner plate. From time to time, he would jot down some kind of numbers and letters, then float off into whatever world he retreated into . . ."

My own thoughts held his words: *Numbers and letters . . .*

He continued, "After dinner, I was invited to accompany some of the other men to his father's study. The doors were closed; the reason for my invitation was made clear. The family was concerned about Anthony's ability to succeed in law school." Richard's eyes stared off into the distance, his voice reflective. "They knew of my efforts with Anthony, had seen his steady progress. If I didn't have to work, I would have more time to help him keep his grades up. They wanted to pay my tuition for school. All I had to do was let them know how much. Anything I needed. Talk about your paranoia—it was like someone handing you a gold brick and saying it was for free."

"I don't know, Richard, sounds like it was a fair deal to me. You were providing a service after all."

"Okay, so maybe I watched the *Godfather* one too many times, but it felt like I was being pulled in somehow. I assured them I would continue to help Anthony and let them know how appreciative I was for all their generosity. However, with all due respect, I would have to decline their offer."

"Well, I have to give it to you, that was a gutsy move. How did they take it?"

"They were gracious and understanding."

"So that was the end of it, right?"

"Not exactly. Things got really different after that. Life got a lot easier."

"I'm not following, how did that make life easier? You turned down a free ride."

"That year when I went to the office to check on my schedule and pay for my classes, I was told it was already paid. I assured them there was a mistake, and I insisted they look at the account again. They assured me the year was paid in full. When I went back to my car, I found an envelope on the car seat. It was stuffed with what to me was an inconceivable amount of money. This went on all the way through law school. Anthony and I talked of many things over those years. We spoke of his family members who were now in legitimate, respectable professions. What a difference a few generations can make. I'll never forget his statement: 'Don't let the suits fool you, Richard. It may be legal, it may be high-tech, but communications along the grapevine runs as smoothly as it ever did.'"

"You went back each Thanksgiving?"

"Yes, and regarding the money, they had no idea what I was talking about. End of conversation. Carla, maybe I learned some things from Anthony that broadened my horizons. There is something about risk-taking that is energizing to a person. There is a fulfillment in being on the razor's edge. Incorporating that into one's life with balance was a challenge."

"How do you mean that exactly?"

"That's a conversation we'll have another day. Carla, give me a few days and I'll get this mystery of yours unraveled and resolved, I promise you." We sat in silence for a moment. As I was about to thank him and tell him how appreciative I was for his help, he said, "There's a lot you haven't told me about yourself, Carla. I've seen your strength, discipline, drive, but I've also seen you back away from people, even close friends. The traits are contradictory."

He was waiting for a response from me. I knew all too well what this meant. In confidence, he had opened up and confided in me. To sustain his trust, I had to give him an equal portion, the dark portion of myself that I had not shared with others.

"Okay, Richard, fair enough. What I have been conflicted about from time to time is the moral or spiritual obligation that I do not invade another person's space. That had not bothered me for years; however, as I was well into my practice, the deeper things came to me.

Where a person really lives began to come into focus. For the lack of better terminology, summoning it up. I became conflicted about the intrusion into the most private, intimate parts of my patients' lives. As time went on, I told myself if my intent was honorable and healing was my goal, then my silent language was a gift. I knew I had been given this gift for the benefit of others, yet to this day I struggle not to cross that line. I've made a distinction between my professional life and my personal life. I realize in my personal life my friends are not coming to me to be healed. I have a responsibility to them, to you, Richard, to be honorable and keep my place. Not to invade their lives simply for my own personal curiosity." *Self-preservation was now questioning honor and place.*

"I do wonder what you think now, Carla. How are you judging me?"

"Judging you?" I knew what I had to say. "I'm not judging you, Richard. We all have decisions to make in life. Things aren't always as they appear on the surface. They're not always black and white." As much as I wanted to know more, fear of what I would find within Richard held me back. He had a calculated agenda, but where was he going with this?

Richard poured more wine in our glasses. "Carla, with all that has gone on—your dreams, the sculpture, Colette's questionable death—something must have come to the surface. What does your silent language tell you?"

He was pounding on the door of my own awareness, reality. I could feel the hair on the back of my neck stand up. Something wasn't right. I could feel myself backing away.

"Not a lot," I said. "And that's been somewhat frustrating to say the least. Just bits and pieces of things I can't make any sense of. Hallways, always going in different directions and water, lots of water. A box of secrets you're not to talk about." I left Jennifer's letters and numbers out. I needed time to analyze that concept myself.

"Carla, this sculpture, where is it?"

"Someplace safe. I just don't want to talk about this anymore."

Richard's voice was demanding. "You need to just give it to me. This isn't a game." He stood up, came over, and pulled me out of the chair. "I want you to give me the sculpture *now!*"

His grip dug into my arm like a steel vise. I struggled, pulled away from him.

"What's wrong with you, Richard? The sculpture isn't in the house. I can't give it to you now."

Richard appeared confused for a moment then reconsidered his position. "How can I help you, protect you, if you don't tell me where it is?" I stood staring at him in silence. Then he abruptly changed the subject. "You need a night out," he said. "We'll celebrate your new office. I've already talked to Ben and Sarah about going out to dinner Friday night at that old Italian place downtown. They have agreed to meet us there." I heard it in his voice: he knew he had overplayed his hand. "Would you like me to stay overnight, Carla?"

"No, I'm okay."

"You could come to my place after dinner. You're exhausted. A good night's sleep would help a lot. I could even be persuaded to serve you breakfast in bed."

So far, he had managed to be demanding, protective, seductive, manipulating, and the personality that was emerging was oh so frightening. There are labels we psychiatrists use when that many red flags go up. I couldn't bring myself to go there. Assimilating that into the rest of the chaos was just too frightening.

"Richard, I'll be fine. I have Kinsey here with me . . ."

"Right, if there was a burglar, Kinsey could hold the flashlight for the guy. I'll pick you up Friday evening at six-thirty, and we'll meet Sarah and Ben at the restaurant."

After Richard left, I built a big, hot cup of coffee, the kind you put sideboards on. I definitely need a good hiding place for that sculpture. The basement walls were made of red brick. One of the rooms didn't have much in it: an old potato bin and some shelves. There was also a small, round hole in the floor filled with cold water. Sarah said it was a small wellspring. Years ago, people put glass bottles of milk there to keep them cold in the summertime. I picked up my toolbox that was sitting by the old kiln. I took a chisel and hammer out, loosened some of the bricks and then removed them. I dug the dirt out from where the bricks had been, inserted the sculpture, and replaced the bricks. However, not without additional labor—Devin had gotten into the hole I had dug out at least three times. Kinsey had managed to turn the bucket of dirt over and then proceeded to walk in it, adding to the cleanup. They were members of the household, after all, and entitled to their curiosity.

Chapter 20

A deliveryman walked into my office with flowers in his hands. "These are for you," he said, setting them on my desk. "Have a nice day." They were beautiful flowers, such a large, colorful arrangement. The card read, "Looking forward to a special night with my girl. Signed as ever, Daniel."

The phone rang. I picked it up and heard Daniel's voice.

"Hello, Carla, just called to confirm our dinner date for Saturday. Everything still a go, right?"

"Yes, right. Your flowers just arrived. They're beautiful."

"Oh, they came then. I'm glad you like them. I'll stop by and pick you up at six-thirty. Is that okay?"

"Yes, that will be fine. Daniel, I'd love to talk for a while, but I have a client waiting and I am really backed up. This is my long day. I'll be working until late this evening."

"I understand," he said. "Not all clients can leave work, so evening appointments are necessary. How late will you be working?"

"I'll be here until around eight o'clock tonight."

"Well, take it easy. I'll look forward to seeing you Saturday." He hung up, and I felt drained. The flowers had come at a good time. If my voice didn't sound quite right, the surprise of the flowers made for a good cover-up.

Marcy appeared in the doorway. "Anything I need to know about? This Daniel person looking a little serious?"

"Too early, the jury is out on that one, Marcy."

"Oh, by the way," she said, "your mechanic called. He can take your car in today. If you want to meet him at Baltimore and Henderson, he'll switch cars with you and have yours back tomorrow morning." My mechanic and I had done it this way for years, "spontaneous" as Colette would have said. "He said he would meet you there in half an hour. From the look of your schedule, it looks like you could make it back in time for your next appointment."

"Tell him I'll meet him there."

I felt my energy level was down about my ankles and headed for my toes. I needed some rest and quiet time. On the way out, I told Marcy that something had come up and I needed her to cancel the rest of my appointments for the day.

"Something came up?" she asked. "The flowers are pretty. We are taking the rest of the day off." She smiled with that all-knowing look.

"Marcy, I only wish I lived in your fantasy world."

"Come on, I've begun to feel deprived. We administrative assistants talk to each other, but I haven't had much to talk about. Their bosses aren't workaholics like *some* people I know. Let's face it, your personal life hasn't been too spicy lately. So let me enjoy this, okay?"

I acknowledged her remark. "My deepest apologies." I stood in complete and total awe, if she only knew. "Okay, Marcy, I'll see what I can do for you."

"Have a nice weekend," she said.

I nodded. "You too."

***

My cell phone rang as I was pulling out of the parking lot. It was Daniel.

"Carla, Marcy said you just walked out the door, so I got you just in time. There are some things I really have to take care of. I'm on my way to the airport. I'm so sorry, I can't make it for our Saturday night dinner."

"How long are you going to be gone?"

"I'm going to be out of the country, and it's going to take some time. I only agreed to do this with the understanding that this will be my last trip abroad."

"Daniel, I take it you have made some career decisions."

"Yes, I definitely have. I'll come see you when I get back. We have some important decisions to make. I promise you there will be all the Saturday-night dinners you want topped with chocolate dessert."

"Daniel?"

"Yes?"

"I love you. Be careful. I know you're not going to tell me where you're going, so I'm not going to know where you are."

"I'll always know where you are, Carla, in my heart. You know how much I hate leaving you now."

"I know. I'll be looking forward to your coming home."

When I hung up, I sat there in the car for a moment. The future that should excite me and fill me with joy for some odd reason was replaced with an ominous feeling that settled into my awareness. It draped itself around me like a cold, damp, foggy night. Was I afraid to be happy? Was that my logical brain communicating with me? That inner awareness was not connecting this feeling with Daniel. I knew analyzing the emotion wouldn't work. It never had. Whatever this was would show up soon enough.

***

5:45 PM
1277 Meadowbrook Drive

Two men in dark clothing slipped over the backyard fence, quickly making entrance into the house by way of the kitchen door. The silence was broken by a clicking sound of toenails on the hardwood floor. Racing down the hallway, Kinsey confronted the two men in the kitchen. One man aimed and fired. Kinsey staggered sideways then fell to the floor. The two men looked at one another.

"Glad they gave us heads-up on that one. He's a big one, isn't he?"

"Yeah, even for a Rottie. What do you think he goes?"

"Rocking a 130 if he weighs a pound."

"What do we do now? Just leave him there?"

The man with the tranquilizer gun leaned back on the counter. "I don't care what kind or size of animal it is. You can't always count on exactly how long they are going to be down. We know the shrink is going to be at work until late this evening. This guy is another matter. Maybe we had better carry him out to the backyard. You pick up one end. I'll pick up the other."

"You think he's really out, right?"

"Yes, he's out."

"Okay, that's your opinion. You pick up the head first."

"Right, you're funny."

***

5:50 PM
Intersection of Baltimore and Henderson

I pulled my Mercedes up to the intersection, and Bob, the mechanic, did also. Today our timing was perfect. We jumped out of our cars, crossed the intersection, gave one another a high five, and exchanged car keys. Everything was done, and we were on our way. It doesn't get any more synchronized than that. I drove back to the house and put the car in the garage. As I went into the fenced backyard, I saw Kinsey lying in the yard. *That's unlike him. He always comes to greet me.*

I came closer and called to him, but he didn't move. Running over to him, I bent down "Kinsey? Kinsey?" There was no response. Grabbing the cell phone from my handbag, I brought up the vet's number. His assistant answered and said he was just leaving for the day. I could hear myself screaming, trying to make her understand she had to stop him. I must have sounded hysterical.

She gave the phone to the vet. "Is he breathing?" he asked.

"Yes, he's breathing, but he's not responding!"

"I was just getting ready to go home. I'll stop by your house on the way. It will only take me a few minutes. Try to calm down. Stay with him." He hung up.

The back door was ajar. Maria had let him out. Maybe she knew something. As I entered the house, I yelled for her. "Maria? Maria!" Then I heard her upstairs. I ran up the back stairway. Halfway down the hall, a sinking feeling hit me. I didn't see Maria's car. The house was quiet, no Latin music. *What is that sound?* Footsteps overhead in the attic. At the end of the hallway, the door to the attic was wide open. Footsteps were coming down the stairs, coming faster and faster.

The door to my bedroom was halfway open. I stepped into the guest room across the hall. As I started to close the door, I saw Devin on top of the armoire in my bedroom. I heard his low growl, that one he made when he had given his final order to Kinsey. I left the door open just a crack. There wasn't a phone in this room to call for help. I had left my cell phone on the ground beside Kinsey.

When the footsteps hit the landing on the second floor, it wasn't one but two men. I could see their shadows on the wall. They stopped and were saying something to one another in low, muffled voices. The one man was pointing toward the back staircase. *They must know I'm in the house.* It didn't take a rocket scientist to figure out what this was about. One of the men would look for me here and the other downstairs. The first man went straight down the hall past all the rooms without stopping. His body movement was like swift, silent water, an indescribable gracefulness. I froze, held captive in this unrealistic scene.

The second man followed, but as he came to the door of my bedroom, he hesitated for a moment. That would be where he would start to look for me. I could see the shiny brass doorknob turn, and the door began to swing open wider and wider. In that moment, Devin leapt off the top of the armoire. The screeching sound Devin made was enough to make one's blood run cold. He was on top of the man clawing and scratching at his head and eyes. The man grabbed Devin and flung him down the hallway. I could hear Devin's body hit the wall. The man ran down the back stairway. To my total disbelief, Devin was in hot pursuit.

Running to my bedroom, I locked the door. The telephone receiver shook in my hand as I attempted to dial 911. One ring, two . . . *For God's sake, pick up.* The police dispatcher came online. She was asking me questions. "Anyone else in the house? Stay with me," she said. "Don't hang up, they're on their way." I told her the back door was open. I knew it had to have been only minutes, but it felt like hours. She kept talking to me, asking questions, relaying information. "They are coming in the back door now," she said.

I heard footsteps then a knock on the door followed by a loud voice. "Police!" I opened the door. "Are you okay, Dr. Van Doran?"

"Yes," I said with relief.

The officer looked around. "Where did this blood come from?" As we looked down the hallway, there were splatters of blood all over the place.

"Well, I would say Devin did a pretty good job."

"Who's Devin?" the officer asked.

"You're not going to believe this one, but Devin is my Siamese cat."

He didn't seem the least bit surprised. "My wife's mother has one of those. Meanest thing I ever saw. From the looks of it, I could almost say I felt sorry for the guy, but then again, I guess he got what he deserved. I'm going to ask you to step outside while we go through the house. We'll call you back in when we're done. Then you can look through the house to see if anything has been taken. One of the officers is out back with your dog. You can join him."

"Thank you, Officer." I rushed downstairs and out the back door, and there was Devin sitting beside Kinsey. Devin was licking the blood off his feet. The officer was keeping a respectable distance. I kneeled down beside Kinsey. He was still breathing. As I looked up, a police officer was escorting the vet into the backyard.

"He says he's your veterinarian," the officer said.

"That's right," I said.

Doc Anderson was looking somewhat surprised at his escort but appeared totally focused. As he started to approach Kinsey, Devin arched his back, evidently still in warrior mode. I picked Devin up and held him close to me. Devin had blood on his coat, and now I had it all over me. The vet made a quick check of Kinsey.

"He could have been poisoned or tranquilized. I'll need him back at the office so I can check him over." He came over to look at Devin but stopped midstride.

"No, the blood's not mine, it's the burglar's."

One of Devin's favorite people was Doc Anderson, so it was not surprising to me that he was more than accommodating as Doc felt over his body. He flinched with pain several times, then a cry of discomfort.

"There, there boy, I know it hurts. It must have been some catfight you were in. Doesn't look like any broken bones." Doc took his flashlight and shined the light into Devin's eyes. "Looks like we might have a slight concussion here. Put him in his carrying case, and I'll take Devin with me. I'll need to check him out a little more from the look of things."

The two police officers carried Kinsey to the vet's vehicle.

I went back to the garage and picked up Devin's carrying case. *Was anything missing here?* Everything looked in place. I put Devin in his carrying case. When I turned around, Doc was leaning up against the workbench. He was a small man with warm brown eyes. He had a soft voice and gentle nature.

"It looks like an attempted burglary," I said. "Devin took exception to their presence. One of the men threw him into the wall."

"After I've finished my exam, I'll give you a call. I think they're going be okay," said the vet.

"Thanks, Doc," I replied with an appreciative smile.

As I was going back to the house, the captain came across the lawn to meet me.

"We've gone completely through the house," he said. "I'll need you to come back in here with me and let me know if you see anything that has been taken or out of place."

The two officers that had helped with the transport of Kinsey were back. One was in the garage and the other standing beside me.

"We just helped the vet with the dog and the cat. They're on their way."

"What did the vet say about the dog?" asked the captain.

"Well, Captain, the vet thinks someone stopped him with a tranquilizer gun. He's not dead."

I could feel the tears streaming down my face. The captain looked irritated.

"That was really insensitive, Kelly," he said with annoyance.

"Oh, hey, ma'am, I'm sorry. I've had dogs all my life. I really didn't mean that the way it came out," he said in an apologetic tone.

"That's all right. I understand. I've had Kinsey for some time. He was a puppy when I first got him."

"He may be your puppy, ma'am, but that's one gigantic puppy. Doesn't look like that old boy has missed any meals," said the officer.

"Captain, if you're ready for me, I really would like to go back inside and check things out," I responded.

"Yes, ma'am, we're ready. The other officers will check the outside." The captain picked up my handbag and cell phone from the lawn and handed them to me. We headed for the house.

"Dr. Van Doran, do you keep money here at the house?"

"No."

"Collectibles that someone could fence easy?"

"No."

"I understand you're a psychiatrist, what about your caseload?"

"Okay, I know where you're going with this, and yes, I do have a diverse caseload, but I don't know anyone that would do something like this."

"That old professor, he lived here before you."

"Yes, that's right. Did you know him, Captain?" I said.

"Yes, I'd see him sitting in his garden. He liked me to stop by and talk to him. The professor wasn't a recluse. He was really quite an interesting individual, you know. I felt the old gentleman was lonely sometimes. He had a sharp mind and a quick wit right to the very end."

"Did he ever talk about his work?"

The captain turned sharply and looked at me, then laughed.

"Are you kidding me? I grew up in this neighborhood. I know people at the university. No one talked to the professor about his work. Even his peers couldn't intellectually summon up enough gray matter between them to purchase a ticket to sit in the ballpark where that old man played. You know what his saying was?"

"His saying?" I questioned.

"You know, what a person says to you more than once and then it becomes a thing between the two of you."

"What was his saying?"

"'If we make of it a burden, we are slaves; if we make of it work, we are men; if we make of it play, we are gods.' Make no mistake, Dr. Van Doran, he was a god in his world. Sometimes he would be gone from the university. The understanding was that he was doing some kind of work for the government." The captain paused for a moment as though he was giving some consideration to other avenue of thought. "That gate over there, the one that connects your backyard to the house where the—"

I finished his sentence for him, "The woman was murdered."

He stood quiet for a moment. I let the seconds pass by, knowing given enough time he would continue.

"In the summer, she came over a lot. They sat out in the garden. She would always bring him a pitcher of lemonade. He brought cookies. The old guy really liked his homemade cookies. He liked the different-colored ones. They were his favorite. He had a name for them, something about church."

I heard my own voice jump into the middle of his sentence. "Stained-glass windows?"

"That's it. They were really good." In his voice was a tone of delight and appreciation. "Did I say the professor was a gracious and generous man?"

I couldn't believe what I was hearing. There was no way this could have been a coincidence. What I hadn't seen before, life's intricate design. Cobwebs shimmering in the morning dew. Patterns began to emerge people, concepts I hadn't previously entertained. The brain now stimulated, racing forward, grasping for reason and logic.

"What did him and the lady next door talk about?"

"Oh, they had lively conversations. He was all about hardcore science. She was more like a sociologist. They met somewhere in the middle between advanced technology and human evolution."

"Can you give me an example?"

He thought for a moment. "The Mayan calendar, she never saw it as the end of time, but a marker, indicating levels of human consciousness and progression. The professor liked that concept. My take on the professor, he saw us as adolescents with technology that could kill us all. Monkeys with grenades. How long would we play with them before we pulled the pin? He felt timing was important. Whatever we did, it was important to be in sync with nature.

"We'll start in the attic," the captain said, "and work our way down."

We went through each room of the house. In the basement one of the officers was checking the windows. "They're locked and secure, Captain."

My own observation of the small room in the basement indicated that nothing had been taken or moved, including bricks. I thanked them for being so thoughtful and quick in their response and of course their helpfulness with Kinsey. The captain handed me a card.

"This is the number for the Detective Bureau," he said. "If you come up with any more information, give us a call." Connors's name was on the card.

I called the vet's office as soon as the police had left. The first words I heard Doc Anderson say was that they were going to be all right.

"Looks like Kinsey was shot with a tranquilizer gun. Whoever did this to him definitely wanted him out of commission for a while."

"What about Devin?" I questioned

"Nothing broken, but he sustained a lot of bruising, so he'll be sore for a while. Bouncing off the wall was probably not a good idea, but he's a tough guy. He'll be okay."

"That's such a relief. I can't begin to tell you how much I appreciate your coming so quickly," I responded.

"I'm glad I could be there for you, Carla. Those boys of yours are both good, healthy representations of their breed and possess a very even temperament." I could hear his demeanor lighten.

"Maybe I need to qualify that with Devin, under normal circumstances," I said. "Can I come get them now?"

"I'd like to keep them both overnight and take another look at them in the morning," said the vet.

"I'll stop by tomorrow evening then."

I walked around the house to check all the doors again and make sure they were locked. As I sat at the kitchen table like a zombie, other than numb, I didn't know what I felt. I stared at my hands as if they were supposed to be doing something, anything, only I didn't know what to have them do. There was nothing to do. *I'll just go to bed and read.* Perhaps focusing on my psych journals would bring me back to some kind of balance.

Starting up the stairs, I was so aware of what wasn't there: Kinsey and Devin following me in their traditional manner. As I stood in the hallway in front of my bedroom door, the bloodstained carpet was a shocking reminder of what I was desperately trying to forget. I climbed into bed and attempted to read some of my journals. Somewhere in the midst of all the chaos, exhaustion claimed my conscious mind. I had fallen asleep.

In my dream, I was in a strange house that looked like a scene from *Doctor Zhivago.* Everything was icy white and looked like shimmering crystal. The chandeliers began to sway back and forth with more and more intensity. Now the whole house was shaking as though there was an earthquake. Knives of ice flew through the air. The breaking, cracking sounds were deafening. A woman's voice shrieked, "No! No, don't do this! What do you want? Why are you here?" Another voice hysterical, screamed, "Run . . . run . . . run!"

I awoke, sitting up in bed, silk pajamas drenched in perspiration. My heart was pounding. It was as though the oxygen had been sucked out of the air. I felt so alone with both pets at the vet.

I definitely needed something to quiet my nerves. Grandmother's tea would do fine. I made my way to the kitchen and reached into the back of the kitchen cabinet to retrieve a tin container. It was labeled appropriately: *Suspension of Consciousness*. The woman was always direct. *Directions: one-half cup*, and in red print: *POTENT*. In a most untraditional way, I heated the water in a cup in the microwave, then put the loose tea in the cup and let it steep. I could only imagine what she would have thought about that. As I picked up the cup, there was a loud rattling sound of glass. I screamed and dropped the cup. It broke and splattered all over the floor. Spinning around I stared at the kitchen door.

"Police . . . police, ma'am, are you all right?"

My voice was hardly louder than a whisper. "Yes . . . " I realized I was just standing there. The police officer wasn't going away. We were looking at one another through the window of the kitchen door. Transformation back to zombie land, commanding my legs to move, answer the door. Taking one good look at him again, I could see his uniform, hear some kind of garbled transmission come through his communicator. With my hands still shaking, I opened the door and he came in. I noticed the leather strap across his revolver had been unsnapped.

"I saw your light on. Were you going downstairs?" he asked.

"You mean to the basement?" I said.

"Yes," he replied.

"No, why would I go to the basement?" I asked.

"Do you mind if I go down and take a look?" he said.

"Not at all. Please, be my guest." I showed him where the basement door was and turned on the light for him. *What was he doing?*

As he started down, I followed him, but he stopped me. "Don't come down until I call you. Go back upstairs."

"Okay." I complied with his instructions as a child would give directions by a parent. I cleaned up the broken glass from the kitchen floor. As I put another cup of water in the microwave, the officer came back upstairs.

"I understand you had some problems here earlier this evening," he inquired.

"That's right. A little like discovering Attila the Hun had unexpectedly come for dinner."

A broad smile crossed the young man's face. "Yes, ma'am, I could see where that would be a little disturbing. Our orders were to keep a unit in the area tonight. It looked like someone was trying to break in through the basement window."

"Oh, great. That's all I need to hear," I said.

"Rest assured, we have this house covered. Try to get some sleep. Things will look better in the morning." He walked out the kitchen door, started down the stairs, then hesitated. As I closed the door and turned the lock, it clicked—a ringing sound in the quiet of the night. He turned around and smiled, nodded and left. *One half cup of tea? I don't think so.* I made a full cup, as strong as I could, and went to bed to drink it.

Sitting at my desk the next day, I found the normalcy of routine comforting. After my last client of the day, I went over to Doc Anderson's office and picked up Kinsey and Devin. Kinsey seemed to be feeling great. Devin, however, appeared to be a bit tender and stiff. Doc gave me some liquid pain medication for Devin and assured me he would be fine in a couple of days. When we arrived home, Kinsey sniffed the backyard in a manner that would have made a blue-ribbon bloodhound proud. We went into the house, and both of them made unusual search patterns. No doubt the smell of different people being in the house had not gotten by their awareness.

I went directly to the basement and checked the broken window. There was Connors's business card. He had written on the back of it: "We're done, you can replace the window now." I checked out the back room again. Everything appeared to be undisturbed. Devin, Kinsey, and I went back upstairs to the kitchen. Pulling a TV dinner from the freezer was the extent of my culinary intentions for the evening. Grandmother's tea called to me. This time I made it according to her directions. Taking the tea upstairs to the bedroom, Devin and Kinsey followed along. After a hot, steaming bath, I could feel the tension in my body slowly melting away.

***

The following day I looked at my appointment book and shuddered. There was no way I had the energy level or concentration to deal with work this week, considering all that was going on in my personal life and the ongoing threats. I needed a vacation. Taking a week off would be just what the doctor ordered. I would have to say something to Marcy, give her some kind of excuse, before she had me on the Riviera with Mr. Hunk, Fantasy 101, compliments of Marcy. I tidied up my desk, went to the front office.

"Marcy, you're working late," I stated.

"Getting some paperwork done, thought I would work over tonight. Next week, I have two grandbabies with birthdays. Oh, I didn't show you the latest pictures." She went to her oversized handbag. Two separate folders came out, one for each grandchild. Her face lit up as she showed me each one. "Sherry can crawl now. That is important, isn't it? They should crawl before they walk?" She didn't wait for me to respond but continued as proud grandmothers often do. They were indeed beautiful, happy babies. One couldn't help but notice how content Marcy was with her life. When she spoke of her grandchildren, her eyes sparkled like diamonds.

"You are truly blessed, Marcy," I said.

Chapter 21

Darkness began to give way to the rising sun. Riding along in the truck Jason looked over at Jennifer.

"I don't know what food Dad has put up at the house. I need to pick up some groceries." He pulled into the parking lot at Walmart. "I'll go in first in three or four minutes then you come in. Pick up some boots, clothing, and whatever else you need." Jason unlocked the glove compartment and took out some cash, handing it to Jennifer. "You check out on one register. I'll check out on another. See you back here at the truck when you're done."

Jason picked up supplies he thought they would need then went to check out. He sat in the truck waiting for Jennifer. Sometime later the little general appeared with shopping bags in both hands. Jason had to laugh, thinking about the shopping trips he had taken with his mother. He thought to himself, *I guess it just doesn't make any difference what the circumstances are. There's no timetable for how long a woman shops.*

Back on the road Jennifer asked, "Are we close to the house now?"

"We've got about twenty-five miles to go. Then we're there, Jen." Jason turned on the radio. They listened to music. Time and the beautiful countryside passed by.

***

The red truck's tires made a crunching sound over the graveled lane. "Jen . . . Jen, we're here."

Raising her head off Jason's shoulder, she stared out the windshield. As her eyes focused, objects came into view. The expansive mountain range spread out before her. The spectacular beauty could only have been created by the hand of a supreme entity.

"I have a place to hide the truck. If the authorities come looking for us, they won't find any evidence we came here. We have camping gear and supplies. Two weeks in the back woods and then we'll come back to the house, unless you want to just stay at the house, we can do whatever you feel comfortable with."

"What about your dad?"

"He's not due back for several weeks. You know, Jen, my dad really loves his work. He has said the patterns on the surface of the earth are a great deal more fragile than people realize. It has always concerned him about how we alter nature's flow. When he gets back and you two meet each other, you're really going to like him, he's a great guy."

"Your dad will be okay with my being here?"

Jason patted her hand, smiling assuredly. "Dad will do whatever he can to help you get things worked out."

As they started for the house, Jennifer noticed two large metal bowls by the front door. She looked at Jason for an explanation.

"Those are for Dad's dog Chip. He found him as a stray puppy in the woodpile, they're inseparable."

"What kind is he?"

Jason unlocked the door then turned to Jennifer. "I think they call his breed a Heinz variety. He's a good dog."

Jennifer stepped into the house with both hands holding on to her shopping bags.

"This way," Jason said, leading her down a hallway. "You can put your shopping bounty in the bedroom. I think there might even be enough room for all of them. I learned all my shopping expertise from my mother."

Jennifer stopped, staring straight ahead, dropping the shopping bags onto the floor.

Jason turned and saw Jennifer just standing there. "Are you okay, Jen? You look like you've seen a ghost."

Jennifer opened her mouth, but nothing came out, visions of her mother's dead body lying on the kitchen floor. Realization engulfed her. She would never shop or do anything else with her mother again.

Jason wanted her to say something, anything, but she didn't. He was aware something was terribly wrong, but he didn't know what. Jason would have to just wait until she decided to tell him.

"It's been a long trip, you're tired. Come with me. I'll put your things in the bedroom. Why don't you just lie down for a little while. I'll fix us breakfast and make some hot coffee."

He walked back to where Jennifer stood, picked up the shopping bags from the floor. Jennifer followed him into the bedroom. At the foot of the bed was a wooden chest. On top of it lay a beautifully designed quilt. The colors were vibrant and warm. Jennifer lay down on the bed. Jason put a quilt over her.

"I'll come get you when breakfast is ready," he said. "Try to get some rest."

***

Later Jennifer sat at the breakfast table with Jason.

"You're a good cook, Jason, and your coffee isn't bad either."

"How about I pour us another cup of coffee and we can take them out to the picnic table in the backyard. The sun is up. It's warm outside. Maybe we could take a walk in the woods later, how's that sound?"

"I think I'd really like to do that, Jason." Jennifer drank a second cup of coffee while the sun warmed her body. The sights and sounds of nature quieted her mind. "What's back there in the forest?"

"I can show you things most hikers never see. They are too busy walking, talking, they miss the life of the forest."

***

Later that morning Jason and Jennifer walked back through the tree line and into the forest. The logging trail gave way to a path that led deeper into the forest. Jennifer could hear the sound of running water as they came closer. She could see a small waterfall and a creek that ran alongside the path.

"Let's sit down there," Jason said, pointing toward a large tree.

"It's beautiful here, so tell me what the hikers are missing?"

"Listen, what do you hear?"

"Water from the falls splashing in the creek. The sound of it is so peaceful."

"Do you see or hear anything else?"

They sat quietly. As time passed, the forest came alive with movements and sounds. A squirrel scampered about the dry leaves, rabbits hopped about in the open, birds chirped their familiar songs, and a deer emerged from a thicket in the distance.

"It's a world unto itself," Jennifer said.

Jason only smiled. "I've found some interesting things in the creek bed, strange-looking fossils in the rocks, even petrified flowers, you can see them embedded into the stone. It's as though in some way the universe wanted those delicate-looking flowers to never be forgotten, to be remembered for all time. Would you like to check the creek out, see what we can find?"

Jennifer stood up. "Let's do that. It sounds like fun. You never know what we might find."

They walked along the creek for a short way, when Jennifer cried out, "Oh, look, Jason." In the water among the rocks was an Indian arrowhead. She bent down, put her hands in the icy-cold water, reaching for the arrowhead, then saw black letters and numbers floating across her hands. Jennifer watched as the current carried them downstream. Picking up the arrowhead, she turned to Jason.

"It's perfect, just like you, Jason."

He could feel his face flush a little, such a sweet compliment coming from Jennifer.

She placed the arrowhead in his hand. "It's my gift to you. Promise me you will always keep it, and when you see the arrowhead, you will think of me as we are now in this special moment, just the two of us here together alone." Her eyes filled with tears. "Promise me, Jason, promise me."

He bent down, putting his arms around her. "I promise, Jennifer, I give you my word." Jason was hoping at this point Jennifer would tell him what had caused her to run. What terrible thing had turned her world upside down. *Had she found out what the black letters and numbers meant? Did she see the man in that Jeep again?*

Answers did not come. Jennifer revealed nothing more to him.

***

Back at the house Jason announced, "I'll make sandwiches for our lunch."

"You're the best friend ever, Jason. I'm starving. While you fix them, I think I'm just going to go in and take a quick shower."

"Take your time." Jason made a pot of coffee, went to the refrigerator, and got out some sliced ham. A familiar sound coming from outside interrupted his thought. It was a Jeep on the gravel lane. Jason went to the front door and looked out. The man getting out of the Jeep was his dad, along with a large yellow dog. When they entered the house, Jason attempted to explain his situation.

"No, Jason, you don't understand, your mother contacted me. That's why I'm here. Son, we need to talk." They went into the kitchen and sat down at the table. Chip took his place on the floor. Jason's dad looked over at the coffeepot. "Smells good," he said. "If there was anything stronger in this house, I would have it. I guess a cup of coffee will have to do."

"Dad, I was just trying to help."

"I know, but I also know there are a lot of things you're not aware of." Jason's dad told him what had happened to Jennifer's parents and what the newspapers had printed. "I know she's here, Jason. If I can put this together, you have to know the authorities are going to be the next knock on that door. I don't know what she did or didn't do, Jason. I do know one thing. She needs help, more help than we can give her."

"Is Mom upset?"

"Some hunter reported seeing your truck in the woods, but no one was around. Your mom is on her way out here now. I'll let her know you're okay. Son, I got it, you were trying to help her, but this one is definitely way over your pay grade."

"What do we do now?" Jason's asked.

"What do you think, what's the right thing to do for . . . what's her name?"

"Her name is Jennifer. I call her Jen."

Chip looked in the direction of the doorway and made a low, soft growling sound. Jason's dad put his hand down on Chip's head. "There, boy, it's okay."

Jennifer stood in the doorway of the kitchen. Her answer was said with certainty: "We both know what the right thing to do is, Jason." Jennifer walked over to telephone hanging on the wall, picked up the receiver, and entered the number 911.

Chapter 22

Monday morning the phone rang. It was Marcy.

"Are you okay?"

"Yes, I'm fine, why wouldn't I be?" Carla responded.

Marcy's voice held an unfamiliar sound of concern. "Okay . . . you're handling it, you're fine, but you do know you're late, right?"

"Late for what?" Carla asked.

Marcy lowered her voice, now a playful questioning inquiry. "You're quite late. Is Daniel really handsome? A hunk?"

"Marcy, you're fantasizing again."

"You promised you'd share!"

"I will when the day comes."

Returning to her professional Marcy demeanor, she said, "Hey, it's beginning to look like LaGuardia International around here. With the other . . . " Then she stopped, as she often did when clients were in the waiting room and she didn't want to mention names or any particular information. "You have two in a holding pattern and another due in any time now. The time frame is getting a little tight. What do you want me to do? I wasn't sure you would be coming in today."

"The first two appointments would be O'Brien and Delong, is that right?"

"That's right," Marcy responded.

"O'Brien is always a half an hour early, that's her pattern, and De Long we will work in. I'll be there in twenty minutes." I hung up the phone, and there sat the empty teacup on the nightstand. My head was clear. I felt like I had indulged in a ten-hour sleep marathon. Hearing my grandmother's voice in my head, "Remember, dear, one-half cup." She was the family and neighborhood's unofficial pharmacist and counselor. Always making some kind of potion, tincture, sleeve, or tonic—a cure for whatever ailment prevailed. They even came to her for advice and instruction regarding their love lives. She was my ally and teacher in a world that only she and I shared at times.

I got ready and knew the morning was going to be an adventure. Normally I had things laid out the night before, but needless to say, that was not one of the routine tasks that I had gotten to last night. I grabbed the first thing in the closet I saw and put it on. Today would be my first attempt at impersonating the girl I used to see on the freeway that put her makeup on in the car. I must have learned something as a commuter. Approximating how many traffic lights I might avail myself to for putting my face on before arriving at the office now amused me.

I raced out of the house and only stopped in the driveway long enough to pick up the rolled-up newspaper before getting on my way. My calculations regarding the traffic lights weren't too bad. Obviously, I needed additional practice time with the makeup application on the move. I quickly began to understand Ms. Freeway Girl could have written a book on the subject. After all, this did appear to be somewhat of an art form.

***

I pulled into the parking lot at work and stepped out of the car. As I looked down, to my horror, I discovered I had on my house slippers. Forgetfulness was one thing, but if my clients saw this along with the mass exodus, they would undoubtedly want a refund. With no other option, I entered the waiting room and began limping. My clients looked on in sympathy. Marcy looked up over her glasses.

"Did you sprain your ankle?"

"You could say that."

"I'll bring you some coffee. I'm so sorry," Marcy said with a sincere tone of sympathy.

I always appreciated Marcy's mothering instincts. Entering my office and closing the door behind me, my inner child giggled and did a pirouette in her tutu. When Marcy brought me the coffee, I thanked her and inquired most humbly if she had anything to go with it this morning. She assured me she did and would bring something in directly. I put my briefcase on the desk with the newspaper on top of it. The coffee was hot and good.

I had no more than settled in and pulled the O'Brien file when Connors appeared in the doorway. He came in and sat in the chair in front of my desk.

"They will have a court order for your files," he said. "You understand time is important here. What can you tell me?"

Marcy brought bagels and coffee for us, along with that concerned look again.

I settled back into my chair. "The runaway would be expected. They'll need Jennifer's statement. Children's Services will do their investigation. Her younger sister, Caroline, is still in the house. Her father will be given an order to vacate the premises. The system will proceed accordingly." I looked up from my file. "But you would know that."

Detective Connors looked frozen in time, bagel halfway to his mouth, which was still hanging open. He looked at the rolled-up newspaper on top of my briefcase. "You really don't know, do you?" There was an unfamiliar darkness in his tone.

"Know what?" asked Carla.

"Marcy said you were late coming in this morning. You didn't have the radio or TV on last night or this morning?"

"Okay, so much for clairvoyance, Detective. It's like this. I had plenty of news in my own backyard last night. Keeping up with the rest of the world's news was just a bit too much. So what do you know that I don't?"

He put down his bagel, picked up the newspaper, pulled it out of its plastic wrapper, and reached over to press my intercom. "Marcy, would you please bring the good doctor another cup of coffee? She's going to need it." He opened the newspaper to the front page and laid it in front of me.

The bold black ink seared into my vision like a flashing neon light: Local Family Murdered. The article went on to identify Jennifer's father and mother, indicating they had been stabbed numerous times. Their bodies were discovered at the residence. Marcy's concerned look now became clear.

"Connors, I just spoke to her father Friday."

"Looks like her parents were killed sometime Friday night."

Connors and I sat staring at one another. "Well, who's going first?" I said.

"There are some things that aren't in the newspaper, Carla. Things you need to know."

"I did notice the absence of one thing. There was no mention of Jennifer being a runaway. Did she return home? What about her younger sister?"

"Her sister, Caroline, was with a friend over the weekend. Her whereabouts have been confirmed. It's Jennifer I'm concerned about. No one has seen her. I know Jennifer's mother had made an appointment for her with the family doctor. We have the doctor and his nurse's statement. I'm worried about you, Carla," Connors stated.

"About me?"

"Yes, and I need to share some things with you. I need your agreement to confidentiality."

"You got it," I said as I felt quicksand sucking under my feet. Connors continued with what the newspapers didn't print. They found Mr. Stevens's body in Jennifer's bedroom. He was on the floor. On the mirror over her dresser painted in blood was the word *THEIF*, with a very large exclamation mark. Jennifer's mother was downstairs in the kitchen. She had just been to the grocery store. The whole thing was a bloody mess.

"Carla, did you ever have a case that was just too perfect? The report was written for you before you ever got there. I don't know if I'm looking for a kidnapper, a victim, or a perpetrator—and none of it feels right."

He sat quietly for a moment. "There's another thing that just isn't right about this case."

"What's that?"

"A ring on Mr. Stevens's hand is missing," Connors stated.

"Well, Connors, maybe it started out a burglary and then somehow something went terribly wrong," Carla said.

"No, doesn't look like that. As far as we can tell nothing else was taken."

"Was the ring of any particular significance?"

"What? Oh, I get it," he said. "No, not as far as we can tell. It wasn't his wedding ring. The ring was on his right hand."

"Was it a signet ring from his university or the military? Perhaps a family heirloom passed down from father to son?" asked Carla.

"His wife had it made for him. We checked with the jeweler. It was yellow gold with one large solitary diamond in the center, not something you could take to the pawnshop easily. The housekeeper said she had never seen him without it. The ring is very important and personal to someone, Carla, I just don't know why. When we find the answer to that question, we will know who murdered Mr. and Mrs. Stevens," Connors said. "You keep your client's cases on the computer, right?"

"Yes, but sometimes not everything from my notes goes into the computer, and I do have security," Carla commented.

"Security, yeah, right. Just accept it—there is no privacy and hasn't been for some time. The bigger and richer the entity high tech searching, the less privacy you have," said Connors.

"Connors, do you think Jennifer was there that night and saw what happened?"

"There is no evidence Jennifer was there that night, but that won't stop the prosecuting attorney's office from scrutinizing your records for a connection. Carla, have you had any new clients you would consider out of the ordinary?" asked Connors. "Think back on some of your old cases. Sometimes it takes years before anger, resentment, rejected love, truth revealed coming to the surface, gets action. Think about it for a minute."

As a child, remembering my father's office the one thing on his desk that captured my attention was the rolodex. The little white cards with information spun around and round. I see in my mind now as if it were electrified on speed racing forward through every client's file I had ever had. Clicking off possibilities, they drop away one by one. Only two names come to the surface of awareness. Like screeching wheels of a vehicle before impact, the realization wrenches at my heart. The genius Jennifer and the veteran, post-traumatic stress disorder, John Clifton, sometimes the irony of life escapes me. Detective Connors looks at me with inquisitive eyes. He wants to know, do I have the answer?

"Well," he said.

"Trust me, Connors, it's a long list."

"Yeah, I get it," he said. "Working at the funny farm. So who's on the list?"

"There are two names at the top of that list. John Clifton, the most likely candidate, but he's in the Veteran's Hospital psych ward. Those who have so much to give and those who have given their all, sometimes the irony of life escapes me, Connors."

He folded his hands almost in the position of prayer. "And," he said.

I took a deep breath. "Our girl Jennifer."

Connors groaned.

"I know, Connors, me too."

"Okay, Connors. I didn't buy a ticket, but I am on this ride with you. Now I have something to ask you. Do you believe some people possess, shall we say, insight? Because I think, sometimes, we have to think outside the obvious."

Connors's eyes lit up, directly holding mine. "Ask any cop on the beat about the full moon. Hospital emergency room attendants, now those people can tell you some weird stories. Is any of it explainable? Oftentimes not, but it doesn't make it any less real." Connor sat forward in his chair. "Jennifer, was she upset with you?"

From him flowed sincere concern, how touching. I truly felt some type of connection with this man, as though our energies of interest had crossed paths before.

"No, it wasn't like that," I assured him. "I don't think I'm a negative issue with her."

"Carla, I know this kid has an IQ off the charts. Do you think someone wants her for what she knows?"

"Actually, what she knows is buried deep. I suspect a triggering mechanism is needed to bring the information to the surface."

Connors cleared his throat. "The human mind is the last frontier. Then they would need confinement. Having her commitment would accomplish their objectives. It's the only thing that makes any sense." He settled back in his chair again. "We . . . they believe Jennifer did the act. It was really a mess, a real act of rage. Nothing surgical about this one." He stared into his coffee cup for a prolonged period of time. "Carla, about your case notes concerning Jennifer, are they up to date in their entirety?"

I looked down at my notepad. My own version of shorthand, years of speeded up hieroglyphics. After analysis, the client's session information would be put into my computer then read as professional language.

"To answer your question, Connors, not yet. If I . . . if I put all her information in my computer, it would be so damaging. Had Mother Teresa been my client with all that information, a jury would have no alternative but to bring back a verdict—guilty as charged. Connors, I get it—what your eyes see your gut isn't buying."

Marcy came in with a note: *Leah called. Jason is absent from the university again.*

"Interesting. A young boy, a friend of Jennifer's, is also missing."

"What's his story?" asked Connors.

"His parents are divorced. Dad lives out west, State Ranger outdoors type. He's not a bad kid. Decision-making and impulse control is getting better, but still an undisciplined puppy dog on a leash. Going one way only to find himself going another. Maturity and time will soften the edges of his path."

Connors shook his head. "Yeah, I know, Dad would bring one of those home occasionally from the inner-city. Good kid, he would say, just needs some help."

"Your dad meant a lot to you, didn't he?"

"He was a big part of my life, good thing too. Maybe I liked a little more edge to my path than was necessary."

"Connors, I think she's with Jason, and I believe they're headed out west." *I didn't tell Connors about my dream of knives flying in the house of Doctor Zhivago. I didn't want to freak him out.*

"Know what the kid drives?" Connors asked.

"A red pickup truck. The university may have the license number."

Connors thought for a moment and then said, "We are cross-checking the blood on your basement window."

"Blood on my basement window? Would you care to elaborate on that?"

Connors shifted uneasily in his chair, took another drink of his coffee. "I read the report from the officer that was at your house last night, the one that went to the basement. They were told to keep a unit in the area. It looked like someone tried to enter the house through the basement window Friday night. Whoever he or she was broke the glass, trying to get in. I thought it might have been Jennifer looking for a place of safety or revenge."

I gave Connors what information I could regarding Jennifer. I explained to him that she was actually a relatively new client of mine, and the circumstances under which she had come to me.

"Did you get everything you need from the basement?"

Connors looked puzzled for a moment and then said, "Basement? Oh, yes, basement. Yes, they're finished."

I could see the wheels turning in his head. He was contemplating the terminology basement rather than basement window. Logical, after all was part and partial of his trade.

"Life can be more than a little maddening at times," he said quietly.

"That's right," I responded.

The pen in his hand clicked back as he closed his notepad. "You know what they call me at the station?"

"What's that?"

"Bulldog." He laughed. "I had just transferred into the department at the time. Guess you could have called it a cold case. Everyone else had let it go, but there was something about that case. I kept working on it even on my own time. I finally put the thing together. I guess the details really aren't important. It was the connection. You know what that's like, Carla."

"Yes, I know what you mean." Any length of time in the business and you knew what he meant. The ones that manage to get past the gatekeepers, the safeguards we put in place. The distancing we do in the name of professionalism. He took out another business card. "I have your card," I said.

He didn't say anything, just turned the card over and wrote down a phone number.

"That's my private cell number, Carla. If you ever need me, you can reach me twenty-four seven, understand?" He was direct.

"Yes," I said, "I get it. You know, Connors, I think we all wear masks. What happens to us in life becomes the thread we weave into our masks. The fibers of our soul, what we show to others. It's the price we pay to come to the party, isn't it? To play on the stage of life." I noticed his eyes were fixed on the sculpture sitting in the bookshelf of father and mother and child.

"I need to find her," he said, "providing she's still alive, and get her story. Those case notes of yours, can you give her time, Carla, just a little more time?" He looked directly at me. I believe it was Winston Churchill that said "In wartime, truth is so precious she should always be attended by a bodyguard of lies." I reached into my desk drawer and pulled out two glasses and a half-spent bottle of brandy. We had our drinks, and Connors left.

Putting the cap on the bottle, I opened the desk drawer, hesitated— whose counting, one more. I poured myself another, took a sip, sat back, closed my eyes, experienced the taste of liquor warm and smooth. Visions of Colette floated across my mind. Bacardi rum and Coke, hot sand, the sound and smell of the ocean breeze. Colette's flirtatious voice as she thanked the cabana boy for her drink. Striving to see color hold the vision, just a little longer. Marcy's voice coming from the doorway shattered the tranquil picture. Back to reality. This weird cycling of chaos that has invaded my life still hovers about me like a predator stalking its prey.

Chapter 23

One week later I had an appointment in the city. A case had been assigned to me by the court. A psychological needed to be performed for a juvenile probationer. His lengthy record preceded him, along with his propensity to warm himself by very large fires. The drive-in had been routine except for the rain that was coming down like a monsoon. Parking in the downtown area was an inconvenience. It always had been. I pulled into the parking lot of my old office, put on my raincoat, and then caught a city bus. The courthouse had been built in the 1800s. Large amber blocks of sandstone, the solid structure a community recognizes as being permanent confirmed its faith in law and order.

I arrived early and sat in a small coffee shop downstairs. The courtroom was on the third floor. I drank my coffee and reviewed the psychological. When it was time, I got my exercise by climbing the stairs to the third floor, with each step attempting to convince myself that I could actually feel that sugar-covered Danish melting away, and sat on a bench in the hall. The wide marble hallway hummed with its own layer of life. Footsteps echoed; some proceeded with confident strides, others hesitated, searching for a particular doorway that would accommodate their needs. Occasionally, the soft, hurried footsteps of a child in tow. Octave levels above the hum, voices conducting business. How could it all appear so routine? In some of those courtrooms, people's futures were being determined. Whole families affected by the decisions that would be made this day. High-powered attorneys with briefcases. The expensive suit that says "Yes, it is costly, but that is what you are paying me for—excellence. I'm the best your money can buy."

Those poor souls in wheelchairs, crutches, and neck braces streamed by. I could hear bits and pieces of their conversation: "It was a con, he wasn't even an attorney . . . he wasn't an attorney." The words hung heavy in the air. *He wasn't an attorney.*

I turned and looked out the window. Across the street sat the building that housed the Supreme Court, where the records of practicing attorneys were kept. I had been to Richard's office, met his secretary, and saw his credentials, framed and hanging on the wall. He did litigation and was out of town a lot. *What am I thinking? I've known Richard for years.*

***

After the court case, I stood on the street corner waiting for my bus, holding the collar of my raincoat closed against the damp wind. The Supreme Court building loomed out of the gray overcast sky, as though it was the only thing on the block. I was here, wasn't I? Across the street was the answer.

I stood in front of the directory. The Supreme Court was on the fourteenth floor. The lady at the desk was older and looked like she had come with the original furniture. She was no-nonsense, strictly business. From her neck hung a Celtic cross with three stones. It was a familiar piece. My grandmother Mary Colleen O'Hare had one just like it. I immediately commented on her cross, telling her of my own memories of the delicate piece and how beautiful I thought it was. We bonded, and she melted into a personality of warmth and courtesy.

"I'm from out of town," I told her. "Just doing some research. I'm looking for an attorney by the name of Richard Dupree."

"Oh yes, such a nice man," she said. I began to feel warm and fuzzy all over. What a relief. "He was such a nice old gentleman," she said. "They don't make them like that anymore. In his nineties when he died. Are you going to be writing an article about him?"

My stomach did an elevator drop to the basement. "Did he have a son or grandson that's practicing now?"

"No, he just had the one daughter. She died so young. Heart disease in a child just doesn't seem natural, does it?"

I felt my mouth go dry. I coughed a little and said, "I'm running late for another appointment. I'll come back later in the week."

Her voice now sounded like it was coming from the bottom of a well. "Today is my last day. I'm retiring, moving to North Carolina. I have family there. But we have an excellent staff here. They will help you."

I managed a smile. "You have a safe trip and a good life in that warm sun."

She smiled politely in return. As I turned to leave, I heard her soft, almost inaudible voice, notes tapping on the door of my own memories: "Light, truth, and crystal, my dear."

I had heard my grandmother give that ancient Celtic blessing at weddings, births, and funerals. I knew the meaning well: "May light free your soul, truth unchain your body, and crystal love gives meaning to the whole." I turned to look at her, my words in kind. "Blessed be."

***

Richard's office building was only a few blocks down the street. There had to be a mistake. Maybe she had confused the names. Just a few blocks, it would only take a couple minutes. I took the elevator to the fifth floor. The door to Richard's office was locked, but I noticed the door across the hall was open. A janitorial cleaning cart sat in the hallway. A woman stepped out wearing a gray uniform. Long, straw-like bleached hair tied back and a face that looked like it had grown old before its time. A hardness reflected in her eyes. In a gravelly voice she said, "Who you lookin' for? Ain't nobody there."

"I . . . I was here earlier today and forgot my shopping bag. There is a gift in it for my husband. It's his birthday today, and I was going to give it to him tonight. Could you let me in, just to pick up my bag?"

She walked over to me and looked straight into my eyes. "Woman, you ain't no good liar, and you ain't been in that office today. Nobody been in that office for some time."

I opened my pocketbook, took out a couple of twenty-dollar bills, and handed them to her.

"I don't see nobody go in, and I don't see nobody come out that door," she said.

"So you can let me in?" I asked.

She unlocked the door and walked in with me. "Ain't never seen no poor attorney in this building, never saw one without clients either. So he's some kind of con man, is he?"

There was that word again. "What makes you think he's a con man?" I asked.

"Attorneys have file cabinets all right, but they have something in them. Those file cabinets over yonder, they don't have anything in them and never did as far as I can tell. Law books on the shelves, everything in this office is plush all right, but it's all on the surface, missy." She was right. The file cabinets were empty and the desk drawers clean. I stared at the red light on the phone.

"Go ahead," she said. "I sure would."

I pushed the button. A man's voice was speaking over some kind of noise in the background. "Richard, it's Kurt, old buddy. I'm getting reports: there's beginning to be too many buffalo in the field. Looks like you need to cull out some of the herd. The window of opportunity is closing. We need to get this to market soon, or we're going to lose our buyer. Get back to me." I leaned back against the front of the desk, facing her as she sat in the chair.

"I checked with the Supreme Court. They don't have his name on record as being an attorney," I said.

The woman looked at me, studied me for a moment. "In this state," she said.

"That's a thought. What if he has a license in another state? But how would I find that out? Oh, you wouldn't know that."

"Don't you be talkin' down to me, missy. May have been behind them bars for a while, but that don't make me no certified dinosaur. Try Martindale Hubbell."

"Who are they?" I asked.

"It ain't *who*, it's a book. Most attorneys are listed there. You can check it out on the internet," she replied.

"I've called him here at his office many times, and he has answered the phone," I stated.

She looked at me with a look of pity and total disbelief. "Haven't had much time to think this one through, have you? Ever heard of call forwarding, caller ID?" She was being kind in the light of my obvious stupidity. "His words rang in your ears, did they? I'll get you justice. Them silver-tongue orators with both hands in your pockets. Didn't help me none either."

As we stood in the hallway, she locked the door to the office.

"Thank you for your cooperation and the information."

She smiled as she put the twenty-dollar bills in her shirt pocket. "My pleasure," she said.

***

In the early morning hour, the shrill ring of the phone jarred me out of what had been a sound sleep.

"Carla?"

"Yes, Connors?"

There was only silence on the other end. In that moment I knew, whatever it was, I didn't want to hear what was coming next. Connors's deep voice on the other end resounded with an undeniable foreboding.

"Carla, I'm so sorry. I'm so sorry I have to tell you this."

"Connors, what is it, what's wrong?"

"It's Marcy," he said.

"Marcy? What about Marcy? No . . . no, I left her at the office, she was fine. Connors, she's fine!"

"No, Carla, she isn't fine. There is no other way to say this. Marcy's dead. They found her body at the office," Connors stated.

"Her body? The office? That can't be," I said defiantly.

"I'm here at the office now," he said. "An officer drove by and noticed the lights on, and when he checked it out . . ."

"I'm coming right over."

"I didn't want you to hear it from someone else. I know there's no sense in telling you not to come, you will anyway. I'll meet you in the parking lot." Connors's voice was solemn.

The rain had continued into the morning. Red traffic lights were nothing more than a blur as I sped through them. There had to be a mistake. Pulling into the parking lot, the wet pavement reflected the police cars' flashing lights. Yellow barricade tape corded off the crime scene. The morgue van was backed up to the entryway. When the gurney came out, her body was covered.

Everything looked so sterile and organized. Men and women in uniform, plainclothes officers—they were all routinely going about their assigned tasks. I didn't see emotion in their faces. They didn't know the victim, the loyal friend, wife, and mother. They wouldn't see her family and friends, the ones standing beside her grave in their sorrow, grief-stricken as they would say their last goodbyes. Her laughter that I would never hear again but in my own memories of her. The scene gripped my heart. Insanity has no logic.

Traffic hummed somewhere in the distance. Life was going on, moving ever forward as though this had never happened. A merry-go-round I wanted to stop, get off, make the motion and the music stop, but it will not. Life marched with defiant intent right past me as I sat there, a spectator on the wheel of time. The car door opened, and Connors sat down beside me. We looked at each other. His face wore the intense helplessness of a well-meaning friend that could not make the situation better.

"Carla, I know how much she meant to you. She was a good woman. She definitely didn't deserve this. It wasn't rape, or theft, but it was either a professional or someone completely out of touch with reality. It had to be someone with the expertise who understood the art of torture. It was hard. They were looking for something. Whatever it was, she couldn't give it to them."

I leaned over and buried my head in Connors's chest, crying with the intensity of a child unable to be pacified.

"Oh, Connors, it's all my fault. She wanted to work over. I should have stayed with her. If I had only stayed with her, she would be alive now."

"You couldn't have known this was going to happen, Carla. If you had stayed, you may very well have been on a second gurney coming out of that office."

"No. No, she died because of me. I should have protected her. I should have done something . . ." My sentence trailed off into uncontrollable sobbing remorse for what I could not bring back.

"I know how you feel, Carla. I've been down that road. I can't tell you the feeling goes away, but I can tell you it gets better. I know it's hard, but I have to ask you the question now. Do you have anyone on your caseload capable of doing anything like this?"

"The only one I can think of that would have the knowledge or ability to do such a thing is in the Veteran's Hospital. John suffers from PTSD. His wife is my client."

"Did he get released or walked out by any chance?" Connors asked.

"Released . . . walk out . . . do they really do that, walk out?" I questioned.

"It's been known to happen," he stated.

My stomach muscles wrenched with pain. "It's my fault she's dead, Connors. I should have told Marcy what John Clifton had said to his wife about her being a double agent. He was clearly out of it. If she had only known, she wouldn't have opened the door to let him in."

"Carla, you're jumping to conclusions," Connors said.

I took the cell phone out of my handbag.

"Who are you calling?" he asked.

"Calling someone that's going to give us an answer to your question." Allen answered the phone. "Allen, its Carla. I need to know about John Clifton. He's still at the hospital, right?"

I knew he had been sleeping, but his voice was alert and clear from years of doctor training. "Carla, yes, he's still with us. Actually, this is one of the worst weeks he's had. We had to put him in restraints and under heavy sedation in the psych ward. He's definitely in the hospital. Why are you asking?"

I tried to explain, but the words caught in my throat. Connors took my cell phone, stepped out of the car, and explained the situation to Allen.

In a few minutes he returned. "Allen seems like a nice guy," he said.

"He is. I spent an evening with him not so long ago. We had dinner and a few drinks. Come to think about it, a lot of drinks."

"Yeah, Carla, I know what you mean. I've had some of those 'lots of drinks' conversations. They can be soul cleansing and gut-wrenching. So what did you learn?"

"How Allen receives his patients. The marquee reads: *Vocation Soldier*. They had been brave young men and women . . . the broken ones, carrying their weapons and armor, with pictures of loved ones encased in love and fear. The brave had carried their comrades off the battlefield . . . parts and whole. Allen, the healer, found them in the darkest of places. I swear to you, Connors, I see him as an altar boy with a candle leading them back."

***

The day of the funeral, the long black hearse led the parade of family, loved ones, and friends. A gray stone archway stood at the entrance of the cemetery. Although it was midmorning, the fog had not completely lifted. Its misty veil added a somber feeling to the day. A Hollywood director would have been more than elated with the setting. My body was there, but my mind was still having difficulty accepting the reality of it all. I saw her in the coffin in her soft blue dress. There were so many flowers, carnations that she loved. It all looked so perfect, so perfectly unreal. Somewhere in this graveyard "Taps" began to play, honoring a brave soldier's passing. The haunting notes vibrated into the space of my own sorrow, then faded into the elusive air. Hearts struggled to hold on to the last note, their loved one, as the bonds of this earthly realm fell away forever.

Standing beside Marcy's grave, all at once the strong scent of her rose perfume surrounded me. In just a few moments she had communicated her peace, a few stitches to mend my broken heart. The rose scent faded away, and she was gone. I thanked her for her love and our friendship that I would never forget. Connors stood beside Sarah and me, words of condolence on his lips, but a harshness in his voice I had not heard before.

After the funeral, I went back to the house feeling as though it was a cave or fortress, somewhere to hide from the world and to look for normalcy. I sat in my chair in front of the fireplace, forcing my brain to slice itself up into small, manageable, uniform compartments: sleep, eat, zone out watching the flickering light on the television screen. In the pain compartment, memories seeped, creeped into my brain one by one, each ending in a black hole of terrifying horror. Scenes played themselves out in my mind, knowing what must have taken place that night in the office. Marcy's inability to give them what they wanted. There was no one there to rescue her.

I retreated to the compartment of sleep again, sometimes my only true refuge. On this dark, lonely sea, no light, magician's white dove, miracle of peace—forgiveness for me. *Dear Lord, grant me uninterrupted sleep.* I mentally compartmentalized my grief. Put it in a folder labeled "Marcy." Alphabetically arranged in a file cabinet, closed the door, duct-taped it shut. *I am in there with Marcy and do not know or care how to get out.*

Somewhere in my brain, reality began to sift in, like filtering light through a sieve. Logic and reason told me I had become a recluse sitting in the dark. I tried to recall what I was doing with all those days and hours, but my mind was blank. I stood in front of the window and pulled the drapes back. The blinding sunlight pounded through the glass. I brought my hands up to shield my eyes from the light of day, from life itself. I knew I could not go on this way forever. *I have to let go. Quit wallowing in guilt.* I could feel depression's teeth chewing away at the very marrow of my bones. *I must grant myself permission to move on and rejoin the human race. There must be a purpose, a mission, worthy of my reentry into humanity. Some kind of redemption for me.*

Who did this to Marcy and Colette? Their deaths were not coincidental. Now the answer came to me so naturally, like a satisfied lover. The one emotion that would release me, redeem my sole from bondage—revenge. Yes, the word floated on my tongue, the taste savory-sweet and so satisfying.

***

Two weeks later, Sarah opened the office. I still wasn't ready, couldn't bring myself to go back. I had become oblivious to time, now operating on autopilot. At 4:55 AM I went about my morning routine. I had on my jogging outfit, running shoes, and was ready to head out for my morning run with Kinsey. As I picked up my water bottle, the front doorbell rang. *Who could that be at this hour? What happened to the rules of etiquette regarding appropriate calling times? Oh, the days of gentry.*

As soon as I opened the door, Richard stepped inside. He didn't bother to say good morning. "You haven't been answering your phone. You haven't been working. Carla, you haven't been back to the office since—" Before he could say Marcy's name, the tears ran down my face. "That's it. You're going upstairs now. Put some things in an overnight bag, we are leaving in fifteen minutes." He put his hands on my shoulders and turned me toward the staircase. I caught a glimpse of myself in the foyer mirror. I must have dropped twelve pounds. The face looking back at me reflected my mental and emotional state: hollow and drawn. No makeup, and my hair looked like it had just exited a tornado. Now we both looked in the mirror. He took a deep breath and injected some sympathy into his voice. "Okay, half an hour."

Chapter 24

I showered and then threw some things in a backpack. I put blue jeans on and found my beloved brown hooded sweatshirt, the one that feels like comfort food tastes. There sat my backpack on the floor. I opened the drawer of the nightstand and took out the gun Connors had given me. I put it in the bottom of the backpack. Yes, I would definitely be taking that along.

"I'll call Maria and ask her to come over and pet-sit," I told Richard.

"We'll take them with us. They will enjoy the outing," he said.

That was informational. Now I knew where we were going: the cabin at the lake, the one his family had owned. It would be a three-hour drive.

"I told Sarah I was taking the week off."

"Great," he said. "That way, she won't expect you back for at least a week."

"I'll call Maria and let her know we are going to the lake. She was going to stop by today."

"It's Saturday morning, let her sleep in," he insisted.

"Okay. I'll leave a note on the kitchen table then," I compromised.

"No," he said, "you can call her after we get there. Let's go. If we leave now, we'll be on the road before the traffic gets heavy. We'll stop at Dockers for breakfast."

Dockers was a restaurant back off the beaten path. Only the locals went there. They served a down-home country-style breakfast before the general population made breakfast out a politically correct statement.

"The carrot before the donkey," I said.

"Well, whatever it takes," was his response. He opened the door for me, and I climbed into his Jeep. He put Kinsey and Devin in the back. "Carla, we will discuss everything that has gone on after we reach the cabin. Is that okay with you?"

I nodded. That was more than okay with me. In view of the early hour, I would be doing good to brush the cobwebs out of my brain, much less contemplate complex concepts.

"Counselor, I would like you to represent my best interest at the next drive-thru. The blessed grain would be greatly appreciated," I said. We got our coffee. I, of course, pleaded for a doughnut to hold me over until breakfast.

As we rode along, we made small talk. For the first time, that was difficult to do. Richard and I had always been able to talk to each other about anything and everything; however, anything and everything wasn't what I wanted to talk about. Now all I wanted to know was what information he had gained on his trip. I had to admit, Richard was right; it would be better to have the discussion later at the cabin. We could discuss everything then.

"Richard, the weather is turning bad."

"Yes, it's beginning to look pretty dark. The weather forecast called for some rain, but it's supposed to be clear and sunny in the south. It will be nice when we get there." The rain began to come down light and steady. "Why don't you put your seat back and take a nap? You'll feel more rested when we get there. We are going to have some decisions to make." He turned the radio on, the music soft and low.

I put my seat back and closed my eyes, but my mind wouldn't shut off. *The people we know, how much do we* really *know about them?* I thought I knew Richard, and obviously that was a mistake. I hadn't known about his dark side, his history, his college roommate. Why hadn't Richard wanted me to leave a note for Maria? It would only have taken a moment. And what about his statement before we left: "Great. Sarah won't expect you back for at least a week."

The picture of Daniel in New Orleans—did Richard know Daniel? I wasn't ready to talk about Daniel to Richard. Ironic, I would now build a wall of secrecy between Richard and myself. Richard was right—in one way or another we are all mask wearers. Even poor Jennifer, living in the perfect home with the perfect parents who were anything but perfect. The music on the radio began to fade into the distance. I felt myself slip into sleep.

In my dream, I saw people sitting around a table. They looked like figures from a wax museum. The tabletop looked like a geographical layout of different countries. It was as though I was floating up above in the air overlooking the table. I could see a volcano in one place and an earthquake in another. The sea was raging and then became a full tsunami. A village in the Alps without people and tornadoes swirling black across the wheat fields of Kansas.

Geometric symbols and mathematical equations floating in the sky.

The wax people at the table began to melt. Their masks began to drop. Within the midst of it all was Colette, again holding a box in her hands, but this time it was different. Written underneath the lock was one word: *Pandora*. Connors was standing beside her. She handed the box to Bulldog, then turned and smiled at me.

My dream came to an abrupt end with the screeching sound of tires. I lunged forward against my seat belt. Kinsey was thrown up against the front seat, his head between Richard and me. We were all looking out the front windshield. There in the middle of the road staring back at us was a very large Black Angus bull. Kinsey looked at me, and I looked at him. We both looked at Richard, who still had a death grip on the steering wheel.

Richard threw up his hands in a gesture of disbelief. He looked around and then pointed in the direction of a field across the road. A herd of cattle glistened in the morning sun.

"Maybe he was on his way over to visit his girlfriend's."

"Right," I said, "but if that's the case, why is he still standing there?"

Richard blew the horn. Romeo snorted and stomped the ground.

"You know, I don't think that was such a good idea," he said, looking at the bull.

"You may be right," I responded.

"Richard, maybe if we backed up, we could go off road and around him."

We backed up slowly. The bull stood his ground. Richard shifted into four-wheel drive. We drove off the side of the road around Romeo and onto the road again. We stopped and looked back. Mr. Bull was still not happy. He snorted and hoofed the road again.

"Richard, I think that bull is coming after us. It looks like he's going to charge," I said, starting to panic.

"That is what it looks like," Richard said as he pulled forward. The bull began to give chase. Richard accelerated down the road, and I began to laugh. The whole picture was just too ridiculous. When the bull gave up and we were safely ahead, Richard turned to me.

"Of course, you would think this was funny. What would have happened if he had caught up with us?"

"Well, then, I guess we would have just become people burgers. Rottweiler sausage and Oriental stir-fry."

Richard pulled over to the side of the road and stopped. "Doc, you are undoubtedly, certifiably insane." We both laughed until our sides hurt. It felt good to laugh, regardless how ridiculous the situation had become.

"I have to ask, Richard, do you think this has ever happened to anyone else?"

"I don't know, but I sure am glad we weren't on bicycles." He laughed.

We arrived at Dockers, had a big breakfast with an extra cup of coffee, and relived our death-defying escape from Romeo.

"Richard, at our Friday-night dinners, you must be the one to tell the story. You do stories so well."

An older man stopped by our table on his way out saying, "That bull you were talking about, that's Henry Stump's prize bull. He's a mean, nasty-tempered thing. However, he is one fine bull. Henry is going to be real upset when he finds out that old boy went dating without payment."

Richard asked the man to sit down at our table, no doubt to get some more local flavor. I excused myself and went to the ladies' room. Once inside the restroom, I pulled out my cell phone. I felt a need to connect with Connors, to let him know my whereabouts. I called his cell phone and he answered.

"Connors, it's me, Carla. Do you know anything more about Jennifer?"

"They broadened the pickup order, it's not just for the state now," he announced.

I told him about the cabin at the lake and where it was because I needed him to know exactly where I was and who I was with just in case something happened to me. "I'll call you when I get back into town." *Sometimes beautiful places can be deadly.*

"If you need me, Carla, I'm as close as that cell phone number," he reminded me.

"Connors, that means a great deal to me right now. In more ways than you know. Richard has the rest of the pieces of the puzzle. I should have it all put together this weekend. When I get back, I think we need to sit down together. There are things I need to tell you."

"Keep your cell phone on this weekend, okay, Carla? And watch your back." There was concern in his voice.

"I will, and I'll see you when I get back." As I hung up, Connors's concerned words rang in my ears: *Watch your back.*

I started to enter the dining room of the restaurant but stopped. Standing in the doorway, for a moment I could observe Richard and the old man at our table. They were deep in conversation. An old farmer, bib overalls, blue plaid shirt, leathery skin. A couple of generations from now, the old homestead independent farmer will vanish from our society. Reflecting their own personalities, barns, neat fencerows, unique in their own way, like a quilt, different in design but uniform in stitch. The stamina and strength of a man, sweat from his brow, only bowing to nature's force. Under the summer's sun, the hands that taught the last generation will one day lay silent as the next gives way to the large co-ops of industry. One man's endeavor, the beginning of our food chain will be but a blot in history's memory. We finished our breakfast conversation then took to the road again.

***

We arrived at the cabin an hour or so later. It was truly a vacation for Devin and Kinsey. As soon as we opened the doors, they both went off to explore. Devin climbed trees and played like king of the jungle. Kinsey ran along the lake and expansive wooded area around the cabin. The cabin, as we called it, was a cozy two-story log home with a front porch overlooking the lake and a dock that generated visions I couldn't allow myself to deal with now.

Roy, the handyman, looked after the place throughout the year. His pickup truck was parked in the driveway. As we approached the front porch, Roy greeted us. He was an older man with a face that wore the character lines of an outdoorsman. Deep wrinkles beneath leathery skin attested to hours of labor in the hot summer sun. A confidence that spoke of a craftsman's skills. His ball cap covered up a receding hairline. He was thin and appeared to work at only one pace—constantly. Roy took care of several of the cabins along the lake and did some routine maintenance and construction work.

"I put the porch furniture back out for the season," he said. He placed them out as he always had. The glider was on one end, and two wooden rocking chairs and a table were in the middle of the porch. "I stocked your refrigerator like you asked," he said. "Anything else you'd like me to do before I go, Mr. Dupree?"

"What about the boards on the dock that we talked about? Did you get a chance to look at them?" asked Richard.

"They're rotten, all right, and need to be replaced. I'm going to be picking up the lumber next week along with some other things," Roy acknowledged.

"Okay, Roy. I'm sure you've taken care of everything as usual," Richard agreed.

"Then I'll be on my way down to Bob Randall's place. They're coming in next week," Roy said as he turned to go.

Sometimes the ritual of routine, knowing the order of things, provides its own comfort. In the morning, Richard and I will come out, have breakfast on the porch, then bathe in the morning sun, and watch the light play across the water of the lake. The woods were alive with wildlife: deer, squirrels, and rabbits. The red cardinals built their nests near the porch. Every season of the year here was scenic.

Richard took our things into the cabin. I stopped on the porch and turned to look at the lake, remembering flashes of our time here together, recalling scenes from memory.

"What, no fish for dinner?"

He had laughed, went to the kitchen, and came back with marshmallows and hot dogs. We took a blanket and built a fire down by the lake, just the two of us in the quiet of the night.

Richard said, "As breathtaking as the night sky can be, it's the sunrise I look forward to the most."

I was the only person he ever brought here. Now I questioned why and who Richard Dupree really was.

"That Roy, he's a good man." I heard Richard say, "He even stocks the refrigerator."

As I turned around, I saw Richard in the doorway with two bottles of beer in his hands and a package of pretzels under his arm.

"You're right," I said. "Roy even remembered my pretzels."

Richard leaned up against the doorframe. We looked at one another for a moment.

"You know, Doc, we always did make a good combination. Beer and pretzels, does it get any better than that?"

"Does it get better, Richard? How much longer am I going to have to endure the secrets, the evil that has been stalking me, invading my life? Sometimes I wonder if I am going to get out of this alive. Is it time to talk now?"

"Yes." He nodded toward the chairs on the porch.

He opened the bottles of beer. I opened the sack of pretzels. We sat in the rocking chairs facing the lake.

"Richard, I need to bring you up to date. Some pretty weird things went on while you were gone." He listened patiently as I filled him in on my encounter with Connors and Jennifer's family tragedy.

I was telling him what had happened to Kinsey when the men broke into my home when Richard interjected, "Yeah, that was an assignment gone awry. One does have to admit though, that was really funny."

"What?" I asked.

He had been listening to me and looking out at the lake. He turned abruptly. "Oh, I'm sorry, Carla. That must have been truly terrifying for you."

"You already knew?" I questioned.

"Yes," he said. "Actually, my dear, it's a very small world we live in, and through modern technology, it has become a lot smaller. Securing the world you and I live in. It takes a particular type of personality to do that kind of work so we can all sleep at night. If we knew what they know, few of us would sleep at all. However, as they say, somebody has to do it."

"Okay, it's my first rodeo. Excuse me, but I'm not following you," I said.

"The thing you didn't tell me about, Carla, was that you traded cars with your mechanic that day."

"What does that have to do with anything?" I questioned.

"The government had a trace on your car. When you pulled up to the intersection, you and the mechanic switched cars. This is where, pardon me if you will, it got amusing in a rather perverse way. Your car went on, you didn't. You came back to the house. Your appointment book and phone transmissions indicated you would be working late that night."

"How would they know that?" Then Connors's words came back to me: *Accept it, Carla, there isn't any privacy nowadays.* "Forget I even question that. Evidently I'm still in the Stone Age."

His lips curved slightly upward as he continued to enlighten the prehistoric girl. "The men that were in your house, they really didn't intend to do Kinsey in. They just wanted to put him to sleep for a little while. They didn't want him to bark and raise suspicion. He was too big and, in their thinking, unpredictable. The easy solution was to let him take a nap."

"What about Devin?" I inquired.

"They didn't know about him, and if they had, they wouldn't have considered him as an issue, much less an adversary." Richard smiled.

"That still doesn't explain why they were in my house," I concluded.

"You know exactly why, Carla, the chip. They had planned to sweep the house top to bottom for it. They were in the attic coming down when they heard you inside the house. At that point, they were just trying to get out. Cover it up as a B&E gone badly. Devin was aware of your presence, and he's territorial. These men were intruders. When the man stopped at the doorway between you and Devin, that's when Devin made his move from the top of the armoire to the top of the man's head." Richard began to laugh almost uncontrollably. "I'm sorry, Carla, but you have to understand. These men are chosen for their physical abilities, mental aptitude, and personality. Profilers researched them in detail. In other words, they are trained to be the ultimate killing machine. Now one of those highly trained killing machines has the dubious distinction among his peers of donning the dreaded name Cat Man. I'm told the guy doesn't have a sense of humor. His comrades, however, are having a field day with this one."

"Did I hear you say our government had a tracer on my car?" I remarked.

"Yes," he said in a matter-of-fact tone.

"Are we talking singular or plural?" I asked.

He took another sip of his beer, turned, and looked at me again. He looked so unstressed by all that was going on around us. "Carla you always were a pretty quick study. Governments, oh, it's plural all right, it's definitely plural."

"What other government?" I inquired.

"Come on, keep up. Remember, *plural*—governments. What you have in that chip is so hot it could totally change the world as we know it. Some technology is still in its infancy but lethal. Very, very lethal."

"What catastrophic disaster is in that chip, Richard?"

"I've known for a long time about your intuition, Carla, or whatever you want to call it. This thing you have, it seems to serve you well. I know at a certain level you have some ideas regarding this issue. What do you know, Carla? Tell me and I'll give you the rest of the pieces of the puzzle."

"Are you kidding me? I've been so traumatized by everything that has been going on. Richard, do you realize my house has been broken into twice? One of my clients, a victim, now thought to be a murderer, and she is nothing more than a child. Then there's Colette and Marcy . . . I can't even . . . " My mouth opened to say the word *sleep,* but nothing came out. The dream I had on the way there before I was abruptly taken out of it by Romeo the bull came back to me. As I recalled the dream, it was still vivid in my mind. I told Richard what I saw. He nodded in some kind of acceptance. "Richard, why did I end up with this chip?"

"Well, for one thing, you live in what was the professor's house," Richard said.

"Of which you facilitated my buying," I stated matter-of-factly.

Richard only shrugged. "The professor worked for the government. A lot of his work was experimental."

"Richard, you knew the professor had completed his theory and it was accurate," I commented.

"Yes, and so did the gardener. He was supposedly one of ours," he acknowledged.

"Ours?" I asked.

Richard raised one eyebrow and continued as though the question was hardly worth a response. "When the dark of money is in play, we can only hope that the research profile people did their homework right. The professor died a natural death, all right. The gardener was in place to find and pick up the chip. The professor had been working on an advanced prototype. He had this little quirk in his personality."

"What was that?" I asked.

"He liked to proceed to the bottom line before presenting his theories. Sometimes they didn't even know what he was working on or how far along he was. He was brilliant but sometimes a bit of a maverick, often working independently."

"So how did they find out?" I questioned.

"When the men took his files and handwritten notes from the house, it was then they realized the professor was much farther along with his theories than anyone knew."

"I still don't understand. What happened to the gardener?" she said with concern in her voice.

"The gardener got greedy. Figured with the down economy his pay wasn't going to be giving him an early retirement. The name of the game then was to get the gardener before he made the exchange and got his payoff," stated Richard.

"Richard, you are working with our government, right?" I needed his answer.

There was a moment's silence. He looked out at the lake. "Why, of course, Carla. Who else would I be working for?"

Indeed, I thought, *who else*. "Where does Colette fit into all of this, and how did she end up with the chip?"

"The gardener realized there had been a breach in his cover story on both sides of the equation. He was trying to get rid of the chip. Claim total innocence and let things cool down. That's the best he could have hoped for. He had seen Colette at the professor's house and thought he might need to use her some time, so he made the connection early on . . ."

"That's interesting, Richard. I had thought it was one of her clients, but he was a lot closer to her, a familiar face she might have seen every week."

"That's right. He dropped the sculpture off at Colette's front door. When he secured what he thought was his way out of the country, it was a trap. Now he was truly out in the cold. They couldn't find the sculpture, but they did find Colette at the top of the stairs. They confronted her. She struggled, jerked away, and that's when she fell. Didn't mean for her to fall. That was the last thing I wanted."

"I wanted?" I repeated back with obvious judgments.

"I said *they* wanted," he continued as though the misspoken word wasn't relevant. His deflection was smooth, flowing as though the question hardly required acknowledgment. If there was one thing my profession taught me, it was to listen when others spoke.

"They would have finished her off later, but because of her fall, she died. When she died, the secret of where the sculpture had gone slipped away with her. She could no longer tell them anything."

"So what happened to the gardener?" I looked at Richard.

His face glowed with pleasure, a cat who had just executed the last volley with the mouse. "They got him, but he couldn't even finance a game at that point. He had nothing to give them. He didn't know where the sculpture was. Years ago, Cecilia's had a saying: 'I no see him anymore.'"

"They killed him?" I said with raised voice.

"Interesting, isn't it? He was a traitor, you need to know how to play with the big boys. He walked right into the trap. Now that's international work exchange. The global market in its truest form, wouldn't you say?" Richard's voice held the sound of pleasure and amusement.

"How safe are we here, Richard?"

"We're okay here. The perimeter is covered, and the house is secure." His voice now sounded cold and distant. "You are now the primary focus, Carla. The competition is out there. The race is on. They believe you have the chip. We need to give them another lead to go chase. My only question is, what did you do with that chip, Carla? Where is it?"

Now I knew Richard was one of the players sitting at the table in the wax museum holding his own masked agenda in reserve, not the team player or the patriot.

"Richard, you told me you would give me the pieces of the puzzle to make the picture whole. What was the professor working on?"

"I don't know about you, but I'm definitely ready for another beer," he said. "Shall I bring you one?"

"Might as well. I've got a feeling this isn't going to be a short conversation." As frightening as he had become, I needed more answers.

Chapter 25

He went to the kitchen and brought back more beer.

"Your dream told you everything you need to know, Carla. The geometric forms and mathematical equations—that was the work of the professor. Do you remember the time when there was all that hoopla about circles in cornfields and so on?"

"Yes," I said. "There were reports, everything from extraterrestrials to hoaxes. What does that have to do with this?"

Richard was somewhat matter-of-fact. "Some people refer to it as the Arc Project."

"Hold up. Excuse me, but is that 'Ark,' as in the biblical sense or alchemy 'Arc,' as in intensification of natural processes?" I asked.

"The latter. In some reports, highly classified of course, one would find it under Apple Orchard," he stated.

My mind was now going fuzzy, and irritation was definitely setting in. "Apple Orchard? What is that supposed to mean? That doesn't mean anything."

"How intuitive," he said with a smug smile.

"How arrogant!" I exclaimed.

"Come on, don't be cranky. It's just fun and games," Richard stated. "Once some of the professor's research papers had been recovered, it became evident to us he had gone down a path in science no other person had ever discovered. Think of it as a new science, something that had previously never been explored. I think the further the old professor went, perhaps the more paranoid he became. When he became aware of the possibilities, the dangers that could lie ahead, it would be enough to give anyone pause to make them think before they unleashed this discovery into the world."

"May I interrupt? And you think my empathic abilities are strange?" Richard raised an eyebrow, and I sighed. "By all means, carry on. So what's happening in the scientific frontier?"

"However the research could produce unlimited energy sources, not to mention expanding space travel. If we could only learn to harness this power, we could truly ride in chariots of the gods. We believe the professor had found the yoke for the phantom neutrons."

Even though Richard had dumbed it down for me, I must have been looking at him like a deer with its eyes caught in the headlights.

"There are those governments' private enterprises throughout the world with power, money, scientists, think tank people, and futurists."

"Richard, you didn't say anything about civilian committees or news media."

"Oh, my lady's brain awakens. If you don't acknowledge the ownership, you cannot be held responsible for the toys you play with or the decisions you make. If you make life in a laboratory but don't disclose your work, the moralist cannot crucify you. The cogs of progress are not stilled," he said.

"Is that what we're calling progress nowadays?" I questioned.

"It doesn't get any bigger scale than this one," he said. "It is the ability to change the weather of a continent; to create hurricanes, droughts, volcanoes, tsunamis; to disrupt commerce and the foundation and stability of a country. Military powers have orgasms in their pants just thinking about the possibilities. Imagine a satellite up above our Earth programed with the proficiency of a neurosurgeon with a scalpel in his hand. That neurosurgeon had to perfect his abilities somewhere, so it was done. Now we have the power and the proficiency to write history. Fields of harvest where drought had once denied the land, where fertile fields gave abundance, now they would lie dormant. Armies would not need to march forward because Mother Nature would deliver disaster via the command of mankind. Imagine, Carla, the generals and powerbrokers sitting at this table of life. No one must ever know that you have any knowledge of this chip. Your life literally depends on it. This matter is settled. You will give me the sculpture. We must figure a way to get that chip into the hands of our government. We need a go-between. In your dream, Colette may have given you the answer. She gave the box to Bulldog."

Before I could stop myself, I said, "I didn't tell you his nickname was Bulldog."

"I know who the man is," Richard said. "He used to work in Washington DC for the government. That's where he met Colette. You know how first loves are. Like I said, Carla, it's a small world. Did you tell Connors what you did with the sculpture?"

"No, Connors doesn't know anything about the sculpture. I told you his involvement has to do with Jennifer and the massacre of her family," I assured him.

Richard leaned forward and stared at me with an intensity that could have cut steel. "Anything *else* you want to tell me, Carla?"

"Okay, Richard, there's a lot more going on. What aren't you telling me?"

"We came up with some interesting background information about the professor. He had a niece, and she was going to be married. There was a freak accident, and her fiancé was killed. No one knew she was pregnant. She went to a small village in Austria and had the baby. A childless couple, relatives from the States went to Austria, registered as the biological parents. They came back to the States with the child. She went back to Germany to the university and continued her education," Richard remarked.

"The professor's house and his estate went to her? She's the one I bought the house from?"

"That's right, but this is where it gets interesting. The professor kept in contact and provided generous support for the child. It took some digging to get this information. We don't know why, but for whatever reason, the professor kept everything cash and carry, no paper trail. What we do know is that there was a definite bond between this child and the professor. Carla, this child was a boy. He was given the name . . . Daniel Walters."

Out of nowhere the information attacked me like the deadly leap of a lion.

"Carla, I would have asked if he had ever divulged any of this information to you, though from the shocked look on your face, I would say that wasn't the case."

I felt vulnerable, naked. What did Richard know about Daniel and me? He might know the surface, but there was no way he could have known the depth of my feelings for Daniel. Richard was right. So much of Daniel was wrapped in secrecy. I took another drink of my beer, thinking it should have been brandy.

"Let's take a walk along the lake. We can talk about your newfound friend Bulldog. Do you think he would make a suitable go-between?" He rose from his chair and held out a hand to help me up. All I could think was anyone knowing of the toys in the toy box was a good target for elimination, including Connors. Richard was planning to clean the slate.

He continued as we began our walk, "Once the assignment has been completed, our adversaries will know we have the basketball. There are other powers on this international court, so there is no slam-dunk, game over in this arena." Richard fell silent. Was he talking only about the sculpture, or was there a weave of crafted metaphor within the statement? "Carla, what does Bulldog know? How much have you told him?"

"Just what I told you and nothing more. Actually, he was just doing some follow-up work involving another client, minor stuff—probation violation, so he did come to the office now and then." I had just lied through my teeth to Richard, and it felt right. I wasn't finding the common ground we had before. His casual demeanor felt distant, aloof, and detached from emotion. It was frightening.

He took my hand as we walked along. I could only hope he wouldn't notice my sweaty, trembling hand. I had wanted revenge, the information that would bring justice for Colette and Marcy, redeeming my own soul from guilt. Now I realized I had fallen into a hole so deep, so dark, light had long since faded from view. The magnitude and scope of his inhumanity is inconceivable.

Richard stopped, turned to me, put his hands on my shoulders, and brought his fingers up around my neck. He was behind me now, forcing me to look at the dock. The memory of the alley and the man in the black leather jacket surged through my nervous system like an uncontrollable seizure. Richard had broken that man's neck so quickly, but I still had what he wanted: that chip. He leaned down over me, his mouth close to my ear, and whispered, "Carla, if you were dying, what would be the last thing you would want to see?"

"Excuse me?" I stepped back.

"It's a legitimate question." He grabbed my shoulders.

"The last thing I would want to see?" I asked as I turned to look at him.

"Yes." He smiled as he looked out into the distance. "For me it would be the sunrise. It's always been the sunrise. All the dreams and plans that can be accomplished in just one day, the footprint you leave behind. And you, Carla, what would you want to see?" Again, his veiled threat had been less than discreet.

"The face of my loved ones so I could let them know love transcends all dimensions. " Seconds passed by with nothing but the sounds of water splashing against the shoreline.

"You're never going to see Daniel again, not ever. You don't want to make me do something to him. Something you will regret. Do you understand what I'm saying to you, Carla?"

"Yes. I understand." He let go of me, and we started walking again.

"Good. Then we will never speak of Daniel again. I always safeguard what is mine. I will never let anything, or anyone, come between us. It's just you and me. We're in this together. Right?"

"Right. But you do understand Daniel is just a friend, there's nothing between us, Richard. No need for drastic measures." I lied through my teeth again.

"You'll never see him again and there will be no drastic measures." Richard had just written extortion into his resume.

The worn pathway beside the lake made for easy walking. Cabins along the lake were few and far between. The owners were mostly professional people coming out for weekends and summer vacations, escaping from the city's rush and pressures of life.

Richard stopped and looked across the lake. "That's Scott and Tammy Brown's place," he said. "Remember last year they said they were going to put in a new boat dock in this spring? That must be the construction workers."

Kinsey came out of the woods and followed along with us, occasionally running off to chase a chipmunk or occasional bird gathering twigs for its nest.

Richard kept his voice low. "With the professor's creative imagination and eccentric desire for completion before acknowledgment of his work, scientifically the most advanced theories on the face of the Earth still remain with us. Carla, experimentation on both sides of the fence is going on. It comes down to who gets it right first."

"Richard, how does this type of thing happen to ordinary people?"

"It doesn't usually," he said, "but sometimes there's a crack in the sky and the rain just comes falling through."

"Well, leave it to me to be standing under the crack without an umbrella. I'm having problems getting my mind to wrap around all of this."

"That's why we're here," Richard said. "So we have time and space to work things out."

Along the south side of the house, the lilacs were in full bloom. We walked across the lawn, and I picked a few from the bushes.

"I'll pick some more later to put on the table," I said.

I loved the smell of lilacs. They were a reminder of our good times here, when innocence and lack of knowledge prevailed. We would walk along the lake and do some hiking on the back paths through the woods. Now white and pink dogwood trees dotted the forest. The pine trees along the back of the cabin appeared even greener. The new yellow-green tender foliage complemented the palette. Today had been an exceptionally warm day. The sun's heat felt good on my body—a healing potion for my terrified mind. The heat I could not absorb I would've liked to bottle and take for another day so the energy of nature could restore me later.

Richard's voice broke through my tranquil moment. "Carla, what is your take on Bulldog, or Connors, as you refer to him?"

"I've got a good feeling about Connors." We walked along in silence for a while. "I've got a question for you, Richard."

"Only one?" he asked.

"When you were down south and took those pictures in New Orleans, you never did really explain that to me. Is Daniel one of our agents, and if so, why wouldn't we use him as a go-between?"

"That's more than one question, and you tell me."

Obviously, my finesse didn't work. Now I was on the chopping block giving my explanation. I could only claim lack of knowledge. We sat down on the end of the dock.

"Carla, do you think you could get Bulldog to come out this weekend? This would be the perfect place to do some brainstorming."

"Yes, I can do that," I said, knowing *Connors could be in danger, but I have no other choice.*

"The phone in the cabin hasn't been reactivated yet," he said. "We'll have to go to the top of the hill."

What Richard was referring to were our cell phones. The cell phones wouldn't work at the cabin; we were in a dead zone. On top of the hill, where the one-lane dirt road meets the gravel road, we could get enough signal to call out and receive calls.

The water of the lake was crystal blue. We could see the clouds reflecting in the water, such a peaceful place. Everyone should be able to come to a place like this without being tainted by such memories as Richard's brother's untimely demise and Richard's veiled confession. We walked back up the lawn to the cabin. Richard picked up his keys as we went through the kitchen and out the back door. We got into the Jeep, went to the top of the hill, and I made my call to Connors.

"It's Carla, Richard and I are at his cabin in the mountains. You said if I ever wanted to talk with you . . . is that rain check still good?"

"Anytime," was his response.

"I know it's short notice, Connors, but could you make it this evening?"

"I can if that's what you want." I could hear a flat tone of concern in his voice, but he was giving nothing away.

"That would be great," I said. "I'll put on a pot roast and you can have dinner with us. We need to discuss something with you. If you can plan to stay overnight, in the morning we will take you to a place that really knows how to serve a down-home breakfast. You may even see a bull named Romeo."

I could hear him chuckle on the other end. "Now that's an offer I haven't heard before." I gave him directions again as though I hadn't previously done so. He went along, no doubt understanding that Richard was close by.

When I was finished, Richard and I drove back to the cabin.

"I'll go to the root cellar," I said, "and get some potatoes and carrots. You check the freezer and get out the pot roast. Cooking sherry is in the cupboard."

The cellar had been one of the features that came in quite handy this far out in the country. It was dug out of the hillside that sloped down toward and along the north side of the cabin. A heavy log door matched the cabin and blended with the overall appearance. I had to admit, it made a nice wine cellar as well. A wooden bar slid across the door. I put vegetables in the basket and picked up two bottles of wine. With both hands full, I pushed the door closed. Richard was always good at helping me in the kitchen. We got the pot roast together and put it in the oven.

Opening the window over the sink, a soft breeze brought in the sweet scent of lilacs. "I'm going to pick some more lilacs for the dining room table."

"While you do that," Richard said, "I'll fix us a pot of coffee."

Devin tagged along and chased chipmunks as I made my selection of lilacs, wildflowers, and a few sprigs of evergreen. Back at the house, Richard stood by the sink and observed as I put the flower arrangement together on the kitchen table. He always had a good body; he worked out regularly, and it showed. His light blue sweatshirt did not hide what was underneath: a well-chiseled body that was physically fit and toned. His blue jeans were tight in all the right places. He walked with the strength and stride of an athlete. I knew no one else that worked out with the veracity Richard did. Now I knew why—machines should be well oiled.

We set the dining room table, and I put the lilacs on the sideboard. It was a beautiful, large arrangement.

"Let's have our coffee on the front porch," he said. I took out two coffee cups, and Richard brought out the coffeepot.

Sitting in the middle of the table was a deck of cards. One hand for him and one for me already dealt out.

"Should I trust you?" I asked.

Without a word, he took a paper napkin off the top of a small bowl, revealing his ace in the hole. Small pieces of chocolate wrapped in gold foil.

"Okay, so I'm putty in your hands."

He looked rather pleased with himself and poured our coffee.

Devin evidently hadn't had his fill of playing king of the jungle. I saw him wander off into the woods again. We played cards and talked of other things. The water of the lake lay quiet, smooth, and clear as a reflective mirror. The distant mountains, now dressed in a soft blue haze, rose to meet the onset of night.

"Richard, have you seen Kinsey?"

"No, and it's getting late. Time to bring him in. I'll take the coffee cups to the kitchen, and you can look for that Rottweiler of yours."

Of course, when Kinsey played in the yard with Richard or rode in the Jeep beside him, Richard miraculously transferred title of ownership. He nodded. "Actually, I think I'm just going to sit here and enjoy the view a little longer. Then I'll bring our things in."

Walking up the gravel road, the scent of lilacs floated on the midst of the evening. Kinsey was on the road just ahead of me. I patted the side of my leg. "Come, Kinsey." He didn't come. Something definitely had his attention. I continued up the steep incline. Kinsey was looking over the edge of the road. I walked over to see what he was looking at. The thickly wooded forest darkened the terrain below me. Stepping closer to the edge, I reached for a branch to steady myself and then leaned forward to get a better look. The ravine was steep. Kinsey continued to whine and pace back and forth alongside of the road. The ground was soft and wet from the spring rains. I could feel the earth beneath my feet begin to shift and crumble. Then I heard a cracking sound as the branch broke free from the tree. Simultaneously the earth, the branch, and I plunged down into the terrain below.

A blur of light and dark streamed past me. Spears of light shot down from the forest canopy. Barberry bushes tore at my face, skin, and clothing. Branches, trees I didn't miss, but hit my body straight on, knocking the breath out of me. Something stopped my descent. I was flat on my back with a piece of wood lying across my body. I picked up the wood and sat up, then realized there was a hand attached to the arm I was holding. The arm was inside a camouflage jacket sleeve. I opened my mouth to scream, but nothing came out. Hanging there with the aid of my own hand, as though it were a part of me, a deformed appendage—I couldn't seem to let go of that deformed appendage. Slowly I looked up the arm to the body, and there lay a man with a gunshot hole in the center of his head.

Something warm and wet crept over my hand as I watched the red liquid flow from his sleeve. The kill was fresh. The sense of the soul, that thing that gives one life, spark, electricity, what I knew as aura, was gone from him. Eyes open without vision, staring up into nowhere. In the distance, I could hear a rustling sound of leaves coming closer. I wanted to turn to look, to see. Where did I want the bullet hole, in the back of my head or the front? Warm, humid air hung heavy over me. I found my next breath harder to take than the one before. Paralyzing fear wrapped itself around me like a seductive boa constrictor; I had become its prey.

The sounds came to a crescendo as Kinsey's heavy body careened into mine. His massive head dislodged the man's arm. Kinsey stood over the man's body and made a low, primal growl. A sense of reality began to slip back into my being.

With Kinsey's strength and four feet on the ground we made it back up the steep ravine. Stumbling and dazed, I felt like a Mack truck had just run over my entire body. We headed back toward the cabin. *I have to let Richard know.* It was as if my whole world had just gone into slow motion. *Richard . . . oh no, was that Richard I heard earlier at the front door, or had it been someone else? Who was the dead man in the woods? Had he been one of the security people, or was he an intruder?* How was I to know the good guys from the bad guys? This game was so far over my head I hadn't even been issued a scorecard.

As we came to the end of the woods by the south side of the cabin, I took hold of Kinsey's chain. We started down alongside of the cabin. There were enough pine trees and lilac bushes to conceal our presence. As we came closer, I could see the front porch. There was a noise coming from somewhere. I crouched down, and Kinsey sat beside me. I pulled back some branches from the pine tree to get a better view of the porch. The table had been knocked over, and the coffeepot was on the porch floor along with the broken coffee cups. *Where are those voices coming from?* I pulled the branches back just a little more, and I could see the dock. Two men, one of them was Richard, were facing each other. The other man had a gun in his hand pointed at Richard. Richard's hands went up in the air. The blast from the gun is muffled but undeniably distinct. Richard flew backward off the dock into the water. He had shot Richard. Killed him.

The man in the black wet suit went over and looked down into the water, then turned and looked back at the cabin. *This can't be happening. I must be dreaming.* I could feel the cold steel of Kinsey's choker chain in my hand and the warmth of his body. This was no dream. *They will be coming for me next. I have to get to the Jeep. It's my only way out.* Another man was going toward the root cellar. Kinsey and I circled back behind the cabin and down the north side. I could see the man pull the door open to the root cellar. *He is looking for me.* One can feel the evil of others. The vibrations that emanated from him saturated the very ground he stood on with bad karma. As soon as he stepped inside, I ran across the lawn, slammed the door shut, and pulled the heavy wooden bar across, trapping him in there.

As I ran to the back of the cabin, I began to pray. *Dear Lord, please let the keys be in the Jeep.* When I opened the door, there they were hanging from the ignition. "Come, Kinsey." He jumped into the front seat. As we turned to go up the dirt road, I could see in the rearview mirror a man running toward the cabin. He had a gun in his hand. It was the same man that had been on the dock with Richard.

On the dirt road, the Jeep slid from one side of the road to the other as I made the turns. In the middle of a sharp curve, I was forced to slam on the brakes. I lost control and slid into the ditch. On the road ahead of me, there it was again. The large log Richard and I had pulled off the road earlier in the day. It was back. *There is no way I can move it by myself. My only choice is to get out of the jeep, get into the woods for cover, and outrun them.*

Reaching into the back seat, I pulled my blue backpack up front with me. I frantically tossed things out, digging into the bottom, but my hand came up empty. The gun was gone. *How could that be?* I hadn't taken it out, and no one but Richard had been with me. He had to have found the gun and taken it out.

Chapter 26

Jumping out of the Jeep, my foot landed in a hole. My body went down; the pain was excruciating. I took a deep breath and tried to get up, but putting weight on that foot was almost impossible. *I have to do this. I have no choice.*

Leaning on Kinsey, we started for the woods. We had just gotten off the road and into the woods when I heard men's voices. They were coming from the wooded area across the road from the Jeep. Two men came out of the woods. Like predators in the animal kingdom, they approached the Jeep. They looked into it then moved on up the road. Kinsey and I sat in silence. We couldn't go back, and we couldn't go forward. I sat frozen with panic.

Out of nowhere, breaking my train of thought, I heard a man's voice, raspy and low. "Keep that dog quiet, or I'll have to kill him." The words fell over me like the sound of breaking glass. Splinters slicing into my skin, penetrating every nerve in my body. Kinsey and I both turned at the same time to see a man crouched behind a tree. He was right on top of us. Had he not spoken we would have been completely oblivious to his presence.

He was dressed in camouflage clothing. Even his face was painted. "Come," he said. "Put your weight on me. I'll take you back to the cabin."

"What for? So you can kill me? Why don't you just do it here? Like you did to that guy in the woods. Like you did to Richard." As I said the words, I heard my own voice, firm and steady. I wasn't afraid anymore. If I had a gun, I would have emptied every bullet into him without a second thought. Not out of fear or panic, but rather out of revenge and rage.

His dark brown eyes were expressionless. A slight smile came across his painted face.

"I understand," he said. "I've found it a little difficult myself when I don't know what side of the chessboard I'm playing on." Kinsey sat beside us. The man patted his leg softly. "Come here, boy," he said in a whisper. Kinsey went to him. He patted Kinsey's head and rubbed his shoulders. "You'll need to loosen the strings on your tennis shoe," he said.

I glanced down at my foot and stared in disbelief. My ankle was already swollen twice its size. As I was untying my shoestrings, I heard the somewhat muffled sound of two more gunshots in the distance. I looked up into the man's face. In that moment I knew he was not the predator that had come for me. We were both playing on the same side of the chessboard.

"Two Black Knights down," I said.

He nodded. "For a novice you don't do badly."

"My second compliment of the day," I mused.

"We're going back to the Jeep." He helped me through the woods and into the Jeep. He cleared the road and with some driving expertise that I obviously didn't have brought the Jeep back onto the other side.

On the way back all I could think of was Richard. I sat in silence. The tears streamed down my face. With Richard gone, so went the answers to Colette and Marcy's deaths, and where did that put me now? Why had they killed Richard?

The man answered my unspoken question. "You have something they want. Richard was just in the way. He was seasoned to the game, knew the odds. That was your question, wasn't it?"

It was, but I had only thought, not verbalized the question. The realization hit me like a ton of bricks. He was doing what I do with my clients: using the tools of silent language. What a shock. We lived in such different worlds, but we used the same tools for our trade. The contrast was stark in its reality.

"Yes, that was my question. You're clairvoyant. An empath."

We sat in silence for a moment. Thinking it appropriate to answer in kind, I touched the sleeve of his jacket, allowing my empathic senses to go into his world. In the military, they would refer to this little exercise we were engaged in as remote viewing, or its equivalent.

"That woman wants to marry you. She wants children. You don't think it would be fair to her because of your work. Thoughts creep into your mind, even when you're working. Concerns about the man at her workplace, fear of losing her to him." Then there were two seconds—a flash of vision: my rescuer's demise. Knowing now what I could not say, I said the only thing I could say: "That man will not be an issue for you."

I could feel the Jeep slow down and then stop. He was looking straight ahead and then turned toward me with the piercing eyes of an eagle. Not the kind that look at you, but through you. A few moments of silence passed between us.

"Have you found this thing we have useful?" he asked.

"Yes," I replied. "Just as you have found it useful in your life."

"Why is it," he asked, "when the answer means the most to us it doesn't always come?"

"Well, my take on that is sometimes we are afraid to ask the question, uncertain if we really want the answer, or we become reluctant to trust the process."

All at once, I felt a searing red-hot pain tear through my shoulder. I gasped for breath. I could feel myself breaking out in a cold sweat.

"What's wrong? Is it your chest?" he asked.

"No."

"Your back?" he questioned.

"No," I gasped.

"Have you been hit?"

"I don't think so," I said.

He leaned over and checked the front of my blouse then leaned me forward and checked my back.

"Oh, don't do that, it hurts so bad. It's not me, it's Richard. He's hurting."

"He's not dead? Where is he?" he asked.

"I saw him go in the water," I said.

"Is he in the water now?"

"I don't know. I can't get past the pain."

"We've got to get back," he said. The Jeep lunged forward. I screamed out with pain.

"I'm sorry, Carla, but we have to get back now. We're not far from the cabin." That was the first time he had called me by name.

"I don't know your name," I said. He didn't say anything. "Mr. No-Name, somehow that's just not working for me." Still no response. "How about I make up one for you? Vincent . . . Vince."

"I like that better." He smiled. "I think that will do just fine."

The Jeep sped down the dirt road. We rounded the corner, and I could see the cabin in the distance. I was sick at my stomach and felt faint. All at once, the picture was in front of me as clear as high-definition television.

"Richard isn't in the water. He's on the couch in the cabin. Someone is with him. He's in pain. What I'm feeling, this is his pain."

Vince stopped the Jeep abruptly. "What are they doing to him?"

"I don't know. The picture is gone now," I said.

He took out a pair of binoculars and looked toward the cabin. "It's okay, those are our people," he admitted.

We pulled up to the cabin. As he got out of the Jeep, he commanded, "Come, Kinsey."

"Kinsey? Is there anything about my life you don't know?"

He came around to help me out. "Your secret uncontrolled passion is dark chocolate."

"You're an insidious man," I said.

"My lady, the most gracious of compliments," Vincent said with a smile.

A man appeared in the doorway then quickly came across the porch down the stairs toward us. They helped me up the stairs and into the cabin. Richard was on the couch, just as I had seen him in my mind's picture. There was a man bent over him.

The man turned and looked up at me. "He's going to be all right. Took one in the shoulder. I've just taken the bullet out."

"You took the bullet out?" He turned his face away from me and said no more.

Richard was conscious. I didn't need to ask how he felt. I knew. Richard looked at me and raised one thumb up—our saying to one another that everything was fine. I sat in the chair across from Richard, watching the doctor as he attended to his various tasks.

The doctor stood up, came across the room, and stood in front of me. Bending down, he took my foot in his hands. His hands were scarred; they appeared to have been burnt. His body was thin, but he moved with ease. There was an eerie quietness about him that somehow calmed the entire room. It was as though the breeze coming through the doorway would have played a melody at his request.

"Do you have any allergies?" I heard him ask.

"No," I responded, then felt a slight prick on the side of my arm. "What was that?"

"Just a little something for the pain." He opened my hand and dropped some pills into it. "These are for later."

"Thank you." I recognized his gift as OxyContin.

Relaxing into the high-backed chair, the room began to swirl round and round. I closed my eyes to make it stop. The weight of the dead man's arm was again across my body. I looked down knowing it wasn't there, knowing he was still at the bottom of the ravine. When I shut my eyes again, his face appeared before me, his eyes staring up into the sky. Eyes without life. His weight was heavy on me, so heavy. My chest couldn't sustain the wait. I could hardly breathe. The sound became deafening, vibrating in my head like a sonic boom. *Richard falling backward. Water cascading over me. I can't breathe.* My whole body was shaking.

Flashbacks, more and more of them, were coming like a motion picture on a theater screen. I was a part of the action, a living nightmare, the mental agony of post-traumatic stress disorder. I could now truly empathize with John Clifton. In the Veterans Hospital, John lingered as a prisoner in the steel coffin of his own mind.

I must make this stop. I took a deep breath and visualized the calming, healing blue light of energy penetrating into and around every muscle and cell tissue in my body. *I can do this.* First my feet, then my legs, surging upward over my entire body. A hot flash broke over me. My concentration was beginning to crumble. I felt my stomach muscles tighten, wrenching. Gasping for air, life-giving oxygen, *where is it?*

I felt arms around me. I buried my face in Vince's chest and tried to hold on to him, but my arms were void of strength. *I'm losing him.* But then I realized it was his strength holding me tight to him. His body felt warm. Inside myself, I knew how the people who had gone down with the *Titanic* must have felt in the icy-cold water. It was unbelievable to think that one's own body could feel subzero.

He rocked me back and forth and spoke to me in a voice soft and low. "It's okay. You're safe now. No one is going to hurt you. I promise." He held me as one would a child, soothing away a terrifying nightmare. His body felt hot. I wanted to crawl up inside him. I don't know how long he held me there in his arms comforting, assuring me. My breathing became more rhythmic. The pictures stopped running in my head.

I needed to make my mind focus, to ground myself. In this case, chase the elusive perception. Questions, I was always good at questions. Inquisitive, unscrambling puzzles, that was my forte.

"Vince, this medicine man that travels with you, what else does he do?"

In a whispered voice, he said, "He builds churches in Third World countries. Every man justifies his actions in the light of day. On a moonless night, it's good to have some anchor for your soul."

"For your soul? Vince, the warrior that would ride the pale horse of the apocalypse, as you take a human life, does this not make you righteous? King the Blameless, circumventing the hand of God?"

Without a moment's hesitation, he said "On this plane it is still the animal realm, with all its unchained emotions and free will. Like it or not, Carla, power rules." If nothing else, his answer brought reality back into focus. "I need you to remember a riddle," he said. My mind was totally concentrated on his presence and his voice. He continued, "You must remember the riddle: The cat had nine lives and a litter of four. The buffalo stands in the field."

"That's a riddle?" I asked.

His face was stern, that of granite rock. "Stay with me. This isn't an English class. Now repeat it with me." We said the little riddle repeatedly. "If the day ever comes when Richard isn't there or you can't reach him, or you feel you can't control the situation." He then gave me a series of numbers. As he said them, he wrote them on the palm of my hand with his finger, as though he was printing them into my brain. "These numbers and the riddle you share with no one, not even Richard. These you carry only in your mind and nowhere else. Put these numbers in the phone. Give the riddle to whomever answers, and you'll be extracted from the situation. Trust me, Carla, people are not always what you think they are, and in some situations, they can't tell you as much as they would like to. You understand?"

"Yes, I understand completely." What I now understood was that I could never go back to my life as it was. Was Vince trying to tell me he was a double agent? This was like living in an uncertain parallel world between yin and yang. Did he get a thrill, a rush, from living in this parallel world? I looked into his eyes. "For you, Vince, this beats paintball?"

He looked surprised for a moment. "It has its ups and downs, incorporating extrasensory perception, remote viewing, however one wants to describe the phenomenon. That brings a unique and interesting quality to the game."

I understood what he was saying. "Yes, that dynamic, energetic force on a subconscious level. Sometimes shadowy awareness, other times crystal clear pictures."

"We just manifest it in a broader scope," he said, "for all the government's research and testing. Exactly how we access this dimension is still a mystery. As far as I know, no one has nailed down a suitable explanation." Vince stood up. "I've got to check on a few things," he said. He left the room.

Richard sat up, his shoulder bandaged, and his arm was in a sling. He looked pale.

"Are you okay to be sitting up?" I asked.

"Actually, I'm not in any pain. Whatever the good doctor gave me must have been some pretty good stuff," Richard said.

Vince walked out of the kitchen. "I turned the stove off," he said. "This area is secure. You're going to have dinner, and then you will be going back tonight." He looked at Richard. "The timetable has been moved up."

As I stood up, I realized the room was now empty except for Vince, Richard, and myself.

Vince came over to me. "I'm going now, Carla. Take care."

I lowered my voice and touched the sleeve of his jacket one last time. "The woman you want so much, she wants you as passionately as you want her." That was as much as I could do for him. What I knew was that I would never see him again, nor would she.

"Thanks, Carla. You take care of yourself." Then he turned and walked out the door.

I got up from my chair, and Richard came over and put his arm on my shoulder. "Carla, I love you so much. I don't know if you ever truly understood how much you mean to me." Not yet accustomed to navigating my weight on one foot more than the other, I winced at the pain running up my leg. "What happened to your ankle? Even under all of that bandage, it looks twice the size of the other."

"I'm okay. I just twisted it in a fall. The medicine man had some potent goodies in his bag. He was most generous with his allocation. Richard, as soon as we get back, you've got to go to the hospital and have that shoulder looked at."

"You know better than that, Carla. Doctors have to report gunshot wounds. That ankle of yours should be x-rayed though. You twisted it on the porch stairs. We'll keep it basic and simple."

"Right, Richard, this sure has been basic and simple."

In our relationship, that authoritarian part of him had always made me feel uneasy. The thing I couldn't put my finger on now came into focus. It was his conditioning, his response to previous training embedded into his being. I recognized Richard for who he really was, a charming, personable, manipulative, risk-taking psychopath.

"Did you enjoy your time in the military, Richard? You found a home, people of like minds, and that would be not only past but also present tense. Right?" I knew better than to challenge him but couldn't seem to stop myself.

He stepped back and looked down at me. "I want you in my life, Carla. However, you do understand, sometimes you can be very frustrating and independent for a woman."

"Spoken like a true chauvinist," I said.

"I think we have had this conversation before," he said. "Do you think you can meet me halfway, Carla?"

"What about the 'present tense and past tense' question. You never answered," I said.

"My photography trips aren't that frequent anymore," Richard insisted.

I thought to myself, *Neither were Daniel's antique dealings.* "The pictures in New Orleans of Daniel, obviously that wasn't a coincidence. Which side of the chessboard does Daniel play on?"

"That's a good question. The stage is set. Sometimes it comes down to only two people after the same thing, playing the game of life and death with so much hanging in the balance. Totally bizarre, isn't it?" His smile was cold and frightening.

I knew what he meant. Now I had to play along and make him trust me. My own life hung in that bizarre balance.

"It's been you and me, Richard, for some time. I think we both understand neither one of us is perfect. Whatever happens we can work it out together."

"That's my girl." My statement appeared to take the edge off and put us back into balance. I had been reckless in my questioning, bringing out in him what neither one of us wanted to acknowledge. He bent down, cradling my face in his hand. "We can have a good life together. I'll make it work out for us. You're always going to be my woman. No one will ever come between us."

I looked up at him, touched his face, and smiled. "In that case, we better begin by trying to figure out how we are going to get dinner on the table. Connors is going to be coming through the door anytime now looking for dinner."

Like two semi-ambulatory patients, we went back to the kitchen and found the roasting pan on top of the stove. We stood looking at the pan, him with one disabled arm and me with one leg to brace weight on.

"Don't you just love it when a plan comes together?" he said. We both laughed at the insanity of it all.

Chapter 27

Connor's voice came from the front door. "Anyone home? I've been invited for dinner, and I'm hungry."

"Come on in," I yelled. "You missed the doughnuts, but dinner's ready." Richard looked at me somewhat surprised and shook his head in disbelief.

"It's okay," I said. "The guy has a good sense of humor. We're back here in the kitchen, Connors." He walked into the kitchen and stopped abruptly. He had a broken coffee cup in one hand and was carrying his jacket over his arm, hand concealed.

"You've been playing a little rough, I see. What happened to you two?"

"Well," I said. "It's a long story and evidently a small world."

Connors was dressed in a khaki shirt, blue jeans, and hiking boots. More casual than I had ever seen him before. His presence filled the room.

"We have a beautiful pot roast here. Actually, you came in on our strategy session," I said.

"Strategy session?" his brain no doubt attempting to put some pattern of reason to things, Connors questioned.

"That's right. A major operation of logistics. How do we get this pot roast to the dining room table?" I said.

Connors laid the broken coffee cup on the kitchen table. He came over to the stove, lifted the lid on the pot roast, and steam rose up along with the aroma. He looked inside. "Looks like enough food in here for the Chinese army. Are you expecting more guests?" He stepped back and looked around the kitchen with a surveyor's vision.

"No. Actually, I think we have had all the unannounced guests our nervous systems can take for one day. There will be just the three of us for dinner, at least in the cabin."

Connors looked at Richard for some acknowledgment or confirmation. Richard was now helping himself to a bite of roast beef, testing its tenderness.

All at once, Richard turned quickly, moving in front of me. He picked up a knife from the countertop. Connors jacket slid off his arm, revealing a gun in his hand.

Richard demanded, "How did you get in here?"

Connors laughed. "The hall monitor gave me a pass. Does that surprise you? We recognize our fellow comrades when we have hunted with them before. Some of the animal kingdom likes their meat raw. Prefer it that way, in a more natural setting." Psych game. Oh yes, Connors was good.

Richard's mind was like the cogs in a finely tuned machine. One could imagine the different scenarios that must have been playing themselves out: *Yep, recognize this one, marh three with his hair on fire.* Bulldog had definitely laid down the gauntlet of equality. Weapons were lowered, and we sat down at the dining room table. Connors demonstrated the poise and patience of a seasoned veteran, awaiting information as to why he had been summonsed. Kinsey took his place on the floor beside my chair while Devin positioned himself on top of the china cabinet.

"Was the road clear when you came in?" asked Richard.

"Yes, Richard, it was. Why do you ask?"

"It was blocked earlier," Richard stated.

"From the looks of you two, I'd say things got a little out of hand around here."

I lifted my bandaged foot onto the adjacent chair. "I wouldn't want to appear as the drama queen of the day, but your assessment is accurate."

Richard turned, looked at me. "Everything is going to be okay, Carla. We just need to get the chip into the right hands. When the transfer is complete, we go back to things the way they were."

"Chip?" Connors said as though he had never heard the word before. His poker face revealed nothing. He sighed deeply and then put down his fork. "Things the way they were? Not exactly, at least not for Carla."

Before I could question Connors's statement, Richard jumped in like a schoolboy who had been questioned by his teacher. "I've got her covered, Connors."

I could see Connors's aura flash red, a total contrast to his physical appearance and mannerisms. There was an intense anger seething beneath his demeanor. Mutual animosity charged the air between them. I had a horrible feeling in the pit of my empty stomach that this night's events were far from over.

"We're not talking about the same thing, Richard. Additional information has come in regarding one of Carla's clients . . . I hate to add more to your plate, Carla, but they picked up Jennifer. You were right, they were headed out west. Unprofessionally speaking, you've got yourself one sick, messed-up kid there, Doc. A hunter found Jason's truck in the wilderness, thought it looked odd no one had been around for some time and reported it to the authorities."

In the midst of all that had gone on, Jennifer had not crossed my mind. Now it was like a splash of cold-water awakening, chilling. "What happened to Jennifer? Where is she?"

"They have her in custody. She's in detention now. The prosecuting attorney wants to try her as an adult," Connors said.

"You've got to be kidding. They're charging her with the murder of her mother and father?" I said.

"That's about the size of it. She has asked to speak to you. As a matter of fact, you're the only person she will speak to. The case will go to trial, and you will be called to testify regarding her mental state. It may be mid-summer before it's on the docket," Connors said.

Somewhere between "I've got her covered" and "You're going to have to testify," I lost my appetite.

Richard came up with an explanation for his need to stay anonymous in regard to the chip being turned over to the government. "Carla and I thought you would be a trusted courier, Connors. Carla, you will need to give the chip to Connors tonight when we get back."

"I can't."

Richard turned sharply. I saw him grip the knife in his hand. "We discussed this, Carla."

"I can't, Richard."

His face became flushed, and the irritation was plain in his voice. "Why not?"

"Not until the bank opens Monday morning," I announced.

I could see the tension along his jawline. "We'll work out the exchange later," he said. "I'll go load the Jeep, and we'll head back tonight."

After Richard left the room, Connors lowered his voice. "Who else knows about the chip?"

"As far as I know, you, me, and Richard. Daniel is involved in this. I just don't know how. I get the distinct impression you know more than I do about Daniel."

His comment was direct. "We are all lethal. Many gladiators, many lions."

"Is there a law restricting the lions to the arena? There were a few times back there I could have sworn I felt teeth marks on my backside."

He smiled. "I understand the gravity of what's going on here and how you must feel."

"Connors, I miss Colette and Marcy a lot. I can't, I won't walk away. The vision of their coffins being lowered into the ground haunts my memories. I said my goodbyes, but they had more living to do, lots more. Call it justice, call it revenge, call it whatever you want. The only thing I know is I have to have it for them."

Connors looked at me intensely for a moment. "Far be it from me to judge you. We are talking degrees here, levels of consciousness. That's life, isn't it—gray areas. We all get pushed up to the line. The question is, where is the line?" Connors moved forward in his chair. "You don't need to have any concerns regarding Daniel. You can put him on the

front lines and then take him home for some R&R with the family. He
doesn't devour his own."

"That's quite a metaphor, Connors."

He laughed. "Yeah, but accurate. At some level one has to admire
him. He's a smooth operator. Make no mistake, he's an ambitious man."

"How do you know this, Connors?"

"That's what is interesting about the world of espionage, my dear.
Observe from the sidelines, Carla. Richard is going to pay for what he
did to Colette and Marcy. I promise you that. You know what Richard
is capable of now. In his mind, anyone who has knowledge of the
sculpture needs to be eliminated. You do understand that, don't you?"

"Oh yes, I definitely understand, but I have a question. In your
opinion, has Richard made any fatal mistakes?"

"As far as I can see he's only made one mistake, but it was a big one."

"What was that?" I asked.

Connors looked out the window toward the lake. "Too many
competitors in the arena always tips the scales, no matter how well
trained the opponent is. What money can't buy will show up at his
doorstep one day."

Now I understood that thread of connection I had felt when
Connors and I first met. What years of experience had taught me: Don't
push the river. It will lead you to your answer in its own good time.

Connors continued, "Richard needs to spill blood, give them
resolution that they want, and at the same time clean up his playpen.
No loose ends. The time is getting near."

"Yes, I know. I also know he's walking a tight rope. He thinks he
has convinced me we are going to have a life together. He believes I'm
still buying his story, therefore, the fantasy world he has created for me
can go on. At all costs he will not lay down his cards until he has the
sculpture in his hands. While we're talking about exposure, Connors,
how did you get that log off the road?"

He took a sip of his coffee. "I had assistance from a mutual friend."

Chapter 28

In the Jeep on the way back, Richard insisted I stay overnight at his house. It was less of a request, more of a command. That night, feeling like the proverbial captive, sleep was elusive and ultimately unattainable. Finally, sunlight began to find its way across the bedroom floor.

I lay there staring up at the ceiling. *He's here.* Richard, lying beside me.

The dichotomy of the man was dramatically intense, dangerous beyond the textbook version of evil. To the untrained eye, he was charming, successful, and even handsome. What every woman looks for in a man. A good lover, provider, and father for her children. Too late she would learn about this soulless man and the cold, damaged genetics that he would pass on to his offspring. The full moon at high tide, the ocean would swallow her up—another helpless victim.

Out of the quiet, his voice broke the stillness of the morning. "What are you thinking about?"

"What?" I asked.

"You were looking at the ceiling as if it were a crystal ball." He laughed that relaxed, warm laugh of his, accompanied by the ever-present smile. "What did you see in your crystal ball, sweetheart?"

I smiled back at him and looked straight into his eyes. "I was just thinking how fortunate I am to have you in my life, Richard. You've always been there for me. We've been through so much as a couple, and it has only served to strengthen our relationship. We do fit together so well."

I could hear the confidence and sincerity in my own voice. I could hardly believe with all my years of experience and training, even I came late to the party, the realization of what lay beneath the surface. My camera lens had been focused, but the development solution was tainted. He was truly a master of disguise. Lying there beside me, he appeared so pleased with himself, thinking he was in total control of his world. On top of his game. An adrenaline junkie strapped to a missile. Oh, he was in his element. I had no choice but to let the ocean waves lap at my feet, perhaps to my ankles, but I must be ever vigilant—aware of the riptide and rogue waves.

He moved closer, put his hand across my breast. When I looked down, I saw a raven's claw. I knew what was next, what he wanted, but I also knew he wasn't getting his way. His appetite in the bedroom mirrored every other aspect of the man, competent and thorough with an underline of edgy dominance.

"How's your ankle this morning?" he asked.

"I think the magic drug has worn off. I'll take more in a little bit. I'm going down to make us a pot of coffee." Quickly slipping out of bed.

"I'm going to take a shower, and then I'll be down to help you with breakfast," he said.

"Richard, Kinsey, Devin, and I need to go home today."

"Okay," Richard said as he got up and put his uninjured arm around me. "We have so much to talk about. Our future has been put on hold for too long. We'll discuss it all over breakfast. Be careful on the stairs." As I left the bedroom, I heard the phone on the nightstand ring.

On my way to the kitchen, I noticed the door to Richard's office was ajar. Stepping inside, I saw his keys and billfold lying on the large antique desk. Dark wood shutters covered the windows and shut out most of the sunlight. His desk was clean and orderly, no files or notepads, nothing of interest—again, déjà vu. I turned to leave but noticed the phone on his desk. Who was calling Richard at this hour? Picking up the receiver, I heard a familiar voice, the same voice I had heard on the answering machine in Richard's fake office the day I convinced the cleaning lady to open the door for me. I sat back down in the chair to listen. There was distinct stress in the man's voice.

***

Richard held the receiver in his hand as he lay back against the pillow. "Could you believe it?"

Kurt said. "I could actually see the golden parachute. Feel the rush of air on my face. Looking down and seeing all that was going to be mine."

Silence filled the air. "Kurt? Kurt, you there?"

"I got the word from the doctor yesterday. Looks like you were right about the cigarettes and that cough. Not to mention our lifestyle. It's cancer. Doctor said I've got six months, if that. Looks like that parachute is going to be taking me down to a wooden box. How's that for bringing the curtain down?"

"Kurt, I don't know what to say. Did you get a second opinion? What about research, do they have anything experimental?"

"No options, old buddy. I guess I just let it go on too long. You were right, I should have quit a long time ago."

"I'm so sorry, Kurt. I mean, man that really sucks. Is there anything I can do for you?"

"Let's wrap this thing up. I'd like to at least see what it would have brought me." His voice cracked. "I've got to go. Talk to you later."

Richard put down the receiver. His mind raced forward: *What a windfall for me. I know all the networking connections. I can have Kurt's portion of the profits. Not like he's going to be needing them. What was it that Kurt had said in his office that day? Oh yes. "I'll probably end up with a few other guys' shares before this is over." That's what he had said. My take could be a lot larger. So what if Kurt had an accident? It would just be putting the poor guy out of his misery a little sooner, doing him a favor even. If the situation were reversed, he would do the same thing. Now a good, hot shower and a little time to convince Carla of my sincerity. I had her convinced for a couple years, and with a little more pressure I'll have that chip out of her hands and into mine by Monday morning.*

Richard stopped in front of the mirror of his bureau and looked at himself. *The execution is in place for Connors after the Monday morning bank exchange. He is just going to quietly disappear. A large bucket of cement will do just fine. I'll have the pleasure of taking Daniel out myself. He will never be in my way again. He will never see or touch what is mine. After a while of the good life, Daniel will only be a vague memory in Carla's mind. All I have to do is paint a beautiful picture for her: A life in the sun. No more worries or clients and their pathetic stories, those weak, degenerate ones. Just the two of us. She'll suck up the happy dream.*

***

More light had begun to filter through the wooden blinds into the office. I gently put the receiver down, got up from the desk, and heard the slight sound of something small falling to the floor. Looking down I found a key, one that just happened to fit the desk drawer. Inside the drawer were a variety of pictures and several passports under various names, Richard's photo on each passport. As I started to shut the drawer, I noticed a piece of paper sticking up from underneath the bottom of the drawer. Feeling underneath the top of the drawer, my fingers found a round button. When I pressed the button, the drawer slid back, revealing a hidden compartment. Inside lay a journal. *How much time do I have before Richard comes downstairs? I have to know what is in this journal.* I went to the bottom of the stairs to listen. Yes, the water in the shower was still running. I hurried back, sat the journal on top of the desk, and began to read.

The journal outlined his assignments, the details of his involvement that had been so extensive. Richard's knowledge of the professor's house that he had convinced me to buy and reports of surveillance. He had known about the chip long before I had shared any of this information with him. He had known about Daniel. I felt my face burn with embarrassment and ignorance. These emotions gave way to rage at how smug and manipulative he had been. He had played me like a puppeteer, pulling the strings as I dangled in the air, dancing to his command. Psychiatrist, trained and seasoned as I was, hadn't caught it in three whole years. The markers were all there. Under a white piece of paper in the bottom of the drawer was one loose sheet of blue paper: a list of names with dates beside each name. At the top was Timothy Dupree, Richard's brother. I ran my finger down the list. *Who are all these people?* The last entry on the paper was Thomas Shankland, I had read his name in the newspaper. He was the man who had found his fate with Richard in the alley behind the restaurant. What I was holding in my hand was Richard's hit list. It had all started so long ago with his brother, Tim. That must have been when Richard discovered the darkest side of himself. One could only imagine what the title of his memoir would be. I put the blue sheet back in the drawer and covered it with the white paper, leaving it as I had found it. Continuing to read, time eluded me.

I was suddenly aware of footsteps and a creaking floorboard that shattered my thoughts. As I looked up, Richard was standing in the doorway, his body still moist from the shower, dressed in a white robe, rubbing his wet hair with a towel.

"Hey, babe, how about I take you out for break—" He stopped mid-sentence and midstride, staring at the open journal lying on the desk. "*What are you doing?*" The shrill tone of his voice filled the room.

"That's it?" I said. "That's all you've got. That's all you have to say." I stood, holding the journal in my hand.

"It's not what you think, Carla." He tried for a smile and failed. "Really, it isn't what you think. I can explain."

Burning adrenaline seared through every fiber of my body. The escalation of energy driven by the desire for the annihilation of another human being. And it felt good. I threw the journal at his face, wanting it to hit his mouth that had spewed so many lies. He dodged the book.

"You sick, narcissistic psychopath! They're dead, and your bloody hands are all over this!"

His teeth clenched and his jaw set. He came to stand close, towering over me. As I looked into his face, it was like staring into the mouth of a volcano ready to erupt at any moment. I expected the clouds of gray, choking ash to rain down on me. Within a split second, his demeanor changed right before my eyes. He spoke in a low monotone voice.

"You don't understand. You really didn't know Colette, you only thought you did. You need to grow up, Carla. Be a part of the real world. Sometimes it gets messy. We can't always put names and cases in nice, neat little folders." A righteousness seemed to overtake him. "Loyalty, commitment is everything, Carla. You have to stand for something bigger than yourself, or you are nothing at all."

He really expected me to buy his self-righteous code of insanity. I wondered if he ever fell off his pedestal, then realized Richard doesn't need a pedestal. Connors was right. Richard was smooth, very smooth, hidden well but nonetheless a booming psychopath rationalizing every move he made. Now he would do so in the name of the greater good. The hair on the back of my neck rose, fight or flight—the voluntary primal command. *I have nowhere to run. I've said too much.* He could see the fantasy world he had created for me crumbling into nothingness.

I took a step out from behind the desk. I wanted to shout at him, *"You killed Colette, and if you didn't kill Marcy yourself, you ordered someone to do it, you're a ruthless excuse for a human being!"* I opened my mouth, but the words anchored themselves in my throat. Every nerve ending in my body was screaming at me, *Get control of yourself, or you'll never get out alive.* Connors's words rang in my ears: *"Be a good actress, Carla. Your life depends on it."*

"Richard, how can you say I didn't know Colette?"

"She had a life before you met her, Carla. A life you knew nothing about. I'm not the bad guy here. She did some things that endangered our country. You have to believe me." He put his hands together as if in prayer. Sincerity dripped from his lips. Oh yes, he was very good.

"What did she do? What don't I know?"

"Colette was involved in things you can't imagine. I'll tell you everything, even get you evidence so you can see for yourself. I'm not the villain you imagine me to be. I just need a couple days. It's complicated. Some things haven't played themselves out yet."

I calculated in my mind—yes, a couple of days until Monday morning when the banks would open. His eyes locked on to mine.

"I know what you're thinking, Carla, so we're going to get this out of the way right now. Marcy, I swear to you I had nothing to do with her death. That whole thing was a different matter. It could have been a strung-out druggie looking for sample drugs for all I know. I feel really bad about what happened to her." The compassion in his voice would have made the devil weep.

"Richard, only a few months ago my life was normal, but now . . . " Taking a page from Richard's book, I laid my hand over my heart.

"Sit down, Carla. You're not going anywhere. Not until you've heard me out. Okay, so I knew about the house and the chip, but you were never in harm's way, I swear to you. I've facilitated a lot of operations. I am experienced and very good at what I do. You really think for one moment that I would let anything happen to you? What happened to Colette could even be considered an accident. Her heel caught in the carpet at the top of the stairs."

"You set me up with the house knowing Colette lived next door, Richard."

He shrugged and sighed as though the whole conversation was all too trivial in the overall scheme of things. "So the house served more than one purpose. Does that make the whole thing wrong?"

"Colette was my friend. She was so innocent and unaware."

"No, Carla. Colette wasn't who you thought she was. She became collateral damage, and that's unfortunate. However, these things happen. Think back, Carla—you knew Colette for two years, don't you think there were things she didn't tell you? You've known me for three years, have I ever lied to you?"

This guy was really good. He could talk his way out of hell. Take the hinges off the door and ask for a refund.

"Richard, this isn't the world I live in or the world I thought you lived in."

"Really?" he said. "While we're on the subject of betrayal, Carla, what about Daniel?"

"What about Daniel?"

"Don't play games with me, Carla. I love you with every fiber of my being. I need to know I have your undivided loyalty. That it's you and me all the way, baby. It's imperative that you understand that. This friendship you have with Daniel, it has to end. I won't have it."

I could see him emotionally step back, restructure his approach. Again, he would present himself as a caring, overly protective lover hurt that I could have considered him as anything else.

"I won't have you in harm's way, Carla."

What I understood was that no matter what I said or did, one moment's mistrust by Richard and my fate would be sealed the same as Colette's and Marcy's—"for the greater good." His. I could feel, taste, and smell it in the air: *I'm next.* There was one difference. I wasn't going to be a vulnerable victim. *I have the chip, and I know how to use it.*

"I know this must be some kind of nightmare for you." He put his hand on my shoulders. "That list you saw in my desk drawer, it's work related. I'm an agent for our government. I do whatever it takes to protect our people. Our country. You do believe me, don't you, Carla?"

I needed to reply correctly, with the right ring of sincerity. I must appear to be that puppet on a string. "Yes, Richard, I do believe you, but this is your life, not mine. I can't live like this. What are we going to do? You have to fix this."

"I understand. I'll take care of you. This will all be over soon. Monday morning when the banks open, you'll get the chip out of the safety deposit box. Connors and I will be there with you. This operation will go as smooth as clockwork. Then we'll take a vacation to Hawaii, just the two of us. You'll like it there. Come on, baby, let's go out for breakfast. If there's one thing you are, Carla, it's logical. Give yourself a little time to think this through and you'll see I'm right. You go wait in the living room while I dress and then we'll head out."

Chapter 29

I sat in the living room, and his words replayed themselves in my head: "*Her heel caught in the carpet . . .* " Connors had made no mention of that fact being in the report. Richard had been the one in the house that night. Colette had confronted him at the top of the stairs. His face was the last thing she had seen. A chill reached down into the marrow of my bones. He killed Colette, and in some way, he was responsible for Marcy's death.

I could make him a nice little cocktail. It would be so easy. I took the OxyContin out of my blue jean pocket. The good doctor had been generous in his distribution, no prescription, and no record. I could crush them up, seasoning for his last meal. When narcissism and polished greed encounter virtue of purpose, there is always a reckoning. Yes, one little cocktail and this nightmare would be over for all of us. Every good action deserves a plan. *Think, Carla, think. When: Sunday, before the banks open Monday morning. Where: Good question, but a better question is, what do I do with his body? How strange it feels, sitting here in my own skin, examining my thoughts as though they belong to someone else.* The room felt cold, traumatized, and void of emotion. *I am contemplating the unthinkable.* I couldn't protect Colette and Marcy, but I could do something about Connors and Daniel.

In the process of cleaning up his playpen, Connors and Daniel would be Richard's next targets. The picture of Daniel in New Orleans—Richard had been investigating, stalking Daniel all along. The plum for his superiors, he planned to serve Daniel up on a spit over the fire.

Philip, my first love, his betrayal had been a demonstration of weakness in character, a reckless moment's decision perpetrated in an afternoon of lust. Richard had premeditated, calculated his betrayal over a period of time. Had he always rationalized our relationship to be one of compromise? Now he would invite me into his world of cloak and mirrors only to hold the dagger of deceit behind his back. *He never planned for me to learn of his part in this charade, nor could either one of us have known what I am becoming capable of.*

Richard came downstairs and sat on the overstuffed sofa with me. We shared that kind of silence one understands as meditative, searching. Exploring mental patterns like ripples in a pond, reaching out further and further, challenging oneself to open doors that had previously led only into the sanctuary of one's own mind. Our own cognition acknowledgment, in some magical way, allows us to see ourselves as a cog in a machine—righteous, sanitary, and clean. If only we were the robots of tomorrow. Only Richard had the capacity to accomplish that. Be without empathy, without soul, without the direction of moral fiber that links us all together as humans. I would play his game of Russian roulette. Again, Connors's words rang in my ears: "*Be a good actress, Carla. Your life may depend on that ability.*"

I turned to Richard, looked into his face, and played to his ego. "There's so much at stake here, Richard. I didn't understand the magnitude of your work, your dedication to the greater good. I only wish you had come to me, confided in me earlier. All that wasted time. You know I've always loved you, Richard. The things I said earlier, I know they aren't true. You're right, I didn't think it through. I guess I was just too close. I didn't stop to realize how hard this had to be for you, and you didn't expect to fall in love with me but you did. I really do want to put all of this behind us, but how do we go on from here?" Just what he wanted to hear. The chip would still be within his grasp.

"You're a beautiful woman. Any man would be proud to have you on his arm. Our lives have changed, but before they changed, we were good together. We can be good together again. If I seemed controlling to you, it was only because I was scared of losing you. Before you, I have never had anyone in my life that I cared enough about to have a lasting relationship with. We can have a good life together. I can give you anything you would ever want, Carla. I can do that for us. When we get to Hawaii, we will get married. It will all work out. We can start over, Carla. There won't be any more secrets. You're my woman, you always have been. You'll give the chip to Connors Monday morning. I'll help Connors get the chip into the right hands. Then you and I can be on a plane right after, anywhere you want to go, just the two of us. White sands, margaritas, and palm trees if you want. You'll see, just trust me."

"Richard, right now white sand, palm trees, and margaritas sound like heaven. Can you do that, get us on a plane for Hawaii on Monday? I just want to forget about all this. Make it go away, Richard, okay?"

"I can do that, Carla."

"Then that's exactly what we'll do, Richard."

I have to save my loved ones from this monster. Only I know how totally dangerous he is. Richard came over and kissed me on the forehead.

"It's going to be all right, sweetie, I promise you. I'll make arrangements now, get the tickets for our trip to the islands. There's a lot to do before we go. I'll have the tickets, everything, ready for us."

"Richard, I need coffee, black and strong."

He smiled that ever-confident smile of his.

"I have instant," he said apologetically. "It's in the cupboard right side of the kitchen sink."

I stood and said, "I'll make us both a cup."

"That's my girl," he said as he reached to squeeze my hand.

I found the coffee, made it strong. The cups sat on the countertop. I reached into my jean pocket and pulled out the OxyContin. My opportunity was staring me in the face. Five, six . . . *No, more. Make sure it's strong enough. Wait to call the squad. He needs to be dead, very dead when they arrive.*

He sat on the couch looking more relaxed than I thought he would be.

"I assume it's all right," he said, "for me to make the arrangements. I have some special places I would like you to see. We'll call it a surprise vacation." His eyes were now studying me. *I know what he's thinking. Is she still buying the game? Richard is in my field of expertise now.* I gave him all the appropriate body language he needed to see. I handed him his coffee cup. Our hands touched. For that moment we were connected. I sat down, took a sip of my coffee. He's running his fingers around the rim of the cup, his manicured fingers like everything else about him—measured, precise, not leaving anything to chance.

"I'll need to know how long I'm going to be away from the office," I said.

He kept holding the coffee cup as he talked. I heard his lies slipping off his tongue, syrupy, sweet and smooth. Somewhere in the inner depths of his being, did he for a flickering moment believe? I want to scream, "Drink the coffee. Drink it now!" My cell phone rang.

"Go ahead, answer it," he said. "I'll start making some phone calls." He sat the coffee cup down and walked out of the room.

Why am I not breathing? I took a deep breath and answered the phone. A recorded message. It's a sales pitch. I hung up. Picking up our coffee cups, taking them into the kitchen. I started to pour the coffee down the sink. Richard's cup was in my hand. *Whose hands are these? A murderer's hands that would hold life's revenge. Who am I? Do I even recognize myself? How many participants do we have in this masquerade of deception?* My stomach wrenched, and I vomited into the sink the breakfast I didn't have.

"Richard, I need to go home and get some things put together."

"Okay, I'll stop by in the morning," he said.

"No . . . I think I'll take Saturday to do some packing, and I think I may want to do some shopping. Maybe a sexy bikini and some new outfits you haven't seen before." There it was, that confident smile of his again, thinking he was in control. "I want to have everything ready to go. Come over Sunday and I'll make dinner for us."

He bent down and kissed me on the lips. *I had just bought myself another day in insanity land. What I hadn't counted on was finding the dark side of myself.*

Richard dropped me off at my front door. "I'll call you tomorrow," he said.

***

Once inside, I locked the door behind me, made a fire in the fireplace, and poured myself a very large brandy. It relaxed my body. The seductive second glass would perhaps do the same for my mind. I held the glass of brandy out in front of me, swirling it around and around. I could see the flames from the fireplace leaping and dancing through the golden liquid. Embers cracked then burst onto the hearth. Separate entities, equations of the same, somehow brighter and more intense than what they had come from.

Like Jennifer and Daniel. Outside normal society, but part of it. As I lowered my glass, the two embers continued to dance on the hearth. They found each other, combined their light, and then slowly faded. The common denominator—Jennifer and Daniel had both known this house, had known the professor. The fire was the body of his work. The chip had a partner, and the partner had the key to the code. There was twisted and then there was just downright bizarre, the child genius and the man capable of carrying out the professor's wishes. Daniel would make a trusted confidant. Jennifer held the knowledge, but it would take Daniel to open Pandora's box. To let out whatever was inside for the world to see. The professor's wisdom, his instructions, what had they been? Was his work to save mankind, or had he ordered his work to be destroyed before mankind, in its adolescent vision, destroyed itself? To think, it only took a doctorate degree in psychiatry, years of practice, and two glasses of very old brandy to figure this one out. Oh, blessed are the ones that sleep in their beds unaware. I went upstairs, undressed, and stepped into the shower. Jet streams of hot water pounded against my body.

When a loud, resounding tap on the shower door startled me, shades of *Psycho* jumped into my mind. I looked through the steam, seeing Daniel. I slid the door back. He was fully dressed.

"Are you coming in?" He just stood there staring at my naked body. "Okay, now you're making me feel self-conscious."

"No, I'm not coming in. This isn't the right venue." Did he say the right venue? The last time I saw him at my shower, oh, it was definitely the right venue. He looked happy. "Come out of the shower. I have a proposal." Odd choice of words. I came out of the shower like a runner one step from the finish line.

"Okay, where is the right venue?"

He scratched his head, looked puzzled. *Now the man was teasing me. Play with my emotions, would he? Oh yes, he would.*

"Let's see," he said. "The kitchen? No, the family room. I like the sound of that, but no, that's not it. The bedroom? Yes, that's definitely the right venue. The bedroom," Daniel repeated.

"Am I dressed properly for the occasion?"

"Yes, what you don't have on will do just fine. Impeccable taste, a classic. I can't think of anything more fitting," Daniel responded.

We went into the bedroom. The blinds had been closed, and my candles were lit. Daniel stood in front of me. He shifted his weight from one foot to the other, swallowed hard, and cleared his throat. He appeared as a grade school child in front of the class preparing to give his first oral report. He finally went down on one knee. It was sweet and touching.

"I'm only going to do this once in my life, so I want to do it right, say the right words. Carla, the first time I saw you, I knew it then you were the one. I'm a good man. I love you. Did I say that? Did I tell you I love you? I do, you know."

"Yes, I think I have the idea," I said.

"I'm not going to be doing any more international work. Strictly an eight-to-five guy now. A good provider." His nervousness seemed to melt a little. "I'll give you beautiful children," he added.

"Well, are you going to ask?" I inquired with zest.

"Ask? Oh, yes." He reached into his jacket pocket and presented me with a diamond ring surrounded with rubies. "Carla Van Doran, will you marry me? I had the ring made especially for you. The rubies are my promise. I knew the ruby's meaning: commitment."

"Yes, a million times over. I would throw my arms round you and give you a kiss, but I'm all wet from the shower. Do you have any idea of how I might consummate my answer?"

His smile was joyful as he began taking off his clothes.

Chapter 30

Juvenile Detention Center
Warrant to Convey: Jennifer Upton

The security officer opened the door for Jennifer. As she walked out of the detention center in handcuffs and shackles, a blue van sat in the parking lot, the one that would take her to the psychiatrist for her evaluation. A man stood beside the open door of the van.

As they approached, the security officer said, "She's all yours. Here's your transport orders." Without another word, he walked back into the building.

Jennifer heard the driver say, "Get into the van. Now!" She looked away from him as he fastened her seat belt. Another man sat in the back seat beside her. The van picked up speed. Jennifer looked at the person sitting beside her. He had on a jacket, the hood pulled up over his head, which was resting against the side window. He appeared to be asleep. She looked down at his white trousers and white shoes, all so sanitary-hospital clean: *we take care of the crazies.*

She looked out the window as the van sped along. City lights and streets gave way to country roads. The silence was broken by the driver's voice that sounded oddly familiar.

He said, "This trip is going to take a little while."

She glanced into the rearview mirror to see his face. The man looked back at her. His dark brown eyes were accentuated by the scar over his left eyebrow. Jennifer could feel her breath stop. He was at the university that night, the one who had tried to get her into the black van. The university police had stopped him, but no one was here to stop him now. It was clear she wasn't going to see a psychiatrist for an evaluation, but where was he taking her? Before her mind could consider the options, his booming voice shattered her concentration.

"What's this!" he said. Looking at the road ahead, Jennifer saw a jackknifed semi-tanker truck. A dark-colored car sat off the side of the road. The van came to an abrupt stop. Two men stood beside the semi. From the body language, obviously they were discussing how the accident had occurred. Heads shaking, fingers pointing, arms up in the air.

The driver unfastened his seat belt and opened the van door. Jennifer watched him as he walked up to the silver-haired man. He did so with a swagger of anger and disdain. Then suddenly he fell to the ground. The two men picked him up, dragged him over to the semi, and put him in the driver's seat. He was slumped over the wheel. It all happened so quickly.

The two men walked back to the van and opened the doors. The silver-haired man looked at the hospital orderly sitting beside Jennifer, reached in, and pulled the hood away from his face.

"He's dead. We'll put him in the front seat."

The other man undid her seat belt, took off Jennifer's handcuffs and shackles. Jennifer looked into his face.

"Daniel . . . Daniel? My Daniel?"

He held her hands in his. "Yes, Jennifer. It's me, your Daniel. You're safe, but there are a few more things we have to do."

The silver-haired man pulled the car that had been sitting on the side of the road up alongside the van. He went to the trunk of the car and lifted out the lifeless body of a woman. They placed her in the van where Jennifer had sat. She appeared to be in her twenties, her body emaciated. The clothing she wore was filthy, hardly more than rags. Written across her hollow face was the story of her life. Her arm fell to her side, exposing numerous needle marks. Drugs had not been kind to her.

The silver-haired man stepped back and looked at her. "Well, this one wasn't in any condition to be a donor." He turned and looked directly at Jennifer. "But her body can serve the purpose of giving a child a new life." He moved the van up by the semi.

Daniel's look was one of deep concern. "You do understand, Jennifer, they're never going to stop coming for you. They want what is in your mind. If they believe you're dead, it ends today. Here and now."

Jennifer could feel tears slip down her face, hear her own trembling voice. "My mother and father . . . ?"

"Yes, I know."

"They think I—"

"I know what they think, and I know you didn't."

"Daniel, when I got there, it was really bad. My sister?"

"In South Dakota with your aunt Mary. Jennifer, you will have to be in a government protection program. Do you know what that means?"

"Yes. I'll never see my sister or any of my friends. It would be for their protection as well as my own. I get it. But can I at least see you from time to time? Daniel, I have missed you." Jennifer continued to hold his hand, her connection to the only person in the future who would truly know her. Jennifer felt her world slipping away second by second.

"And I've missed you. I promise we'll work things out," he said. As they drove away, Daniel said to the silver-haired man, "Nicholas, I owe you one."

"I'll take my regular payment. The beer is in the fridge, right?"

"Yep."

Daniel took out his cell phone and pressed some numbers. A loud explosion followed. Jennifer turned around and saw black smoke, flames climbing into the morning's clear blue sky.

Chapter 31

The sun's rising lit the bedroom with a soft, warm glow. The empty pillow beside me held a note: *Needed to pick up something from the store. I'll be back shortly. Love, Daniel.*

As my feet hit the floor, I realized the need for another OxyContin. Once I got to the kitchen sink, I downed one and put the others in my blue jeans pocket. Craving a sense of normalcy, routine—what I imagined a domestic diva to indulge in daily. I flung myself into a frenzy of domesticity, cinnamon rolls hot coming out of the oven. The aromas of breakfast floating seductively in the air: Canadian bacon, toast with apricot jelly, coffee, of course, along with my favorite French vanilla creamer.

Reminiscing of the summers I spent with my grandmother, no one surpassed the woman's culinary arts—it was her passion. She tutored me in regard to my gifts, application, and responsibilities. *"You must learn the elements,"* she insisted. *"They are not always easy. Men, on the other hand, are not so difficult. Choose wisely, feed them good, and bed them well. They will then flow in harmony with you."*

A knock on the kitchen door, it was Daniel. He stood there with a box of chocolates and a large bouquet of flowers. Handing the box to me, he asked, "Legal tender for breakfast?"

"What are the flowers for?" I inquired.

"I was feeling romantic," he said, "so I guess I went a little crazy."

After breakfast, we sat on the sofa with our coffee, just like ordinary people. On television, a reporter was giving updates on an earthquake recovery. I sat sipping my coffee and wondering if the world had any good news. Across the screen, people in the water were trying to save beached porpoises. Daniel laid the morning newspaper down on his lap as he watched the scene unfold. The newscaster reported, "We don't know why they are doing this."

"Right," Daniel responded.

"Okay, Wonder Boy, what is causing them to beach themselves?" I asked.

"Well, let's just call it a miscalculated moment," Daniel said.

"I don't think so. That's not much of an explanation, and trust me, Daniel, I have found an interest in the importance of detail."

He had started to pick up his newspaper but put it back down. "Testing imperfections. Shall we just say sometimes things aren't where you think they are? Or too much of a good thing just doesn't work out well."

"So much for gibberish. Elaborate," I said.

"You really want to know?" Daniel responded.

"Absolutely," I demanded.

"Submarine Satellite Geometric Cession Session." He sat waiting for a response.

"I believe I have heard about the technology somewhere before," I said.

"Very few people have. You truly are in a selected minority."

"Yes, yes, I feel so entitled. Now all I need to know is how this Trojan horse works."

"You and a lot of other people, what comes out may yet be an uncontrollable commodity," he said.

"You're kidding, right?" I stated.

"Nope. They have the technology, that's in place. Another satellite has gone up to upgrade the program. Basically, what you're looking at is a satellite system through which the Navy activates geometric succession, transmitting to the satellites symbols and equations. We can use this technology in a variety of degrees."

"Varying degrees?" I questioned, wanting more information.

"This is where it gets a little tricky. Unseen vibrational forces in the atmosphere, quantum mechanics neutrons oscillation. Election neutrons don't have a definite mass. The scientists needed some working models. Some of the technology they have down to a fine science. They can literally draw on the landscape. That was kindergarten. Nature is a broad spectrum, Carla."

"Care to clarify that a little? What are we talking about here, global warming, sea levels, what?"

He looked at me and shook his head as though what I had said was so far off the mark it didn't even deserve a response. *I think I've been here before, and I've just been demoted from kindergarten to preschool.*

"Carla, are you sure you want to know?"

"Yes, but I don't think I like the way this conversation is going. Why do I feel like a little starving furry creature staring at a cheese-baited mousetrap?"

"Okay, which do you want first, the good news or the bad news?" he asked.

"The bad news then the good news. I always like to finish on a high note. There is good news, right?"

"Guess it depends on how you look at it."

Snap, I had just bought the cheese.

"A solar storm could be catastrophic. Particles called a coronal mass ejection, or CME, can travel six hundred thousand miles per hour and can reach Earth in approximately eighteen hours. If it hits the Earth straight on, the power grid goes down, no electricity. Lights, food supplies, gas, water can't be pumped to industry or houses. Refrigeration of medication, phone, internet, all gone. Some of these backup generators have a few days or a couple weeks. You get the idea. We're not even going to go into the water supply for cooling pools at nuclear power plants."

"What are the chances of something like that happening?" I asked.

"Some scientists think we are due for one soon. The CMEs seem to be in sync with the eleven-year sunspot cycle," he stated.

"So much for the bad news. You did say there was good news, so what is it?"

"Defense systems and preparation for prevention," he said.

"Okay, Daniel, let's take this from the top. What defense could possibly be in place?"

"Some of the observation monitors we have put out there in space, they can give us information and warning time. They can project when a CME might strike and the measurements of electrical surges on our power grid. They can also tell how the CMEs might affect Earth's magnetic field. On the prevention side of the equation, temporary transformers are being developed that can be moved on trucks. For surge protection, there are some new gadgets out there on the market for further consideration."

"So who is dealing with coordinating all of this?" I asked.

"Government, Homeland Security, the scientific community, and private interest groups with money," Daniel said.

"Private interest groups, what's with that?" I asked.

"Holding the world hostage, now how much fun could that be? Carla, with what you now know about the Phantom Neutron Project, you can understand the professor's concern."

"You're telling me the timetable is coming closer to intersect?"

"On Earth, we humans are but a speck on the timetable. Our planet has experienced cataclysmic events. Scientists have told us continents have risen and fallen. Climate changes have occurred. The magnetic fields here on Earth have changed over time. We know different species, even the strongest, have come and gone. We can only hope to have defense, preparation, and maturity when the time comes. It's not a matter of if, but when. The more scientific knowledge we possess, the more likely to survive as a species we become."

"Daniel, I have never prescribed to the right hand not knowing what the left hand is doing. It is inherently against my nature to follow blindly, regardless of the purity or righteousness of the act. There's something I need to tell you, Daniel. I know the professor was your uncle."

Daniel looked more than surprised. He jolted upright in his seat and studied me intensely for a moment. "I'm impressed. That's information the government doesn't even have, and there is little they don't have. May I ask how you came by that information?"

"A friend of mine, Richard Dupree," I said.

"Richard Dupree, that man is resourceful but hardly your friend, Carla. Yes, my uncle was the professor. I could tell you a great deal about him, more than anyone's research into his life and work could ever tell them. I knew what the man thought and why," Daniel said.

"So that's why you're here?" I said.

"Not exactly, but I can't say I didn't position myself to be in the right place at the right time. Now I'm here for my own reasons," Daniel said.

"And what are they?" I said.

"To see the professor's wishes carried out. He never did accept that scientists should do their work and not know how their creation would be utilized. He felt an obligation to himself and society to honor his work and its application. His passion and philosophy of life, that was what he taught me," Daniel replied.

"Did he also teach you to kill with righteous passion?" I asked.

Daniel smiled. He got up from his chair, came across the room, and sat down beside me. I could feel my own heart pounding in my chest.

Nothing was what I thought it was. The only thing I was certain of was Daniel. He was not being deceptive.

He leaned back, put his arm across the back of the sofa. "To answer your question, my dear, no. Actually, your taxpaying dollar secured such an exotic education. That's right, your government at work. In your field, Carla, you're an accomplished professional. In the world you were manipulated into, your naivety blanketed their agenda and served them well. The person you thought was your protector turned out to be a Judas. Love triangles, they are never simple, are they?"

"You knew about Richard?" I asked.

"I've always known about Richard. Connors, now that guy is a piece of work. When those two stars cross, and they will, my money's on Connors," Daniel stated with certainty.

I knew whatever he said next was going to shake my world to the ground. My stomach muscles tightened, and every part of my being felt wired. I couldn't have been more alert if I had been on speed.

"Carla, when did you figure out that Richard knew all along about the chip? This house and what would come to be your relationship with

Colette—it was natural after all. Your professions being so similar, quite a stroke of genius, I might add. However, I would have never used you like that, Carla. Not ever!"

"I should have seen Richard for what he was earlier on, but by the time realization sunk in, I was committed on more than one level to see this through. Daniel, why did you show up at Leonardo's that night?"

In a soft voice, he said, "I came solely for another reason. I already knew what Richard, the assassin for hire, was . . . even the government didn't know the whole story. The chip had only half the information they were looking for. What I hadn't prepared for was falling in love with you. I wasn't looking for a relationship. In my world, personal relationships only make things more complicated, or so I thought. However, I have come to realize that obsession and passion ignore that premise altogether. I gave you my word, Carla, I keep my promises. When this is over, there'll be no more traveling. There's a chair behind a desk waiting. The eight-to-five man is long overdue. I'm really looking forward to a life together with you, Carla."

Perhaps my mind was just fried. I was getting answers, but logic wasn't following. "I need to ask the question, Daniel, what other half were you talking about?"

He reached over and ran his hands through my hair. His touch was soft and gentle. He sat back against his pillow. "Pour us both a glass of that aged brandy you have."

Standing at the sideboard pouring the brandy, I found my hands were unnaturally shaky. When I turned around, Daniel was in front of me. He put his arms around me and pulled me to him. He leaned down and put his face next to mine.

In a voice so soft I could hardly hear him, he said, "What I am going to tell you will clarify so many things, but you are not necessarily going to like what you hear. You must know that in all my life I have never exposed this part of me or my work to anyone. You must promise you'll never divulge what I am going to share with you."

I looked up into his face and found the need and desire for the first time in his life to share his life. We sat on the sofa. I took a sip of my brandy followed by a deep breath. Daniel began to reconstruct reality as I had known it.

"I always knew who my uncle was. In fact, I came here often."

I was amazed. "You came here, to this house?"

"Yes. As I became older, my uncle and I had long talks about his work. The guiding principles of Western science clashed with his view of humanity and our responsibility to our fellow man. Was it Sir Francis Bacon who said knowledge is power?"

"If you came here, you had to have seen and known of Jennifer?" I questioned.

He swirled his brandy around in its glass. "That's why I was at the restaurant that night. I had to know if any of her mental capacities had been breached. What had she told you, remember? The only way to find that out was to make the connection with you."

My mind raced forward, reexamining everything I had ever known about Jennifer. The first glaring light that hit me: she was a gifted child, excelling off the charts in science.

"She knows?"

"She knows nothing," he said.

"How can that be?" I asked.

"One could say the silent observer holds the equations and I hold the key. We government boys are hardwired to find something physical, the thing that is going to give us the answer. The chip in reality is nothing more than a red herring. Granted, it holds some of his work but not its conclusion. I had questioned my uncle about his decision to place his life's work in such a fragile vessel—two souls on the planet Earth. He was unyielding in his decision. The professor was concerned about our timing, of science's interaction with nature. To him, that was the pivotal issue. He felt it was imperative for science and nature to be in harmony. Our reward for lack of respect could be extinction."

"Daniel, I work with sick people every day, and I think I can fix them. The professor's situation had to have been conscience riveting. What a legacy to leave . . . just think about all that potential. I was once told that he was concerned about our intellectual development. He considered us teenagers with a grenade."

Daniel laughed out loud. "Carla, I don't know who told you that, but yes, that's about how the professor would have seen it."

"Daniel, there's just one thing I don't understand," I said.

"Just one thing?" he said.

"Okay, make fun of me. I'm still in catch-up mode. Jennifer has issues, I'll give you that, but being Mata Hari isn't one of them. She's just a child. How could she hold such information?"

"Hypnosis is an interesting little phenomenon. Talk about your paradigm shift. I gave her numbers, she gives the equation. By the way, in case you were wondering, we don't believe Jennifer murdered her mother and father. We think men went into the house that night. They were looking for Jennifer. Don't know what went wrong, but whatever it was, it went down bad."

I nodded. "You distanced yourself from her until the necessary time arose, until the need to retrieve the professor's conclusion."

"That's right."

A small child's voice echoed in my mind like sound waves, "*Numbers . . . numbers? Letters, jumbled and tumble and they all fall down.*" I had not given her numbers, so the letters jumbled and tumbled, and all fell down into Pandora's box awaiting the master key.

"So the professor, the crafty fox, had been providing his little protégé a mentor in absentia. Through hypnosis the silent observer holds the key, secured in a code that only you, Daniel, know?"

"I told him I thought it was risky, but the professor wouldn't relinquish his position on the matter. Did I ever tell you the old guy really loved horse racing, particularly the thoroughbreds?"

"What, no photo finish?" I asked.

"Now you're getting the idea." In a casual manner, he added, "An additional update. Jennifer was being transported for mental evaluation, and it appears she died in an auto accident."

My mind apparently had a little more agility and some capability for thinking outside the box. "You arranged her escape, didn't you, Daniel?"

"Yes," he said.

"Where is she now? Is she safe?" I questioned.

"Better than safe. She's going to have a life without the scars of her past. We have erased that for her: no dramatic memories, a new identity and face. A new family, the only one she will remember. She will excel and live in the world that her brilliance was meant for. You do understand, Carla, we couldn't risk her being institutionalized. There was just too much at stake."

"Daniel, do you realize how fragile Jennifer is, a teenager taken from her parents, her friends. How is she taking all of this?"

"It gave her comfort to know she will still see me from time to time. There was one thing she felt the need to hold on to from her past. She mentioned a locket the professor's wife, my aunt, had given to her which she lost.

"A locket?"

"Yes, the locket meant a great deal to her. It represented another loss in her life, which Jennifer had to bear."

"Daniel, did the locket that she mentioned by any chance have science symbols inscribed inside?"

Daniel stared in disbelief. "Carla, you know about the locket?"

"Daniel, I have the locket." Pulling a necklace chain from inside her blouse, she unhooked it, handing it to Daniel. "This belongs to Jennifer. Please give it to her to help soften the transition.

"What about Jason? They were together," I asked.

"It looks like things have worked out for him as well. He's out west with his dad. His mom flew out to be with them. They're going to go through some marriage counseling and try to work things out," Daniel said.

Daniel moved closer to me and laid his head back on the high-back pillowed sofa. My mind felt like an unleashed windmill, broken loose spinning faster and faster. When the blades come down, where would they land? How deep would they cut? Every step of this odyssey had brought me deeper and deeper into a world I never wanted to see, much less live in. What sinister price was to be paid? The ticking of the grandfather clock in the hallway was the only thing that filled the void.

"Carla, what are you going to do with the chip?" Daniel said.

I knew now what the professor would have wanted me to do, whose hands the chip was meant for. "I'm going to give it to you, Daniel. I know you'll put it in the right hands."

"I was certain you would say that, Carla. I've made some arrangements and put some safeguards in place," Daniel said.

"I told Richard the chip was in the bank and that I couldn't retrieve it until Monday."

"I know," Daniel replied.

"You know?" Before he could answer, the back doorbell rang. My heart skipped a beat. "Daniel, Richard can't see you here."

"I'll take care of this, Carla," Daniel assured me.

"No, you don't understand. Richard really isn't right. A dark evil possesses his soul. He is dangerous in so many ways. Daniel, he wants you dead."

"Come on, Carla. It will be okay."

As we walked toward the kitchen, I realized that Daniel had a gun in his hand.

"Where did that gun come from?" I asked.

Daniel didn't answer. His total concentration was on the kitchen. At this point, I felt I had become insensitive to surprises. Stepping in front of me, he looked through the glass window in the kitchen door. He stepped back, smiled, and put his gun behind him.

As I opened the kitchen door, Connors stepped in. "Hey, Daniel. Saw your car parked in the back. Been moving any more logs lately?"

Daniel laughed. "Gave it some thought but decided I really wasn't cut out to be a lumberjack."

"So you two know each other?" I looked at Connors. "Daniel was the mutual friend you mentioned at the cabin, the one that helped you take the log off the road?"

"We go back a ways," Connors said, remembering his time in Homeland Security working with Daniel.

Two men came in behind Connors. Daniel stepped forward.

"Gentlemen, perhaps you would like to show Dr. Van Doran your identification."

They simultaneously reached into their jacket pockets, revealing some very heavy artillery as they pulled out their shiny badges with appropriate picture identification: Homeland Security. I took the men downstairs, opened the door to the small room, and showed them which bricks to remove.

They completed their task and were gone in a matter of minutes, but not before one of the men delivered a message: "Carla, someone said to tell you, 'Take comfort in the knowledge that the white knights still play on the chessboard.'" I knew that would be Vincent's last message to me.

Daniel and Connors sat at the kitchen table. Daniel said, "With or without the professor's research, our government will go forward. I have set up a chain of connections worldwide. If the day comes when this needs to be exposed to the public, it can be. The moral issue you and the professor were concerned about has been resolved."

Connors looked at Daniel. "By the way, there is still this little matter involving a case of mine, a missing girl?"

Just as casually, Daniel replied, "Connors, I wouldn't be too concerned about that. I have the feeling she's just fine."

Connors nodded. "That's good to hear. What about Carla?"

"We'll be taking a military flight out this afternoon," Daniel said.

"I could stick around, drive you to the base," Connors said.

"No, but thanks for the offer. I have a military officer coming in. I even made arrangements for Kinsey and that mountain lion she refers to as a cat."

Connors said, "I've heard about his inhospitable personality."

Daniel smiled. "Oh, by the way, some investigative reporters are going to be given a few turkeys to go chase. When the spotlight gets bright, some of our unsuitable playmates are going to have to set up business somewhere else. When it gets hotter, they may start distancing and eliminating their own."

Connors extended his hand to Daniel. "Take good care of her."

"I will," Daniel assured him.

A young military officer, by the book, spit shined and polished, came in as Connors was leaving. He positioned himself in the hallway.

The rest of the morning consisted of arranging for the trip with Daniel. Devin and Kinsey were put in crates and taken away.

"We're going to be gone for a couple months," Daniel said. "I'll go down and turn off the lights in the basement. You make one last check upstairs and we're ready to go."

I went upstairs, closed all the blinds, and came back down. I sat in the kitchen and waited for Daniel to come back up. The house was so quiet. I walked out to the hallway, but no one was there. The officer must have gone to the basement with Daniel. Starting down the stairs, "Daniel . . . Daniel?" I called. He didn't answer.

As I reached the bottom of the stairs, I saw Daniel's body on the floor. I felt a presence behind me. I didn't have to turn around. "Richard . . . " Something covered my face. I struggled and tried to pull away, but his grip was too strong.

I felt my body going limp, and somewhere in the distance I could hear his voice: "You betrayed me, and you're going to pay with your life. Believe me when I say it'll all be over soon, Carla."

***

A knock on the kitchen door, then another. Connors pushed the door open and stepped in. "Hey, I brought you a bon voyage gift." He sat the bottle of champagne down on the kitchen table beside Carla's handbag and keychain. "Hello?" Walking into the hallway again, he called out, "Carla . . . Daniel?" Silence engulfed, cascaded over him.

A sinking feeling gripped his stomach. His breath became softer, deeper, as he reached for his revolver. Entering the family room, he gave it a quick overview. The morning paper was lying on the footstool. A vase of flowers sat on the end table with a note to Maria: *Take them home with you. Enjoy them. I'll contact you later. Love, Carla.* He turned to walk away, but something in his peripheral vision caught his attention.

There, on the floor behind the sofa. He moved forward to get a better look. Boots, then the crumpled body of a young man in uniform. Connors made a quick check of the entire house. Carla and Daniel were gone. As he passed by the basement door, he noticed it was slightly open.

Moaning sounds floated up the stairs. Connors descended the stairs, the light hanging over the workbench swung back and forth, casting shadows over objects and into corners. Daniel was sitting on the chair in front of the workbench, his head down on the bench. Connors pulled Daniel up. His body was unsteady.

Supporting his weight, Connors looked into his eyes. "Daniel, hey, man, you in there?"

"Carla," Daniel responded.

"No, Daniel, it's me, Connors. Where's Carla?" he asked.

"She's right here. She called to me. My head hurts. What happened?" Daniel moaned.

"Oh yeah, you're in good shape all right. Evidently Carla interrupted the proceedings," Connors said.

"Proceedings, what proceedings?" Daniel repeated.

"What can you remember, Daniel?" Connors asked.

"My head hurts." Daniel held his head with both hands.

"Think, Daniel. What can you remember?"

Daniel sat there trying to clear his head to remember. "It was Richard. We struggled, and then I heard Carla. She was calling to me, coming down the stairs. I think he hit me with something. Where's Carla?"

Connors and Daniel looked at one another for a moment. No words passed between them. Daniel struggled to get up, stand on his feet.

"Connors, Richard has Carla and he'll kill her. She has nothing now to give him but her life. We have to find them, and I don't even know where to begin."

"How much lead time do they have on us?" Connors questioned.

Daniel looked at his watch. "I'm not sure. Maybe half an hour."

"We can get to them," Connors said. "I got a little bored the other day, had some time on my hands, so I put a tracer on Richard's car."

"Connors, you did what?" Then a slight smile came across Daniel's lips. "Never really out of the game, are we? They called you back, didn't they?"

"Yeah, just recently got an official invitation to the party," Connors said.

"Welcome aboard officially. Now let's go find Carla." Daniel pulled himself up and staggered toward the stairs.

Chapter 32

Where am I? Lying here looking up at the patches of blue sky. Tree limbs swayed above me in the breeze. I could tell it was late afternoon. The smell of pine trees surrounded me, creeping into my awareness. The mind attempted to find some sense of reality. A sound in the distance beckoned.

Attempting to sit up, my hand slides across a smooth surface. Looking down, I see the black plastic I was lying on, *a body bag*, then the Jeep. A flash of memory floated to the surface: Daniel lying on the basement floor.

That constant sound again, where is it coming from? I stumbled to my feet, footsteps staggered, dazed as I walked toward the sound. The constant cadence became louder. Movement and rhythm with each stroke, metered like a beat of music. As my mind began to clear, a figure came into focus with each shovelful of dirt. The forest quiet but for the preparations being made for my final resting place. The beauty of the wilderness now took on a black cloak of horror. Isolated from humanity, I was on my own as no human being should ever be, totally alone. No one to know I had ever been here.

My own survival would be in my hands and mine alone. *I have to find a path, a way out.* Going back to the Jeep, maybe I could go out the way the Jeep came in. I followed along, looking at the tire tracks on the ground until I came to a fork in the path. Statistical data supports the fact given a choice the higher percentage of people will turn to the right.

If they find my body, what will my colleagues say? She let her professional guard down. Let some psycho client too close.

The police would go over my files, look for a suspect. Richard, the ex-fiancé and longtime friend, would probably make every effort to help them and give them information. He would delight in the deception, the game he would play with them—his charisma getting inside information. His leading them astray would no doubt further inflate that enormous ego.

I know he will be coming for me. I can feel his presence in the air. Instinct, the ancient part of our being: acute smell, hearing, a mind firing on all primitive senses, awakening survival alertness. Richard was no amateur predator. Turning to my right, I scuffed up the ground with my foot, continued up the path, and made a few more marks on the ground. Stepping off the path, I backtracked down along the left side. *Perhaps I can buy more time if I'm lucky.* He wouldn't find evidence I had gone this way.

Coming to a clearing, I could see a farmhouse ahead of me. The sun in its last vestige of light illuminated the world, making everything more vibrant. Wildflowers scattered across the field standing tall. The Blazing Star flowers of purple and white appeared as soldiers standing vigilant defending a forgotten fort. Crickets announced their awakening from the thickets and awaited the onset of shadow and darkness.

I could feel my heart pounding in my chest. Sharp, razor blade pain with each step. I reached into my blue jean pocket and pulled out another OxyContin, the mind ordering the body to run faster, *faster*. As I looked up at the house, a horrible sinking feeling took my breath. The house was dark with broken windows. Weatherworn wooden slats, peeling paint. The second-floor shutters over the windows were partly gone. One side of the wrought-iron railing around the widow's watch torn off and lay on the ground. The front door was half open. It was as though the house was screaming in its own pain: "I have been abandoned!"

This house would be a place of hiding if only until dark. Entering the house, one could feel the cold, damp emptiness. The sunlight came through the open windows like fingers searching across the empty walls for any sign of life. In the kitchen, pieces of a broken chair lay on the black and white squares of the linoleum floor. On top of an old wooden table, beneath the dust of times past, lay a bouquet of wildflowers: a faded rainbow of color. My hand reached down; white-tipped French fingernails softly touched the dry delicate petals only to see them crumble into dust. They wouldn't be held a moment longer. One black-and-white photograph lay beside the rainbow of memory, a beautiful lady from another era. Perhaps the flowers were lain there in her memory.

I opened the door and looked down the stairs to what appeared to be a basement. Again, flashes in my mind's vision of Daniel lying facedown on the floor. A musty smell floated up to greet me. The thought of being down there, trapped, made my whole body shiver and shake, giving *claustrophobic* a completely new meaning. A rustling sound. Was someone down there? Then I saw it in the corner, hanging from a wooden rafter, the bat fluttered its wings. A rush of air as it flew past my face, shrieking its way to freedom.

Taking the stairs to the second floor, some of the steps creaked. A board cracked and broke under my foot; the old wooden steps groaned. Looking out the upstairs window, I saw movement at the edge of the clearing. *It can't be him, not so quickly.* The figure emerged, coming across the field. It was Richard. An alternative reality, mechanical man, unchained and pursuing me. I ran from room to bare room, but they were empty. There was nowhere I could take cover.

Down the stairs, entering the kitchen, I started for the back door. The front door opened, *He's in the house.* How could he do that so fast? Was this man part cheetah? I stepped behind the kitchen door and froze in place. One could hear the calling of the crows as though, somehow, they understood danger had entered their world, stalking its prey. His footsteps stopped, hesitated for a moment.

If only it could be a moonless night and I could hide within its darkness, fade into the plaster of the wall. *He's standing on the other side of the kitchen door, so close to me.* His heavy breathing was clearly audible. My ears close to explosion from the hammering, pounding sound of my own heart. *Can he hear my heart's panicked pounding?* My legs like concrete, my feet nailed to the floor. I knew his hesitation lasted only a second, but it felt like an eternity. He turned to walk back down the hallway. The creaking sound of the stairs echoed against the bare walls. *He's going to search the empty rooms.* His footsteps thudded overhead.

Running out the back door, there's an old barn at the back of the property. A rusty shovel propped open one side of the barn door. *Maybe I can find something to defend myself with.* Stepping inside, the barn is dark but for a few holes in the roof that let light through to the dirt floor below. Pieces of the slate roof lay scattered about. Large, heavy wooden beams, tongue and groove style, supported the loft. An old sickle and pitchfork were hung on the wall. I took the pitchfork off the wall, stepped back into the darkness, and waited.

I could see him now in the doorway. He went over to look behind the stacks of baled hay. *He's coming out. It's now or never.* I was so close to him, close enough to feel the heat from his body, hear the rasping sound of his breath. The air held the intensity of an electrical shock that encompassed the entire barn, saturating the very ground we stood on. The tingling sensation ran up and down my spine like a pianist playing the *Flight of the Bumblebee.*

Richard spun around. His eyes locked on to mine with wild surprise. Flashes of anger and rage filled the air between us, seared white light.

For Colette, Marcy and Daniel justice and redemption for me. The time had come. With the fierce aggressiveness and speed of a feline, I sprang out of the shadowed darkness to the prey that was now mine. The pitchfork's sharp, pointed arrows sang through the air, swift— direct into Richard's body through his shoulder into the barn wall, pinning him like a captured animal in a trap.

Richard screamed in agony. As our eyes met, his flashed with fire.

I ran from the barn, ran until I thought I couldn't put one foot in front of the other, gasping for air.

Just ahead of me, the trees broke into open land. *There could be a road, cars, people, someone to rescue me.* The ground sloped down, and beyond the drop was invisible. Coming closer, approaching the edge of the clearing, I looked down. There wasn't a road, only a cliff that went straight down to the rocks below. I could feel the pounding vibration in the ground beneath my feet. Footsteps like a telegraph line pulsating, surging up my legs to my brain. *He's coming. Richard is coming.*

Something deep within me that had no words of expression, evocation of all knowledge and awareness of one's own demise. I looked toward the sky. *Dear Lord in heaven, if this is my time, powers that be light my path.* I turned and saw Richard coming toward me. Blood saturated his shirt. It gushed from his shoulder, dripping down his arm. It's over now. There was no way out. I was trapped.

The sun was setting, bright fluorescent red. He walked past me to the edge of the cliff and looked down. It was as though time stopped. When he turned around, I could see the anger, rage, in his face. His voice was barely audible.

"You betrayed me. Lied to me."

I could feel my own anger rising up in my throat. "You said we needed to get the chip into the right hands, well, now it is, and what a price I had to pay. You took everything from me, Colette, Marcy, even Daniel."

"I told you to stay away from Daniel. Did you really think I wouldn't find out? We could have made it work, Carla, but you fouled what was good between us. Letting Daniel touch you, put his hands on what was mine. You allowed him to take in the sweet taste of your body." His eyes slithered over me like a cold serpent. "I can see it all now," he said. "You are lying there in his arms, and he can smell the scent of your lovemaking. That was inexcusable, Carla. No man takes what's mine. Now let me look at you one last time." His face took on an eerie softness. Across his lips, a sneer masqueraded as a smile. He looked for a reaction before delivering his final blow. "Yes, I killed him, you know, your Daniel. I killed him. Left him lying in his own blood, bleeding out. The knife slid so smoothly across his throat."

Richard studied my face, stricken and drawn, that felt like it had turned to stone. The transformation was only exceeded by the deep wounds of pain and disbelief I knew showed through in my eyes. Eyes I knew he had seen before in the downed deer before the final shot. It was time now for him to finish this, but had he gone too far? Would I now welcome death so as to deprive him of my fear as I fell from the cliff? Second by second, my body plunging in descent. He wanted to hear my screams, the smell of fear. He wanted it all.

Suddenly, Richard looked past me as though I wasn't even there. Stepping backward, his heel went down into an uneven crevice in the rock. He appeared like an ice skater attempting to regain balance. Each step backward became more animated, frantic. His hands of raven's claws reached out for me.

"Carla!" he called out. "Carla!"

His eyes, windows to the soul, housed only a dark abyss. His mouth opened wide, a gasp of breath. The instinct to reach out for him did not even cross my mind as he disappeared from my sight. I wondered if Colette reached out for him in those last moments at the head of the stairs. Had Marcy begged for her life? Did Daniel know what was happening to him as he took his last breath of life? For Richard, had he seen the sunrise this morning?

Looking out over the empty edge of the cliff, two men's shadows spread across the ground in front of me. Their silhouetted hands elongated into the shape of guns. I spun around to see my executioners.

"Connors?" *Who was that standing beside him? No . . . no, I can't let my heart accept what my eyes are seeing.* The gift of vision this time was cruel beyond belief. I heard my own voice crying out in agony and pain.

"You're only an illusion. You're not real! You won't stay. You can't. You'll only leave me," I shouted.

As Daniel stepped toward me, his voice reached into every cell of my body. "I told you I would always know where you were, Carla . . . in my heart. I'll never leave you." He put his arms around me, solid, warm, and so alive.

Burying myself in his chest, hot tears ran down my face. I heard Colette's voice like a song in the wind: *I'm telling you, girl. If you find that man, tell him you love him, and you will never let him go.* I looked up into the face of the man I knew I would spend the rest of my life with.

"Daniel, I love you, and I'm never letting you go."

We walked over to the edge of the cliff and looked down. Connor's voice, void of emotion, cut through the silence.

"Go on, get on that plane. I'll take care of the rest of what's down there. You weren't here. I wasn't here. Colette and Marcy can rest in peace now."

Below lay the crippled mass of a human body. The ancient rock formation stretched out a bed, soaking up the oozing red stains of life. One broken link in the chain of damaged DNA.

Humanity's survival, a silk thread—with decades yet to go.

The End

Epilogue

Seventeen Years Later

Jennifer, now known as Christine Baker, has a personnel file representative of a very intelligent and stable scientist. She possesses one of the highest security clearances in the government's Apple Orchard Project.

On vacation, her car winds up the mountain road to that place she has been so many times before, a place of solitude and beauty. She sits looking out at the mountains watching the clouds float lazily across the sky. Glancing down at her sterling silver ring, she runs her finger over the onyx stone and presses open the secret compartment. The diamond from her father's ring sparkles in the sunlight. She hears the whispered raspy voice of Aaron in her ear: "It's okay, Jennifer. The diamond is perfect. The only perfect thing you could find about your father. This stone symbolizes your strength and will to survive. No one will ever see his blood on your hands."

A half smile crosses Jennifer's face as she closed the top on the onyx ring.